DENTON COUNTY, TEXAS
AUGUST, 1982

We was in the field drinking. We argued for a long time and it was hot. I took my clothes off and laid down on the blanket. Becky took her clothes off except for her bra and panties. And we kept on arguin', cussin' each other.

Finally she must hit me in the side of head and before I knew what was happening, I just stabbed her with the knife. I just picked it up and brought it around and hit right in the chest with it. She sort of sat there for a little bit, then dropped over. She was the sweetest thing that ever happened to me and I just killed her . . .

Frieda "Becky" Powell was fifteen years old when Henry Lee Lucas killed her.

She wasn't his first victim — and wouldn't be his last.

ZEBRA'S TRUE STORIES OF SEDUCTION, SEX AND MURDER

MASQUERADE   2833, $4.95)
by Lowell Cauffiel

To teen-age hooker and drug addict Dawn Spens and her pimp boyfriend John "Lucky" Fry, he was Dr. Al Miller, the most generous sugar daddy they'd ever known.

But to the upscale Detroit community where he lived and worked, he was Dr. Alan Canty, a respected psychologist with a successful practice and loving wife.

So why did he disappear, only to be found with his arms, legs and head severed? What tragic event would have led Canty to such a bloody and gruesome death?

Award-winning journalist Lowell Cauffiel brilliantly unravels the bizarre world of double identities and lies that led to Canty's lurid death at the hands of Fry. Cauffiel goes beyond the brutal facts of the case to recreate one of Detroit's most famous and grisly murders.

"A COMPELLING WORK OF TRUE CRIME, OBSESSION, AND GROTESQUE TRAGEDY." — *Detroit Free Press*

MISSING BEAUTY   (2755, $4.95)
by Teresa Carpenter

Brilliant Tufts University research scientist, Professor William Douglas regularly cruised Boston's porno district looking for sex. And when the devoted husband and father of three met commercial artist and high-priced call girl Robin Benedict, his life changed forever.

Overwhelmed by the passion of their sexual encounters, Douglas would do anything for Robin — including embezzling university grants to pay for her time. But something went wrong: Robin disappeared, and the last person to see her alive was the professor. Was Robin dead? Did Douglas murder her? Pulitzer Prize winning writer Teresa Carpenter uncovers the dark secrets of "the call girl and the professor" in this Hitchcock-like true crime masterpiece!

"AN EXTRAORDINARY TALE OF OBSESSION AND MADNESS." — Joe McGinnis, author of *Blind Faith*

HENRY LEE LUCAS:

The Shocking True Story of America's Most Notorious Serial Killer

DR. JOEL NORRIS

ZEBRA BOOKS
KENSINGTON PUBLISHING CORP.

For all of the victims, including those murdered, others whose careers have been jeopardized, and even Henry Lucas himself who suffers from a culturally inflicted disease. But especially, we honor all those who insist upon the truth, without distortion or bias, no matter how discomforting or unexpected those facts may be. And for the personal supporters: Marguarite Jones McKinney, David Melvin Maurer; Don, Don Jr., and Julia Cuba.

ZEBRA BOOKS

are published by

Kensington Publishing Corp.
475 Park Avenue South
New York, NY 10016

Copyright © 1991 by Dr. Joel Norrisand and
Shadow Lawn Press

First printing: August, 1991

Printed in the United States of America

Acknowledgments

Sheriff Jim Boutwell; David Bowen; Richard Burgheim; Max Call; Phil Carlos; Warren Causey; Brad Darrach; Paul Dinas; Dr. Stephen Egger; Enrico Ferorelli; Dr. Jay Fogelman; Det. Sandra Gallant; Dr. Dale Griffis; Dr. Stephen Harms Jr.; Doug Hawthorne; Donald Higginbotham; Carolyn Huebner; Dr. Jonathon Indik; Dr. Tom Kubiszyn; Father Emil LaFranz; Dr. Anton LaVey; Zena LaVey; Laura Little; Dr. Venon Mark; Dr. Paul New; Captain Bob Prince; Pat Pulling; Boyd Rice; Det. Jerry Semmandle; Nicholas Shreb; Clayton Smith; John Taliaferro; Dr. Bill Walsh; Dr. Phillip Williams

And a special note of thanks to Nan Cuba, without whose efforts and talent this book could not have been written.

Introduction

Finally, The Whole Story

147 dead — 250 dead — 360 dead —
2,000 dead — 3 dead — 0 dead.
Devil worshiper — born again Christian.
Abused child — sociopath — liar.
Heterosexual — homosexual — bisexual
Serial killer — con-man extraordinaire —
    pathologica fantastica.

How does one prove any of the above? Since we met in June, 1984, Joel and I have been perplexed by this dilemma and yet felt compelled to look for solutions. Motivated by society's proliferation of violence and our nagging suspicion that continued work on the Henry Lee Lucas story might contribute information which could help counter what has become a cultural disease, of episodic violence we persisted. In spite of criticism, disappointment, and the gruesome nature of the material, we pieced together testimony and data we hope will ultimately calm and heal. Our experience has been a battle against illness, injustice, and misinformation.

Our journalistic and biopsychosocial research began while Joel was completing "An American Tragedy," a *Life* magazine article with Brad Darrach and editor Richard Burgheim on the serial killer phenomenon. In late June, 1984, with two weeks left to work on the piece, news began appearing over the wire services about a man named Henry Lee Lucas who was confessing to scores of mutilation murders he claimed he committed with his running mate Ottis Toole. The descriptions of violence were so extreme, Joel believed Lucas was a con-man titillating Texas lawmen and media. Lucas should not be included in the article, Joel insisted. Then an editor at *McCall's* magazine sent me over. I had a history as a journalist and access to Lucas. Two weeks before, I had been offered an interview with the professed killer, but had turned it down, certain I wanted no connection with such lurid material. But Joel and I each trusted the integrity we observed in the other; so, tentatively but well intentioned, we began. Once we heard the facts in Lucas' story firsthand, he became the lead for the *Life* article, the subject of several more, one of five case studies in Joel's *Serial Killers, The Growing Menace,* and finally the focus of this book.

About a month after our initial meeting, Joel came to Georgetown, Texas, to meet Henry. As we sat in one of the jailhouse offices, 8:30 a.m., Henry walked by in the hall, led by jailers to his day's first interview with some law enforcement official suspecting him of a murder crime in a different jurisdiction. Although his jailers seemed to dwarf him, he looked crisp, alert, aflush, dressed in jeans and a red-checked shirt. He glanced at us smugly and grinned.

At 10:00 a.m., apparently on a break between inter-views, Henry exhibited a shift in affect: he appeared wilted and irritable. He scowled. By 3:00 p.m. he was pale and wrinkled, with a very low affect. He was belligerent as he denied us our scheduled interview. He resented the *Life* article, he said, because the sheriff and Texas Rangers, his co-workers in the on-going crime in-vestigation, hadn't been presented fairly. No, he wouldn't see anyone who mistreated his friends.

Then just as unpredictably, an interview with Sister Clementine, the jail minister and confidant to Henry, was arranged instead. We talked to her and looked at her collection of the killer's paintings, but Joel became im-patient with the delays. I told him I was encouraged, felt sure we'd soon get to see Henry. I'd been through this routine several times before. And indeed, we were pleased when Sister Clemmie invited us to accompany her while she delivered the infamous prisoner his dinner of cantaloupe and chicken.

We sat across a table from them while Henry ate. He was still pale but now calm, sometimes childlike with Clemmie as she fed him slices of cantaloupe with her fingers, both of them afterwards giggling. All day she had been telling us stories of Henry's training in a death cult, and that night, as Henry chuckled and smiled at his closest friend, she continued with more details about rituals, kidnappings, and signature markings on corpses. Law enforcement wasn't acting on Henry's in-formation quickly enough, she said.

She was referring to Sheriff Jim Boutwell and Texas Rangers Bob Prince and Clayton Smith, who had been given charge of the nationwide Lucas investigation. They worked in their small, county jail, which like the displayed series of large, framed photographs of bearded sheriffs from past years, had the polish of pride, similar to a simple but gracious home where the well-used silver is glistening clean — unpretentious and ordered.

Boutwell, nicknamed "Snake," was a typical Southern macho sheriff. He was a man of few words, kind and the father figure a child in trouble would want to take charge. He felt both burdened by and attracted to the media, often chatty and as forthcoming as time would allow. And Prince worked hard at crediting Boutwell with the leadership role, while the Texas Ranger had moved to Georgetown from Waco solely for the purpose of overseeing Lucas and his interviewers. Prince was easygoing but never varied from prescribed procedure, his John Wayne-like frame filling his small, central office.

That night as we left Georgetown, we discussed how these two men together with Sister Clemmie, without realizing it, had set up a therapeutic community. By giving Henry a modicum of respect, they had turned chaos into order, facilitating an attitude of camaraderie that kept the serial killer in line. Now in retrospect, we sadly understand Henry's reason for later turning against them, claiming they had eagerly blamed him for murders they knew he hadn't committed. We realized the last thing anyone should want is for a serial killer to love him/her, because that affection eventually turns into hate. He actively participated in an attempt to ruin the reputations of his former law enforcement buddies. But in spite of several difficult years, these men's careers are still intact.

Soon after Joel left Texas, we began discussing the

possibility of an in-depth study of Lucas. Through a friend, I arranged for Henry to undergo an all-day series of tests and examinations at Presbyterian and Baylor hospitals in Dallas. Prince and Boutwell eventually agreed to fly him five hundred miles by private aircraft, and the doctors and staffs donated their services. After seven postponements, which included Henry's fluctuating moods and the worst snowstorm in Texas' history, he underwent the testing on January 28, 1985. The CAT scans and psychiatric evaluations were mailed to Joel's consultant, Dr. Vernon Mark, then director of neurosurgery at Boston City Hospital and president of the Center for Memory Impairment and Neurobehavioral Disorders. Small abnormalities were discovered in the frontal lobes, temporal lobes and in the parts of Henry's brain that are related to emotional control. Dr. Bill Walsh, a Chicago biochemist analyzed locks of his hair, and found a cadmium concentration more than thirty times the population median value, placing Henry well within the levels of dangerous biochemical imbalance.

With the completion of these tests, which combined the efforts of several medical specialists with those of legal experts, the barriers of "linkage blindness" (a term coined by criminologist Stephen Egger, but originally referring only to law enforcement's reluctance to interact during investigations) were broken for the first time. Our efforts had produced benchmark results. Still, our primary discovery was that for each question answered, there appeared ten more questions.

So, while I published a few articles on Henry and then embarked on a career of academia and literary writing, Dr. Norris traveled the country accumulating more research into the causes of the phenomenon of extraordinary violence. He interviewed several killers, including Charles Manson, and began refining his ideas for a serial killer profile.

During his talks with the inmates, he heard repeated tales about satanism, and this became a second area of investigation for him. But after additional conversations with such people as the Louisiana exorcist Father Emil LaFranz, Satanic Bible author Dr. Anton LaVey, LaVey's associates Boyd Rice, Nicholas Shreb, and Blanche Barton, cult crime specialist Dr. Dale Griffis, and San Francisco Detective Sandra Gallant, Joel discovered documented criminal activity with "outlaw" satanic groups but no proven crimes connected to organized religious satanists. Still, some of the killers claimed their motive was some version of satanism while others said they murdered as born-again Christians. Ultimately, he realized their pathologies, more than their belief systems, linked them.

Meanwhile, Henry began his recantations. He didn't kill nobody but Mom, he said. And people believed him, including the Texas attorney general. But because Joel had witnessed Henry's personality changes, he wasn't completely surprised at this reversal. He likens Henry to a kaleidoscope whose chips of glass shift and settle, then resettle according to the current viewer's whim, but the colors remain the same. Henry, like other serial killers, learned the skill of transformation and adaptation at an early age in order to survive.

There were many victims in the scandal surrounding Henry's recantations. The Texas Rangers became old-West cowboy bullies whose leaders, Prince among them, needed stringing up at the nearest live oak. Boutwell got trampled in the rush for bigger game. Joel and I dueled with journalist Hugh Aynesworth over Henry's guilt or innocence while several attorneys who volunteered to represent Henry bit the dust one by one under public scrutiny. Victims' relatives, already traumatized over the loss of a loved one, spent their money and emotional energy taking sides in the shootout; a definitive answer was required for them to cope with their tragedies. The religious sector quarreled over whether Henry was the devil, someone assisted by God to remember details of numerous murders, or a pitiful drifter victimized by evil law enforcement officials over-eager and callous to the underprivileged. One district attorney, who led an eventual grand jury investigation into the authenticity of Henry's confessions, later, himself, came under indictment for charges of bribery. He was ultimately acquitted. The Texas attorney general, using his association with the recantation theory as his way to look crime-tough, lost his race for governor.

Meanwhile, Texas adopted a new law mandating an automatic death sentence for anyone proven to have committed a murder as a serial killer; this legislation was nicknamed the Henry Lee Lucas Law. And Henry, in spite of eleven murder convictions, one death penalty sentence, six life sentences, two seventy-five-year sentences and one sixty-year sentence, received a stay of execution, ironically because neither the prosecution nor defense raised the issues of his childhood abuse and eventual medical problems.

Currently he is being tried for four more murder cases in Florida; Ottis Toole and Frank Powell the brother of Henry's murdered common-law wife Becky are testifying against him. All in all, the Lone Star State has looked downright silly. This mess is one of the rea-

13

sons it is important not only to include the psychological and medical findings in this book, but also to educate the public, hoping, ultimately, it will influence policy makers who can insure that such confusion won't be repeated.

Henry Lee Lucas has become mythic, the subject of several TV spots, one movie, and several books. His experience has served as a benchmark in psychological, legal, and media circles. This comprehensive study takes us for the first time into the depths of his primordial mind and lets him tell us everything, including his fantasies and delusions, through which always runs a thread of truth.

Nan Cuba
San Antonio, Texas
August, 1991

Chapter 1

"Orange Socks"

Interstate 35 cuts like a chainsaw straight down the United States from the western tip of Lake Superior to the Rio Grande just west of the Mississippi. It slices through Texas on an angle from Oklahoma southwest to Laredo, lopping off east Texas from the rest of the state. Back in 1979, you could still do upwards of 90 miles an hour just to keep the eighteen-wheelers from breathing down your neck, especially after you cut west south of San Antonio. They'd loom up out of the black specks on the horizon of your rear view mirror. Sometimes it was a hundred miles between gas stations, so you'd be smart to stop wherever you could to top off your tank and visit the bathroom before heading back onto the heat of the asphalt. Even in late October, the road was hot and tar-like as you headed south from Waco toward Georgetown in East Texas.

That's where the hitchhiker was going.

The reddish-brown-haired girl in the tight white tank

top, short cutoffs, and bright pumpkin-colored socks was thumbing south on 35. It was the fastest way to get wherever she was going. She was a hitchhiker ambling south on no particular schedule when she met the sad-faced, one-eyed stranger near a truck stand outside of Oklahoma City. She was a loner—a drifter in her mid-twenties heading into Texas maybe toward the border; he was a drifter, too, willing enough to give her a ride without asking any questions. He said he had no destination in mind so he'd take her as far south as she wanted to go. Whatever she was running from, his ride was as good as they get in this part of the country, and she would've been a fool to turn it down. She believed she could take care of herself.

They two drove for hours until they crossed the Texas line. Then they stopped, the one-eyed man would tell the Williamson County Sheriff five years later, and had sex. He wasn't really satisfied after having sex, but he figured he'd have more later. Then they drove on. Stopping at truck stops for food and pushing on into the night. They stopped at a truck stop just south of Waco for breakfast and the one-eyed man marked to himself that the girl spent an awfully long time in the bathroom.

She reappeared in the restaurant and they pushed on into the hottest part of the day. They were on one of the most isolated parts of I-35 when the one-eyed man felt himself getting tired and ornery. He wanted sex again.

"I want to have sex," the one-eyed man said, barely taking his good eye off the road. "I want to pull off and do it now."

"No," the girl said. "I don't feel like it."

They kept on driving. The one-eyed man let the subject set for a few miles but brought it up again.

"I want you to know that I really do want to have sex with you. We had sex before."

"But not right now," the hitchhiker said. She didn't say no this time, the one-eyed man marked to himself, only not right now. That wasn't good enough.

"Do you want to have sex later?" he finally asked. Sex was the only thing on his mind, and when he felt the need to have sex, that was all he could talk about. Everything else would fade away into shades of gray and the thing foremost in his mind would be the craving for sex that had to be satisfied.

The driver looked at his passenger, getting a fix on her as he continued to talk about having sex. The hitchhiker edged away from him toward the door, repeating "not now" over and over again. Then the hitchhiker began looking at the door as if she were measuring it, and in a sudden movement she lunged for it with both hands, yanked on the doorhandle, and tried to leap out of the car.

She was almost out the door and to safety when the driver took his hands off the wheel and grabbed the back of her neck, hauling her back into the car. Hooking his arm over her shoulder, the driver pressed the hitchhiker into him, trying to control her as she struggled against his grasp by pushing off his chest. She was a fighter, the one-eyed man said to himself, a devil of a fighter, and he'd have to quiet her down before she killed the both of them.

The girl fought for control of the wheel, swinging away at the driver while lunging for the gear shift as the car swerved across lanes. The one-eyed man fought the hitchhiker and the car as he yanked back on the wheel and elbowed her hands away from the transmission lever. Finally, in desperation, he jerked the car over to the right shoulder and stood on the brakes. He held her to him as tightly as he could, wrapping his arm around her neck and across her throat. He bent her backwards as he steered to a stop. She kept on fighting him until he turned to face her, brought his left arm around, and choked her until her head slumped forward and she relaxed.

By then the one-eyed man was feeling cold chills through his entire body. The car began to reek of the foul-smelling perspiration that had drenched through his shirt and pants. The hitchhiker stirred and the one-eyed man watched her for a minute as she fought to regain her breath. Her thighs twitched as she started to regain consciousness, maybe her eyelids even fluttered, and then he lunged at her, squeezing and wrenching her neck with an instant surge of violence like an electrical charge. The hitchhiker's body went into a lurching spasm, and then she died.

The one-eyed man was seized by a familiar passion as he yanked the dead girl's legs out from under her and threw her over into the back seat. Then he climbed on top of her, pulled off her tank top and cutoffs, bunching her pumpkin-colored socks down around her ankles, and had sex with her corpse until there was no violence left in him. He fondled her breasts and had sex with her another time before he was spent. Then he climbed back behind the wheel and drove along the shoulder of the interstate until he came to a culvert in a desolate area where he stopped the car. It was dark by now. He opened the back door to the car and dragged the nude corpse out of the back seat, rolled her over to the edge of the embankment, and dropped her into the culvert. Then he closed the door and drove south into the night.

The following day, Halloween, a motorist along I-35 found the nude body of the strangled girl sprawled face down, hugging the dirty concrete. Later that day, both he and Williamson County Sheriff Jim Boutwell noticed the incongruity of the stretched pumpkin-colored socks that were bunched up around her ankles. Sheriff Boutwell dubbed her Orange Socks. Looking at her as if she were sleeping on the ground, he promised himself that he would find her killer.

Orange Socks was just one of a score of unsolved homicides that had been taking place along I-35. Over the next two years, Sheriff Boutwell had helped form a task force with other sheriff's officers and Texas Rangers from jurisdictions up and down the Interstate. In 1981, Boutwell had coordinated a meeting in Austin with the assistance of the Department of Public Safety, the Texas Rangers, and the state's crime analysis section. Twenty-nine officers came together from agencies along a 500 mile stretch from border to border along I-35 that wound from Gainesville to Laredo and Fort Worth. For a full day the investigators examined photographs, compared M.O.s, studied police reports and evidence, and searched for some lead or some explanation for the trail of dead bodies.

The victims were teenagers, young hitchhikers like Orange Socks, elderly women taken from their homes near the road, vagrants, business people, and women with car trouble. They had been shot, beaten, strangled, dismembered, and there was even a hit and run. Yet there were no similarities, no common M.O., and nothing jelled at the meeting. The victims were as varied as the types of weapons that were used.

Must be truckdrivers, the officers decided — the only logical conclusion. The police believed that truckdrivers had a logical easy access to all of the victims, and the different M.O.s were easily explained by a variety of offenders. If these cases were to be solved, they'd be solved case by case and not by finding a single killer. Or there'd be no solution at all.

That's what Sheriff Boutwell believed until he got a phone call from his friend, Sheriff Bill "Hound Dog" Conway over in Montague County nearly two years later.

Hound Dog had an inmate in his jail who would plead guilty to the murder of an old widow and who would probably be found guilty of the stabbing murder of his traveling companion. Even at his arraignments, this one-eyed drifter named Henry Lee Lucas had talked of numerous murders he'd committed across the state and in Georgia and Florida. Hound Dog had an idea that Lucas might know something about the Orange Socks murder. Conway also thought that Lucas might have leads for some of the other I-35 murders that had taken place since the late '70s.

Boutwell made the trip to Montague County just after Lucas was arraigned. He chatted with Lucas for awhile, nice and relaxed, offered him a cup of coffee, then read him the Miranda warning and showed him a photograph of Orange Socks' face. She was lying on the ground, her eyes closed after death. But Jim Boutwell was careful to cover the neck area so that Lucas couldn't see how she had died. Henry stared at the girl for a minute and then said, "Yeah, that one was a hitchhiker, and she would have been a strangle."

This was too good to be true, Boutwell thought to himself. He hadn't even seen the abrasions on her throat. Then Lucas described the Orange Socks case and several others from around Austin. He provided Boutwell with descriptions of about 156 homicide cases nationwide. When the sheriff returned home, he rushed to check much of the information Henry had given him and decided that Lucas knew what he was talking about. Now, anxious to clear his Orange Socks case, Boutwell brought Lucas to Georgetown for arraignment in the Orange Socks homicide, hoping to get a solid confession and ultimately a guilty plea.

Boutwell brought Lucas and Don Higginbotham, Lucas' court-appointed attorney, to the culvert where Lucas said he dumped the girl's body. It was here, Lucas said, right here, that he committed the murder and threw the girl out of the car. It was now time to confess. Boutwell set up his video camera, and as the eighteen-wheelers whizzed by them on the highway, Lucas described the events leading up to the murder of Orange Socks. He confessed to a case that had plagued Boutwell for four years.

"I picked her up in Oklahoma City," the drifter began. "Then we drove around awhile; we stopped and had sex . . . voluntary. That one time we had sex, I wasn't satisfied. She put her clothes back on, and we stopped and ate at a truck stop. We started to go back south. We took 35 south. And after we came back on 35, why, I asked her to have sex with me. She said no."

Higginbotham interrupted the confession. In his strongest terms, he advised Henry to go no further in his confession. "Henry," he said. "What you say can put you in deep trouble. You are confessing to a capital crime—talking yourself into life in prison or even a death penalty. I advise you strongly to go no further and say nothing else." Higginbotham wanted to point out that in Texas, a defendant could receive a death sentence only if he had murdered someone while committing another crime such as rape. Henry was confessing to felony murder.

"I got to confess," Henry Lee Lucas said. He explained that he'd tried to live with whatever it was that had been torturing him for 33 years. "I've tried to get help for it," he said. Lucas said that he'd already tried to kill himself to escape what was torturing him. If he couldn't do the job, he might as well let the state kill him, he said. Then he continued his confession.

He told how the girl tried to jump from the car and how he kept her inside while the car swerved. "We drove for a little piece further than that, and I pulled off the road because she was fighting so hard I almost lost control of the car and wrecked."

Then the sheriff asked him why sex wasn't satisfying to him. "The last time, it was the Kotex; she had a Kotex on . . . It just wasn't good sex to me."

The missing fact, Jim Boutwell said to himself. The missing fact that nobody but someone who had actually penetrated or examined Orange Socks could have known. The young girl was in the middle of her period and bleeding heavily. She had stuffed bathroom tissues into her vaginal cavity in order to staunch the flow. That was why Lucas wasn't satisfied by the sex and why the woman didn't want to have sex with him a second time. Boutwell knew he had his killer.

Lucas was sent back to Hound Dog's Montague

County jail house. He eventually pleaded guilty to the murder of the old woman, "Granny" Rich, was sentenced to 75 years for the crime, and was found guilty of murdering his traveling companion, Frieda "Becky" Powell, whom the police called his common-law wife. He was sentenced to jail for life for that homicide. After his convictions, Lucas was put on trial in San Angelo for the murder of Orange Socks. The jury, seeing his videotaped confession, found him guilty and the judge sentenced him to die by lethal injection. Lucas, despite many appeals and automatic stays, is still waiting for that sentence to be carried out.

The Orange Socks case would have been almost cut and dried had it not been for a second videotaped confession by another self-professed serial killer who was purported to be in company with Henry Lee Lucas at the time he committed his notorious spate of killings across the south. This man's name is Ottis Toole, currently in prison in Florida, who claimed to have been Henry's other half in a "killing pair" that murdered for a violent Satanic group called The Hand of Death.

In Ottis' videotaped interview with Texas authorities and Sheriff Boutwell in Georgetown, a very different version of the Orange Socks murder emerges, a version that played to a skeptical audience a full three months before Lucas was brought to trial. It was a confession that the jury who sentenced Lucas to death never heard.

Boutwell read the Miranda rights statements to a scruffy, bearded, heavily overweight Ottis Toole who sat back, smirking into the camera. Ottis appeared hulking. He mumbled his answers, his movements were sluggish as if he were on sedatives or barbiturates, and he stared at Boutwell without recognition. It was as if he were unable to focus his vision or his concentration on the goings-on around him.

He and Henry did pick up the hitchhiker in Oklahoma, Ottis confirmed, and they did indeed stop for food at a truck stop before heading south to Georgetown along I-35. It was true, Ottis continued, that Orange Socks and Henry had sex with one another. In fact, Ottis watched them having sex, got turned on and masturbated. Henry was his lover, and it excited Toole to see Henry having intercourse. Then Ottis got jealous because Henry had enjoyed himself too much. When they were back in the car, he said, Henry got behind the wheel and he got in the back seat.

"I was sitting in the back seat and I leaned over and choked the shit out of her," Toole confessed to Boutwell.

"Did Henry choke her any?" Boutwell asked Ottis.

"I'm real sure that he did," Toole answered. "Then Henry got out of the car and fucked her . . . he decided to fuck her after she was dead."

"Do you recall anything that was different than, say, somebody that he'd normally fuck?" Boutwell asked.

"Oh," Toole answered, ". . . he'd fuck any woman as long as she got a pussy."

"What made you decide to strangle her?" Boutwell asked again.

"Well, I was jealous," he said. "I didn't like him fucking with her."

They'd never believe this guy, lawyers for Lucas thought as they watched the tape of Ottis Toole confessing. He didn't even seem to know where he was, to whom he was talking, or what he was talking about.

Some of them watching the video tape joked that he might not even know he was on the planet earth. No, they couldn't use him. Toole, they thought, would have no credibility whatsoever with a jury. Yet Lucas' own lawyer, Don Higginbotham, still could not fathom the seeming paradox of Henry Lee Lucas. He claimed that he really couldn't grasp the meaning behind the confession of a person who he believes could not have been individually responsible for the murder of Orange Socks, yet who willingly assumed the guilt for the crime. On the surface, it made no sense, but very little made sense when it came to the mysteries surrounding Henry Lee Lucas.

Those mysteries began in June of 1983 when Henry Lee Lucas sat in a small room in the jail of Montague County, Texas, facing a huge sheriff determined to convict him of murder. He was the stereotypical beaten, downtrodden, lawless drifter with whom it was difficult to sympathize. His one dark eye darted to and fro. His left eye, the artificial one, drooped eerily away, expressionless, seeing nothing. His black hair was tangled and greasy, matted from the road dirt, sweat, and grime that he had accumulated on his travels across the south. He was thin, pale, and dirty. His hands shook as if in a tremor. He was a man who had scrabbled his entire life together out of a meager existence of cigarettes, coffee, candy bars, booze, and dope, and had failed at everything he tried to do. His voice was soft, bitter, unassuming, and self-deprecating. He almost cried.

Henry never looked up. He kept muttering into his hands "I've done me some terrible things." He began telling the sheriff of murders, rapes, mutilations which, if true, would mark him as the single most savage killer in America's history. But now it had all come to an end for him in jail. "Maybe some of the others I killed," he said to the sheriff. ". . . Maybe their families love them and want them to have a Christian burial, too."

In June, 1984, just a year later, Henry Lee Lucas was a picture of health and confidence. He leaned back in a chair at the scarred work table that was his desk, smiling, ebullient, smoking, joking, laughing as he freely confessed to being "the worstest killer in history." He eagerly admitted to the most bizarre and demented of murders.

"I've killed every way known to man — strangulations, stabbings, shootings . . . everything except poison. I never poisoned nobody," Lucas proclaimed, almost gleeful as he faced down his accusers. His good eye flashed, challenging and mocking the array of police officers around the room. He was confident. His hair was washed and combed, he was 35 pounds heavier than the shell of a man who had faced police a year earlier, and his complexion was clear. He granted or denied interviews with law enforcement officials, psychologists, psychiatrists, and journalists on his own whim in what he called his "office," an interrogation room at the Williamson County jail.

Less than a year later, in April, 1985, another Henry Lee Lucas confronted the police. He was a terrified, paranoid little man who accused, scolded, cajoled, and pleaded with his friends to help him out of his predicament. Then, in the very next breath, he denied that he even had friends, proclaiming that everyone had abandoned him. He insisted loudly that he was what he claimed to be: a killer of staggering proportions. But, he said, there were people out there pressuring him to recant. "They" had threatened to take away from him forever his beloved jailhouse confidante and minister, Sister Clemmie. "They" had promised him tennis and privileges at the best institution in the "Club Fed" system if he recanted.

His good eye reflected his desperation; his hands shook, he fidgeted, he cowered as far back in his chair as he could get. He renewed his habitual complaints of stomach problems. He begged people to fight for him. He cried for acceptance of his bizarre recantations, for his betrayal of those same friends he had just berated. First he despised his former friends, then he lamented what he had done to them. Lucas cried that he had been captured by a death cult who had threatened to kill him if he did not go along with their wishes.

"I'm here and have no one that I can get help from," he said. "Since I came up here they got their captain to say that I am only a liar. That made me feel that they have betrayed me, so I went on TV and told that I never killed nobody but Mom."

He was moved again to the McLennon County jail and began an odyssey that embarrassed agencies in legal jurisdictions throughout the country, humiliated prosecutors who made pilgrimages to his jail cell for scraps of information about missing persons in their counties, and even called into question the reputation of the fabled Texas Rangers. During this period, doctors said that he was sick and emotionally unstable, Sister Clemmie said that she was afraid he was going to commit suicide, and a federal grand jury was empaneled to investigate the grand jury that was investigating

27

the original task force investigations. The Lucas case had become a media circus.

However, by January of the following year, Lucas had again regained his composure. He was confident, albeit less ebullient, calm, logical, reasonable, and credible. He faced the cameras of CBS' "60 Minutes." He was the very picture of a wronged man telling his story to an audience that seemed willing to hear it. Lucas played well against Harry Reasoner, telling him what Lucas knew would make the kind of story 60 Minutes liked to air: a story of subterfuge, governmental misconduct, bureaucratic incompetence, and a legal system out of control. Lucas himself was controlled; he was neither confrontational nor cowed. Rather he was open, forthcoming, and entirely convincing on national television. In three years Lucas had transformed himself from the filthy terrified drifter incapable of looking his interrogators in the eye to a sobered, healthy, sanguine interviewee in the visitors' room of the El Paso county jail. He had a new set of friends and he reflected the image of trustworthiness they created for him. Lucas had played out one of the greatest hoaxes in the history of the criminal justice system, he said. He embarrassed the system and played off opposing political forces against one another. He would soon die, but he at least had the grace not to laugh into the faces of his executioners.

Such were the four faces of Henry Lee Lucas: which one was real?

Is Lucas a savage monster who prowled the interstates preying on unsuspecting hitchhikers? Did Lucas invade homes and businesses in the still of the night to rob, rape, torture, and kill? Did he torture and mutilate his victims, cutting off the hands and genitalia of his living, crying, pleading victims, while he was insane with terror, fury, and pain? Was Lucas the demonic agent of a "thrill-kill" cult called The Hand of Death, committing murders to satisfy a monthly death quota and abducting little children for lives of sexual slavery, torture, and death? Or was Lucas a willing pawn in a game played by police interrogators desperate to close unsolved homicides? Was Lucas clever enough to convince hundreds of professionals that he was something he really wasn't? Was Lucas intelligent or cunning enough to toy with Texas Rangers, prosecutors with Ivy League law school degrees, experienced judges, and savvy reporters? Did those who paraded him in front of the cameras know more about this man than the other professionals he had burned so badly with his original tales of murder, his recantations, and his recantations of recantations? Is he still playing this game today? Who is Henry Lee Lucas, and why are people still so fascinated with his exploits?

Lucas, in fact, is everything that he has been portrayed to be. He is a chameleon, an individual with little or no sense of his real self but who reflects the needs and wants of other people around him. Lucas adapts so readily to his surroundings that he begins changing before the very eyes of his audience into the creature they have come to see. If he does not do this consciously, then he does it on an instinctive level the way most serial killers adapt to their surroundings just to survive. This is what has made it possible for Lucas to go from a destitute Appalachian drifter and serial killer to a prime-time star on 60 Minutes.

It is only after people understand and appreciate Lucas' uncanny abilities to discern what others around him want that they understand what he has managed to pull off. Lucas has abilities that place him well outside the norms of civilized individuals. He has killed his own mother, killed his common-law wife that he raised since she was nine years old, killed an old woman who had been kind enough to provide him and his traveling companion with food and a place to live, and he has killed at least one police officer in West Virginia. Most of the institutions that Lucas has come into contact with have been the courts and the prisons, and they simply processed him through.

Over his years in custody, Lucas has confessed to more than one thousand murders, slightly more than two hundred of them attributed to him by law enforcement officials, and then has denied them all. At one point he had convinced law enforcement authorities that he was the worst serial killer in history. In less than a year, however, he had convinced other professionals, including many in the media, that he had perpetrated one of the greatest hoaxes in history. By the end of that year he had law enforcement officials in states across the southeast at one another's throats as they defended and attacked his confessions and recantations.

It may well be impossible to ever know the entire truth about Lucas. But one thing is certain: whether he killed five, fifty, or five hundred, he has an amazing ability to strangle the truth to death. He has manipulated, cajoled, twisted, and distorted events, the truth, and people from the time he was first arrested in 1983 on a weapons charge until he appeared on 60 Minutes. And in perhaps one of the most amazing twists in an already twisted tale, Lucas has both used people and been used himself. Those who wanted him to clear unsolved murder cases from the books have used him as have those who wanted him as subjects for numerous articles, professional papers, medical studies, and even books. Even people who faced serious political problems in their home states used him to deflect the heat or to provide clues into painful missing persons cases. But as confidantes, friends, police, lawyers, and police interrogators took their respective turns at using Lucas, Lucas used them in turn. But rarely has anyone honestly confronted the paradoxes in the Lucas case.

Perhaps the most frightening aspect of the entire affair is that through cunning, an innate ability to manipulate, and a seizing of the moment — all traits that enhanced his abilities as a serial killer — Henry Lee Lucas has become more important than he should be. His reputation may have far exceeded his actual crimes. If Lucas killed half the people he once claimed, he is one of this country's most prolific murderers and indeed the mad dog he says he is. At a minimum, he is a sociopathic liar who has told so many lies that neither he nor anyone around him can determine the truth.

Serial killers are accomplished manipulators. It's another skill they learn in order to survive and persevere in their hunt for victims. Once in captivity, however, serial killers become manipulators. In fact, the more notorious the felon, the more accomplished the manipulator he usually becomes once he's behind bars. Lucas is no exception and has, along with Charles Manson, become one of the most skillful in this system. He has manipulated institutions as well as people. Law enforcement has received a black eye trying to fathom the real Henry Lee Lucas. Similarly, psychiatrists and psychologists have stumbled over themselves to find meaning in Lucas and have demonstrated only their lack of understanding. Even religionists have seen both Satan and salvation in Lucas, only to find him twisting their words and their precepts. The press has been misled by the swaying winds of Lucas' confessions, recantations, and convolutions. Reporters from print and broadcast media seem to have been all too willing pawns in Lucas' games. Some of them have been collaborators in misleading the public to get the best press on Lucas.

The only way to reach some type of understanding of Henry Lee Lucas is to review his effect on the people and institutions he has touched and to look at the horror of his life and his upbringing. No one comes away from a confrontation with Henry Lee Lucas since his incarceration without being changed. Before his capture, the lives he scarred, mangled, or ended in terror are the subject of rampant speculation. After his capture, he has become a serial murderer of professional reputations and careers.

Chapter 2

"I Hated All My Life"

"I hated all my life," Henry Lee Lucas once told a psychologist in a prison interview. "I hated everybody. When I first grew up and can remember, I was dressed as a girl by mother. And I stayed that way for two or three years. And after that I was treated like what I call the dog of the family. I was beaten; I was made to do things that no human bein' would want to do. I've had to steal, make bootleg liquor; I've had to eat out of a garbage can. I grew up and watched prostitution like that with my mother 'till I was fourteen years old."

Henry was born the last of nine children on August 23, 1936, in rural Montgomery County, Virginia, nine miles from Blacksburg in a wooded cleft hard between Brushy Mountain and Get Mountain. His father, according to birth records, was Anderson Lucas, a longtime alcoholic and double amputee aptly nicknamed "No Legs." He had lost both legs when, in a drunken stupor and miserable that his wife, a prostitute, was having sex with a customer right in front of their young son

Henry, staggered out into the snow and fell under the wheels of a slowly moving freight train. "He hopped around on his ass all his life," Henry said of his father. "Skinned mink for a living and sold pencils at the skating rink after that until one night he got so sick of what she was doing he laid out in the snow for a whole night, drank, caught pneumonia, and died."

Henry's mother was named Viola Dison Wall Lucas, an alcoholic half-Chippewa native American whom Henry describes as the bane of his existence. One of Viola's granddaughters described her as a "dirty old woman who chewed snuff, and the kind of person you would not want to be around." Henry says she often beat him, his brother Andrew, and the legless Anderson indiscriminately and for no reason. "Some people say they gonna give a whipping with a switch or something," Henry has said. "She'd use sticks! She didn't know what a switch was," he remembers. "When she went and got a switch, she went and got a handbroom stick. She'd wear them out."

Their home was a four-room, dirt-floor log cabin up in the hills of rural Virginia, two miles from the nearest neighbor, that had no plumbing or electricity. The Lucases only lived in three of the rooms. They were an extended family, of sorts: Henry Lee, his brother Andrew, old Anderson the "father" who has also been described as a former boyfriend allowed to live in the cabin because he had nowhere else to go, Viola, Bernie, Viola's pimp, who was also her manager and boyfriend, and all of his invited customers who beat a path to their rural cabin door. They all slept in the same room, and Henry didn't just peek at his mother having intercourse with strangers, but, he has said over and over again in interviews, was forced to watch. Viola even made her husband bear witness to her licentious ways. "She made us just stand and watch," Henry says. "Stand in the house, or she would beat my brains out if I didn't."

Viola beat her son mercilessly with any weapons she could find. Her cruelty was such that she wouldn't even let him cry. After beating him and telling him that what she had done was for his own good, she would prophesy that he had been born evil. She even went on to predict that he would someday die in prison, a prophesy for which a Texas court has already set a date only to have it adjourned on appeal. Viola's continuing violence began to infect every level of Henry's existence. Henry Lee's earliest memory, he claims, is of his mother finishing up with a customer then pulling out a shotgun and shooting the man in the leg. The blood spattered all over him in the process. This traumatic scene may very well have set the stage for his own fascination with spilling the blood of others.

Henry says that his mother neglected her children and her home, having deserted a previous family of four daughters and three sons. "It was just about as bad as any house that I've ever seen," Henry says. "I have been in a lot of hog pens that stayed cleaner than our house did." The boys did all the chores and made and sold moonshine. One of Henry's specific chores was to "mind the still." Viola, he says, absolutely refused to cook for the children but did prepare meals for herself and Bernie. Henry, his brother, and Anderson scrounged for their own food, which was usually foraged from garbage cans, stolen from other homes or from stores in town nine miles away, or bought from what Anderson could make begging or selling pencils. Whatever they had, Viola always made them eat from the dirt floor.

He has vivid memories of growing up in the cabin. On an average day, "Lots of times I'd spend in the woods. I'd go out to play in the woods or I'd go walk nine miles into town. I'd walk to school, drag in wood, carry in water for half a mile. That was my average day." But all during his childhood, his mother berated him, beat him, and acted as if she hated him.

He even says he called her "Vi" or "Viola," refusing to say "Mom" because at the time he believed he "really didn't have a mother." He says he put a shield around his emotions since he was not allowed to complain or cry because in this way, although he says he was never happy, neither could he be hurt. He explains that Viola nurtured this sickness and even called him a "bad seed."

"I was worth nothing," Henry says. "Everything I had was destroyed. My mother, if I had a pony she'd kill it. If I had a goat or anything like that, she killed it. She wouldn't allow me to love nothin'." He remembers a pet mule that he kept. His mother, seeing him take pleasure in the animal, asked whether he liked it or not. When he replied that he did, she went into the house, reappeared with shotgun, and killed the mule. Then she beat him because of the expense she'd just incurred in needing to have the mule's carcass carted away. "She wanted me to do what she said, and that's it. That is, make sure the wood is in, the water's in, make sure the fires are kept up. The dishes when you get through eatin'— I'd have to wash 'em. Work! That's it! And I'd have to stand and watch her have sexual acts with a man." Incidents like these were responsible for Lucas' fear of loving and for his lifelong inability to feel empathy for other living creatures. Whatever he loved as a child was destroyed.

Therefore, he learned not to love. In fact, he learned that there was no value to life and that people were no different from any of the thousands of inanimate objects that populated his world.

The child abuse that Henry endured was so serious it left him with permanent lesions on his brain. He recalls one incident when he was seven or eight years old in which his mother beat him savagely with a piece of wood and left him to languish in a semi-conscious stupor for more than a day before Bernie became worried that the child would die and drove him to a hospital. "I wouldn't go out and pick up a stick of wood," Henry says about the incident that precipitated the attack. "And she took a two-by-four and knocked my brains out with it. It made the bone and all wide open. I stayed out for about 36 or 38 hours before I came to. Bernie was worried that I wouldn't wake up." He says that Bernie kept talking about how the police would come if he died. Finally, Bernie took Viola and Henry to an emergency room. "She told the doctor that I fell off a ladder, and the doctor went ahead and accepted it." Years later this story would be confused with another story about young Henry in which he alleges that he fell off a ladder and had a nail driven to his skull that had to be removed by a doctor.

Viola Lucas also liked to outfit Henry in girls' clothing. Lucas remembers that on his first day of school his mother curled his long blond hair and made him go to school in a dress. Annie Hall, his teacher, who became one of the few people in official positions of authority who came in contact with Henry Lee Lucas during his youth, was shocked. She took the responsibility for cutting his curls and dressing him in pants. Viola, Henry remembers, stormed into school in a fury and verbally abused the teacher. Miss Hall was not afraid of Viola, fortunately for Henry, and as the term progressed, the teacher began feeding the malnourished youth sandwiches during school lunchtimes and took him to her home where he would receive the only hot meals he ever ate as a child.

"She brought my dinner, or if she didn't bring it, she'd take me home and I'd eat there. And she'd bring me some old clothes that she could dig around to get. I think she was responsible for my first pair of shoes," Lucas remembers. "She took me out of a dress and put me in pants." Years later, in a rare interview, Hall described Lucas as one of the many impoverished and desperate Virginia hill children in her classes. But, she revealed, he was especially dirty, smelled very bad, and was constantly tormented as an outcast by the other children.

Henry also remembers the man he called his father as a pathetic but kind human being who would sneak him money from his moonshine operation to go to the movies. "Maybe it was a nickel, maybe a dime," Henry remembers. "But it was all the money I had and he'd give it to me from the still or from beggin' on the street." Henry also remembers how he had gotten some money from Anderson and instead of going to the movies, he stole a battery-operated radio from his next-door neighbor a couple of miles away from the Lucas cabin. That afternoon, Henry and Andrew hid in the woods and basked in the episodes of "The Lone Ranger" and "Sky King." The boys dreamed of leaving home.

Anderson was one of the handful of people who was actually kind to Henry. He taught the boy how to work the makeshift distillery and in the process encouraged Henry's taste for liquor. At the age of ten Henry began drinking regularly and is a diagnosed alcoholic today. Henry remembers that the legless man was as much a victim of Viola's brutality as anyone else in the cabin. "He couldn't do anything about it either," Henry has said. "She'd knock his brains out as soon as she would mine. He drank just to get away from it. He'd go out and lay in the snow just to get away from watching her. That's what made him die. He laid out in the snow and caught pneumonia, and he was drunk and died."

Psychologists at the Ionia state mental hospital in Michigan, where Henry was sentenced in 1961 after his repeated suicide attempts in a Michigan penitentiary, described a different portrait of Viola's mountain cabin. Lucas was serving a 25 year sentence in Michigan for murdering his mother. "As previously stated," the report indicates, "the patient's earliest recollections seem to center around a dirty, filthy log cabin in the hills of Virginia wherein the entire family, including the mother's current boyfriend, all slept in the same room. One of these boyfriends in the patient's early life he remembers as a dirty old man with both legs amputated who used to sit on streets and beg for a living." The report makes no mention of Viola being a prostitute, but describes Lucas as a severe, chronic schizophrenic.

When he was seven, he remembers, Viola took him into town and pointed to a strange man walking on the street. "That there's your real father," she purportedly said to him. Lucas recalled the incident to the psychologists at Ionia and still remembers it today. He says that he never stopped feeling deceived and tricked by his mother.

Lucas kept on getting head injuries right through his childhood, which severely exacerbated the damage he'd sustained from his mother's beatings. A year after Bernie took Lucas to the hospital in a coma, Henry's elder brother, Andrew, accidentally sliced into Henry's left eye with a knife, injuring the optical nerves so severely that for months, Lucas could only see shadows and phantom images. "I was making a swing with my brother and he accidentally pulled up with the knife to cut the grapevine in two. And I was holdin' it still, and the knife slipped through the grapevine and hit me in the eye. And that's what started it and then I was in the hospital, and it healed back up so I could see a shadow."

His peripheral vision was seriously impaired as well, causing him to walk sideways so that he could see what was on his left. He was eventually returned to school, where the teacher who had shown him so much kindness when he was younger purchased a special reader with large type so that Lucas could keep up with the rest of the class. Even this level of progress was interrupted when another teacher at the school, Mrs. Glover, while striking out at another student, missed and accidentally hit Henry instead. His wound reopened and caused him to lose the injured eye completely. It was replaced with a glass eye that he still wears. Mrs. Glover quit teaching altogether after that. "It was an accident. I didn't mind, but my mom did. She almost beat her brains out."

The beatings and head traumas took their toll. Lucas experienced periods of shock and disorientation, and he recalls having had recurring seizures and periods of physical dissociation for long periods after the assaults. "What I remember was that it was like somebody layin' down and stompin' you, and you keep fightin' to get away from 'em. I didn't know anything happening around me. I couldn't hear, really. It was like being in a different world. I used to float through the air when I was a kid, too. I used to be layin' in bed, just felt like you're floatin' right off the bed up in the air. Just feel like I could fly. It's not a nice feeling. It's a weird feeling."

Lucas also has recurring auditory hallucinations that intrude into his very shaky sense of reality. He recalls hearing voices and animal sounds ever since his severe concussion and coma when he was eight. "Sometimes I hear stuff when there's nothing around. I've heard my name called and there ain't been nobody with me. I've heard all kinds of noises and stuff and there been nobody around — people, animals. I've gotten up and gone outside in the daytime to go and look, but I can't see anything. I can't find it."

When he was just thirteen, about three years before his first arrest on a breaking and entering charge, Lucas claims that he was having a wide variety of sexual experiences. His half-brother also introduced him to bestiality. They trapped small animals whose throats Henry would slit open in a private ritual designed to arouse them sexually. "It satisfied me," he said years later. "It was just sex, that's all. It was just to have sex." Lucas often trapped animals and skinned them alive for pleasure. At about the same time he began stealing for food and money. He also stole for the pleasure of it. "I stole almost as soon as I could run," Lucas says. " 'Cause I didn't want to stay at home. I figured if could steal, I could get away from home and stuff."

Lucas claims to have committed his first murder in 1951 when he was fourteen. He says he cornered a seventeen-year-old girl at a bus stop, bludgeoned her until she could no longer resist, carried her up an embankment, and attempted to rape her. When she awoke struggling and screaming, Lucas began strangling her. "I had no intention of killing her. I don't know whether I was just being afraid somebody was going to catch me or what. That killing was my first, my worst, and the hardest to get over. I just couldn't take what happened. I would go out sometimes for days, and just every time I turned around I'd see police behind me. Everywhere I'd go, I'd be always watching for police and be afraid they were going to stop me and pick me up. But they never did bother with me."

Lucas didn't kill for the thrill of killing, he explains. He did it because it was the only way he could have sex. "Sex is one of my downfalls. I get sex any way I can get it. If I have to force somebody to get it, I do. If I don't, I don't. I rape them. I've done that. I've killed animals to have sex with them. Dogs, I've killed them to have sex with them — always killed before I had sex. I've had sex while they're still alive only sometimes. Then killing became the same thing as having sex."

In 1952, Anderson Lucas died from pneumonia after spending all night in a drunken stupor outside in the snow. Henry blamed Viola directly for Anderson's death. And afterward, Henry was left alone to face his mother's brutality and the violence of her johns who often turned their anger on him. Henry says that he felt no attachment to Viola or to the cabin after Anderson died. He remembers that no one cried or even spoke at Anderson's funeral. After it was over, Viola went home with Bernie, and Henry swore he was leaving the cabin and his mother forever.

His older brother soon left to join the Navy, and Henry began roaming the neighborhood, looking for trouble and getting into scrapes. There were reports of his peeping in windows, and he himself says that he often stole food because he was constantly hungry and slept under houses because he was afraid or unwilling to go home to face Viola.

Henry's first serious brush with the law came in 1952 when he was charged with breaking and entering and petit larceny. He was sent to the Beaumont Training School for boys in Virginia. He liked Beaumont, he said in an interview years later, because it was the first time he had lived in a place that had plumbing, electricity, and television. Institution records tell a different story. Lucas made frequent attempts to run away and trips to juvenile detention. He himself says that he made his first real friend at Beaumont, a black youngster, troubled like Henry, who sometimes ran off with him on his escape attempts. The two youths became inseparable and the institution's psychological records of the juveniles cite the possibility of a homosexual relationship.

The Beaumont records describe Henry's background from the point of view of the social workers assigned to his case in 1952. They say that Henry's father, Anderson, was "illiterate and had a reputation of being a bootlegger." Mrs. Lucas, they say "drank heavily and admits that she has bootlegged in the past." The Beaumont records describe Viola's cabin as a "small shack in the Craig section of Montgomery County. The home is furnished with only necessities and is not clean or neat. There are four rooms, one of which houses two goats that belong to a roomer who is a half-witted man who owns a half interest in the house."

The records continue. "Henry has one artificial eye which drains at times. He states that he lost the eye when playing with his brother, and the knife with which they

43

were playing went in his eye. Henry thinks the glass eye is too small. He was to have an eye examination while in detention but this had to be cancelled when he had to appear in court."

Strangely enough, in August, 1952, just eight weeks after his commitment to Beaumont, an evaluation describes Lucas as "very spoiled and wants his way quite a bit." This, the evaluator says, is true despite Lucas' "good personality." "He is truthful," the report says. "And has good personal habits. Henry's behavior has been good in jail in all situations as well as his attitude in work, and the company. One of his major drawbacks is the fact that he needs close supervision for any job that he undertakes. His adjustment is borderline and Mr. Nelson feels it is quite difficult to get to know Henry. It seems that he has somewhat of a wall around him and will not verbalize his problems." However the rest of the record describes numerous escapes and AWOL hearings before the school's disciplinary committee, and notations that Henry seems to have two distinct personalities.

"Mr. Smith reports that Henry's personality is puzzling to him since at times he is pleasant and other times he is so quiet that you just can't tell. He shows some initiative and has a good attitude. Mr. Smith states that he is getting settled again, but doesn't believe that he is ready for a trust. He also notices that Henry appears emotionally upset at times ands especially so after the last visiting Sunday." Yet a month after this report was written, Henry was reported AWOL again, brought up before the disciplinary committee, and sentenced to "Corporal Punishment and Force" indefinitely.

On July 16, 1953, Dennis Taylor, Henry's caseworker

at Beaumont, wrote Kate Bolton, the Superintendent of Public Welfare for Montgomery County, that Henry was ready for release. "We feel that Henry has reached his maximum adjustment here at the school and when the Placement Committee meets on September 7, 1953, we plan to recommend that he be released from the school." Although, the letter admits, Lucas generally appeared happy and cheerful, "it is difficult to learn this boy's true feelings about anything as he does not relate very well." Again, the caseworker indicates that as a teenager, Lucas had developed two distinct sides to himself. One was cheerful and outgoing, but the deeper Lucas did not relate at all to his surroundings, was closed up, and very guarded. Dennis Taylor describes this dual nature in greater detail in another part of his letter: "Although Henry has not taken the initiative to better himself in our program, he has done that which has been required of him. He has not entered into any phases of the program with any enthusiasm. He has, during recent months, abided by the rules and regulations more willingly and it is felt that he has been truthful, but he has not become involved in any more situations where it was necessary for him to alibi his way out."

Generally, this was a positive report despite its admission that Lucas remained a custody problem throughout the program and required close supervision. The report really cannot determine whether or not Henry was rehabilitated, but stipulates that he met the requirements for release and "deserves another chance in his community."

Lucas was discharged from the reformatory in September after a year-long stay. This dual nature described by the Beaumont psychologists and caseworkers—his personality that was sometimes friendly and outgoing and at other times closed up and guarded—would remain an aspect of his character for the rest of his life. He himself has often described the "two Henrys," the one Henry who would ingratiate himself with women and the other Henry who would cold-bloodedly kill, rape, and mutilate them. Lucas claims that shortly after his release he raped his twelve-year-old niece, although there is no independent verification available.

For a while he worked as a farm laborer or yard hand. He did odd jobs and outdoor construction work. "I had different jobs," he says, learning skills and picking up whatever training he could. "I worked for the state highway department, I worked for the federal. I worked for several different people." But by June of 1954, just nine months after leaving the Beaumont school, he was again in trouble. A state criminal court convicted him as an adult of breaking and entering burglary, and he was sentenced to the Virginia State Penitentiary for four years. He was 18 years old, and, he says, Viola never even showed up at his trial. While he was in prison, Henry worked in the chair factory, at the tailor shop—he says he liked sewing—and with the road gang manacled to other prisoners. On May 28, 1956, Lucas and another inmate bolted from a chain gang during a rest period along the side of a rural road under construction, stole a car, and drove to Ohio. When they ran out of gas, they stole another car and slipped across the Michigan state line into Monroe where they were finally arrested after two months. During this period, Henry says he met and fell in love with a girl named Stella who, ironically, was to be the cause of Lucas' second confessed murder.

Lucas was arrested in Michigan on a federal charge of transporting stolen property across state lines and sentenced to serve thirteen months in a federal reformatory in Chillicothe, Ohio. At the federal reformatory he served his time as an elevator operator, after which he was transferred back to Virginia to complete his original sentence with time added for the escape. He was finally paroled in September, 1959, when he was 23. He made his way back Tecumseh, Michigan to join his 43-year-old half sister, Opal. She was his favorite sibling after his older brother Andrew. Lucas has said that after his release from the Virginia penitentiary, he was frightened, angry, and mean. He was also drinking heavily at the time. "I'd drink seven days a week if I was able," he later admitted.

While he was staying with Opal in Michigan, Henry asked Stella to marry him. She agreed, and the two of them became engaged. But shortly thereafter, Viola came to visit her daughter. She also had another agenda: she wanted to take Henry back home. She told Opal that she was old, tired of doing things for herself, and wanted Henry back in Virginia to take care of the cabin. On the night of January 12, 1960, she followed Henry to a bar in Tecumseh to tell him to come back with her and call off his engagement. She came upon Henry and Stella happily celebrating their engagement and making plans for their wedding. Viola quickly put a stop to that by starting a fight with Henry and Stella. Soon the three of them were screaming at one another at the bar, and Stella, realizing that she was at the center of a mother-son feud, called the marriage off and stormed out of the bar.

For Henry, this was a replay of his entire youth.

Whatever he loved, he remembered, whatever he felt belonged to him, his mother took away. He was an adult. He'd been tried, convicted, and served prison time as an adult. And now he'd just been told by the woman who had repeatedly beat him with sticks and clubs when he was younger that he wasn't allowed to get married because he had go back to the filthy log cabin to take care of her. "She was cussin' and everything else. I was sittin' when she came in and started cussin'." When Viola saw that she couldn't change Henry's mind, she attacked Stella and drove her off. Now Henry was alone again, bitter, full of hate, and drunk. He became furious and to keep from getting violent, he drove back to Opal's apartment.

Viola followed him, burst into the apartment, and the two of them began drinking while they continued the fight. It was getting later and later, and Viola became her abusive self all over again. She started cursing, accusing him of all types of deviant behavior. She insisted that he come back with her. She gave him orders, told him that he was no good and would come to no good. And finally, he remembers, she told him that she knew he was having an incestuous love affair with his own sister. Then, in a sudden and violent fit of rage, she picked up a broom and smashed Henry across the head with the handle. It was suddenly the Virginia cabin again as Henry, reduced to a seven-year-old child, reeled from the pain and ferocity of the blow.

"I guess it was about 12 o'clock in the night when she hit me. She took a broom handle and hit me over the head and face. I was so mad that I hit her back," he said about the incident. "All I remember was slapping her alongside the neck, but after I did that I saw her start to fall, and I decided to grab her. But she fell to the floor, and when I went back to pick her up, I realized she was dead. Then I noticed that I had my knife in my hand and she had been cut. I got scared and turned out the lights and went outside and drove back to Virginia. I only stayed there one day, and I started to worry about my mother and wonder if she had been found. I left Virginia and started driving back to Tecumseh to give myself up. I was picked up by the police in Toledo, Ohio, and was later returned to Tecumseh. It was a terrible thing to do and I know that I have lost respect of all members of my family, but it was just one of those things, and I think it had to happen."

In later interviews, Lucas has said that he never really blamed his mother for his life of crime that followed. By the time they had their last fight in Opal's apartment, Henry says, any of the feelings he may have had for his mother were completely dead. "She done pushed me beyond the limit of my caring," he has said. "I don't say it's her fault. It's her life. I was just stretched to a point where I wasn't going to be pushed no further."

Actually, the wound alone would not have proved fatal, but Henry's sister didn't find Viola until the next day, almost fourteen hours later and too late to save the woman. Opal brought Viola to the hospital, but the woman was old, weakened because she was an alcoholic, and the complications resulting from the wound and her prolonged period of hemorrhaging had made her injuries critical. It was impossible to save her, and Viola died in the hospital. The records said Viola died of a heart attack precipitated by the knife wound. She had simply bled until she went into shock and could not be restabilized. For Henry, it was a charge of murder in the second

49

degree. Years later he maintained that he was falsely accused of murder when he was only defending himself against her attack. But he pleaded guilty to the charges and was convicted by a Michigan court that sentenced him to the State Prison of Southern Michigan for 20 to 40 years.

"My mother always told me that I was going to die in prison," Lucas said. "And she had all of this control over me, and she wouldn't let me leave and she wouldn't let me get married because she wanted someone to do the bootlegging for her. She even told my sister that I was going to die in prison. I always felt I was always under the curse of her. And then when I was found guilty for murdering her, and I knew I did not, and went to prison, I felt she was controlling me, even though she was dead. And I had this nervous breakdown, and was in prison for six years."

Chapter 3

Prison In Michigan

"She did it!" Henry says of his mother. "She got me into prison by dying of a heart attack after I hit her and then once I was in prison, she kept talking to me inside my head." Lucas has described his experiences at Southern Michigan as a nightmare that would not end. In the dead of night, the voices would come to him. There would be different voices, a multitude of voices intruding into his consciousness, arousing him from sleep and tormenting him during the night. Lucas felt he couldn't resist the voices pushing him into destructive behavior.

"How could your mother be responsible for your problems in Michigan when she was already dead?" he was asked by psychologists in Texas.

"I kept hearing her talking to me and telling me to do things . . . and I couldn't do it," Lucas says. "Had one voice that was tryin' to make me commit suicide, and I wouldn't do it. I had one tell me not to do anything they told me to do." Lucas realized that the voice was in his imagination, but it sounded as if were real. "Now I know it was my imagination, but back then it was just as real as if I had sat there and heard it. I wouldn't see things. It was just sounds."

The voices, he says, were literally driving him crazy. He was getting no sleep at night and no peace during the day. The voices surrounded him in his cell and followed him through the cellblock. They hounded him, urging him, ordering him. It got so bad that he began looking for help from anyone who would listen to him, even from his own family. In his second year at Southern Michigan, Henry wrote a letter to his sister Opal saying he was going to kill himself. He kept hearing his mother's voice, he said, telling him to do "bad things" and reminding him of his destiny of death inside prison walls. He says he told the prison doctors and guards about the voices telling him to kill himself and hurt others, but they wouldn't listen. They either ignored him, he says, or laughed at him. But the voice kept telling him not to do what the guards told him to do and to kill himself. So first, he refused to obey orders.

"I got in a fight with one of the officers. He ordered me to go in my cell and I told him I wasn't going in it, and we started fightin' there on the gallery. So the guy on the tower, he shot me through the shoulder, and we was still fightin'. So they called the goon squad out. And the goon squad come in and they tried to break us up, and three or four other guys got into it, and we eventually all got tired and quit. Everybody got locked up. They had a big investigation."

That was the beginning of Henry's attempts to get the prison administration to notice him.

He also attempted suicide on two occasions. He sliced his wrist with a razor blade, and later cut across his stomach. The prison doctors placed him in the Ionia State Mental Hospital where he remained for four and half years. Those first six and half years in the Michigan penitentiary and state hospital were some of the most difficult prison years Lucas says he ever experienced. "It was the worst six and half years I've ever seen in my life. I've seen people stoned, kicked, burned to death and everything else in prison."

Lucas says that he did not receive humane treatment in the Ionia mental hospital. "They didn't have no therapy there. You had to walk around on the floor and shine the floor with your feet. They put these cloths over your shoes on your feet, and you'd have to walk the floor, shine the floor. Had to. I'm not kiddin'. They'd beat your brains in if ya didn't."

Lucas was medicated heavily with depressants, antianxiety drugs, and antihallucinogens to control his moods. "They gave me Thorazine. They had me on Benadryls. They had me on Benadryl tablets and had me on liquid Thorazine for a long time. The drugs really didn't help any. To me the Thorazine just made me feel more quiet. It didn't keep me less active. It didn't stop the voices at all, which is what they wanted it to do. It also made me more apt to hurt someone."

As scary as the drug therapy was to Lucas because it was beyond his control, he would face even worse experiences at Ionia. "After the Thorazine, they gave me shock treatments. The only thing I remember about them is what I was told. They kept giving them to me over and over again until I couldn't do nothin' for myself. Then they took me back to where I was just a baby. And they had to relearn me to eat, to walk, everything. There was nothin' I could do."

In fact, Lucas became a guinea pig at Ionia state. He was subjected to behavioral therapy designed to break his will and make him compliant, drug therapy designed to alter his moods and temper his anxiety so as to make him more passive, and painful shock treatments which ultimately were supposed to make him more compliant to the system. At first, the shock treatments were administered, according to Henry, without any mediating drugs. He says that he bore the full surge of electricity which sent him into convulsions and then unconsciousness. Without the muscle relaxant sodium pentothal, the treatments were a painful experience, leaving him rigid and tremorous after each shock. Eventually, the doctors relented and by administering an anesthetic, they allowed him to escape some of the pain associated with the trauma. Nonetheless, the types of shock treatments that were routinely performed in the early 1960s were a violent and painful form of invasive medicine that left patients disoriented and suffering from memory lapses.

These crude psycho-medical procedures made Lucas mean and determined to get back at the doctors who had, in his words, "tortured" him. "I was locked up in one cell for six and a half years. Talked to the doctors once in a while. I described to them several times the things I had done in the past and what I would do if I got out of prison. I told them that if I got out I would go back to killing. And that's what I done."

His psychiatric transfer summary from Southern Michigan State Prison to Ionia describes Lucas as "compliant," although the evaluator, Phillip Bannan, writes that Lucas describes "deep feelings of depersonalization which in his words seem to be an empty feeling and a recurring impression of just drifting on air. He further states that he daydreams of being somewhere else and during these experiences it is though he is really there." The report states that Lucas has a significant inferiority complex and a general lack of self confidence, self reliance, will power, and perseverance. It indicates further that he is a schizophrenic with only a "fair" prognosis for recovery and recommends an immediate transfer to Ionia.

Lucas' August, 1961, admittance form to Ionia State Hospital describes the patient as "potentially dangerous, no outside privileges."

Lucas says that the treatment he received in Ionia transformed him. First of all, he explains, none of the doctors in attendance seemed to understand that he fully intended to kill upon his release from prison. Second, he remarked that he was so brutalized by the conditions at Ionia, the drugs that he had to take against his will and his being strapped into a chair and convulsing in pain from electroshock treatment — as if he were being electrocuted — that he learned what it was like to be tortured. Henry says he learned to follow the rules, and he knew that no matter what he told the doctors at Ionia, he would soon be getting out.

In 1966, the psychiatrists at Ionia transferred him back to the State Prison of Southern Michigan, and one official wrote to the parole board suggesting "I would say that he is making good progress. I am impressed by his growth." Another report stated, "He is grossly lacking in self-confidence, self-reliance, will power, and general stamina. He does not have the courage to blame others for mistakes or misfortunes or to engage in aggressive social behavior aimed at alleviating some of his discomfort."

Henry himself says that he had learned true viciousness from his experience. "I learned to be mean. I learned every way there is for law enforcement. I learned every way there is in different crimes, I studied it," Lucas explains. He told the psychologists who interviewed him years later that he wanted to learn how crimes were committed so that he would be proficient at it. By studying police procedures, he said, he intended to avoid being caught. "After I got out of that hospital, they put me in the records room. And every record that jumped through there, I would read it, study it, and see how what got who caught. I intended on doing these crimes when I got out. I was planning to kill."

Years after he told psychologists how he learned police procedures in prison, he told a television interviewer how he eluded police searches. In prison, he said, he discovered that police routinely did not coordinate their searches. Homicides in one jurisdiction, even vicious homicides, would not necessarily be reported in another jurisdiction. And even when police reported them, there was little cooperation among the agencies. Once he committed a crime—usually a spree of robberies and felony homicides—he knew that he had merely to jump across a state line to avoid being caught in a police dragnet. After he committed a spree of crimes in the second state, he would be in a third state before police in the first two states realized they were looking for the same perpetrator and coordinated their efforts. He would be gone from the third state before any connections were made to the first two sprees and across the country. In this way, he would brag, he would follow his own headlines from the safe distance of two or three states away without the worry that the police would try to track him down.

Henry Lee Lucas served four more years in Southern Michigan before severe overcrowded conditions in the cell block forced the warden to begin early release procedures. But, Lucas maintains, he didn't want to leave prison. He says he told the officers who notified him of his early parole that he wasn't ready to leave, he hadn't been rehabilitated, he was still a killer. "I told them all—the warden, the psychologist, everybody—that I was going to kill. I told them I was serious. When they come in and put me out on parole, I said I'm not ready to go, I'm not going. They said it was too crowded. They said 'you're going if we have to throw you out'." Lucas made them a grim promise. "So I said 'I'll leave you

57

a present on the doorstep on the way out.' "

Lucas bragged several times years later that he had told the Ionia officials that they should not release him or he would kill again. He was released in June of 1970 and claims to have left the prison and killed two women almost within sight of the walls. He says that he left one of the bodies within a block of the prison, but law enforcement officials have been unable to confirm the murders. "I told them I would kill if they let me out and I did. I did it the same day, down the road a bit. It wasn't too far away from the prison. I killed a woman down in Jackson, Michigan. I took her up to next to the prison and killed her within walking distance of the prison. They suspected me, but they couldn't prove nothing."

Lucas says that he didn't kill for sexual reasons, he did it for revenge. "I gave them something they gonna remember! Then when I cleared it up here a while back, they said, 'Well, I didn't think you were going to do that'. They know now, that I meant what I said. I was bitter at the world. I hated everything. There wan't nothin' I liked. I was as bitter as bitter could be."

A little over a year after his release from Southern Michigan, Lucas was arrested in Lenawee County, Michigan, for an attempted kidnapping of a fifteen year old girl waiting for a schoolbus. According to psychiatric records from the State Department Medical Center for Forensic Psychiatry in Ann Arbor, Lucas was trolling in his car alongside a young girl on her way to school. Lucas stopped his car beside her and said "Get in or I'll shoot you." The young woman refused to get into the car and tried to walk away but Lucas got out of the car and confronted her. "Your boyfriend told me to shoot you because your going out on him," Lucas said. The girl asked Lucas what her boyfriend's name was and Lucas couldn't answer. When the schoolbus arrived, Lucas told the girl she was lucky this time, but that he'd catch up to her later. He drove away. She later filed a criminal complaint with the county sheriff and Lucas was arrested, held in the county lockup for seven weeks, and transferred to the Center for Forensic Psychiatry for bail evaluation.

The district attorney raised the possibility that because of Lucas' previous mental history, his years at Ionia, and his suicide attempts that preceded his transfer to Ionia, he was probably not competent to stand trial. Newton Jackson, the Center's evaluator, wrote that despite Lucas' "disheveled, unkempt, and dirty" appearance, his "schizoid sort of smile," and his "poor insight," he was competent to stand trial. He felt that Lucas might be judged not guilty because he had a history of being maintained on the drug thorazine which he was not taking at the time of the attempted kidnapping. Further, Jackson wrote, although he couldn't specifically recommend against bail because of Lucas' clinical condition, it was probably unlikely that Lucas would return to the court for trial. "It is very likely," the psychologist wrote about Lucas, "that further difficulties with the law will be encountered by him in the foreseeable future." Dr. Jackson's insight was highly prophetic. Henry Lee Lucas was ultimately adjudged competent to stand trial, and was convicted of the attempted kidnapping of the fifteen-year-old girl in Lewanee County. He was eventually found guilty of a parole violation as well.

Chapter 4
Henry and Ottis

In 1971, Henry Lee Lucas was back in prison again. He spent four years in a Michigan state penitentiary for the attempted kidnapping of a teenaged girl and for violating his parole by carrying a gun. According to a variety of records and interviews, Henry was released in late August, 1975, and took a bus back east to Perryville, Maryland, where he was met by his half-sister Almeda Kiser and her daughter Aomia Pierce. Henry said he wanted to "hole up" for a while and make some money.

He didn't. The ensuing thirteen years eventually turned into the period of the greatest controversy in his life. Did he become a hopeless drifter who worked at odd jobs here and there, mooched off relatives, and generally did very little while accomplishing even less? Or, as law enforcement agencies believe, did he set out on one of the longest serial killing sprees in the annals of American crime? Having killed once, with certainty, and having said that he killed at least two more times subsequent to his release from Southern Michigan State Prison, did he kill again and again? After his arrest in Montague County, Texas, he told police that he wandered from state to state, murdering people at random, that he met up with Ottis Toole in Florida and entered into a homosexual relationship with him and that the two of them with Toole's niece and nephew set off as a rag-tag band of vagrants robbing their way across the southern United States.

Records from the McLennon County grand jury investigation do show that Lucas stayed at the Kiser home in Port Deposit, Maryland, for about three days before moving in with Aomia Pierce and her husband, Darcell, in Chatham, Pennsylvania for about three months. While he was living with the Pierces, Lucas drifted through four or five jobs, one after the other. During this time, he also began dating Betty Crawford, the widow of one of his nephews who had died in an electrical accident while he was working. He considered her family, and originally began seeing her as a friend. On December 5, 1975, Henry and Betty were married.

According to records, immediately after they were married, Lucas, Betty Crawford, and Betty's three children stayed with Pierces for a few days while they looked for a place to live. Henry found them a house which they rented in Port Deposit where they lived for a short time while Henry looked for a place with more room. He finally wound up buying a used mobile home which they moved to lot C-3 at

Benjamin's Trailer Park in Port Deposit in January, 1976.

Lucas could not hold down a steady job. He did some car repair work whenever he could find it, collected and sold junk. Henry also helped out his brother-in-law Wade Kiser by stripping out junked cars for scrap, for which he was paid a small hourly or daily wage. Lucas only brought a minimal amount of money into the family. Their primary sources of funds were Betty's Social Security check, public assistance, and food stamps. Lucas tried to reopen an old public assistance file he had started back in 1970, adding Betty and the children to the family, but they were rejected for everything except the food stamps.

During this period, Henry also began buying, fixing, and reselling several junk cars which he was able to drive on Wade Kiser's wrecker tags. Wade was a salvage and wrecker operator who was able to put state license tags on the vehicles he was salvaging and transporting. Lucas used that to drive around the cars he was trying to resell, thus avoiding the need to pass them through state DMV registration procedures.

Lucas has told a slightly different story about this period.

From time to time, Lucas says, he sought to escape from the relentlessness of holding down multiple jobs and the responsibilities of managing the house while Betty lived off his labor. He complained to her, he has told interviewers. He tried to get her and her children to take care of the house and pitch in with money while he was working, but nobody would help him. Even Betty's attitude seemed strangely distant, as if she'd married Henry for the work he could do and the money he could bring in. Part of him believed that it was almost like being back in the Virginia hill cabin with his mother. Henry was getting restless and unhappy.

The McLennon County report says that the Lucases and the Ben Plaskis, a family they met at the trailer park, left Maryland in June, 1977, for Hurst, Texas, where Betty visited her mother and Henry looked for work. He couldn't find a job so both families drove to Illinois, pulling everything they owned behind them in a U-Haul. The Plaskis decided to stay in Illinois while the Lucases returned to Maryland.

Within the month, Henry and Betty separated and Betty went back to using her husband's name. However, years later investigators claim to have learned that Lucas began to molest Betty Crawford's daughters sexually throughout the time they were living together. The investigators do not know whether Betty knew about the sexual molestation while it was happening, or whether it was the sexual molestation that led to the breakup of the marriage.

Other sources say that Lucas would occasionally leave Port Deposit to go on drinking sprees. But there are no arrest records concerning him or any other information detailing his whereabouts until

1977. In July, 1977, Betty Crawford accused Henry of molesting her two daughters. Lucas denied the charges completely, but left his wife, Betty, and her family in Maryland on July 7 and headed south toward Florida. He was never charged with child molestation.

The McLennon County report says that after Lucas left Betty, he moved in with relatives Opal Jennings and Nora Crawford. While living with Opal, Lucas traveled to a family reunion in West Virginia with his brother-in-law Wade Kiser. They left Port Deposit on July 28, 1977, but got held up in a traffic line when they hit bridge construction over Harper's Ferry, West Virginia. While waiting on the line, Lucas and Kiser struck up a conversation with a stranger with whom Lucas agreed to travel to Shreveport, Louisiana. Kiser said that while he was enroute to Louisiana, Lucas stopped off in Lindhurst, Virginia, to visit his half brother, Harry Waugh. He then continued to Shreveport before he headed back north.

Henry's sister Almeda Kiser says that Henry called her collect from Knoxville, Tennessee, and again from Bowie, Maryland, to tell her that he'd been stopped by the state police for hitchhiking. Her husband, Wade, said that Henry and the stranger went from Harper's Ferry to Henton, West Virginia, and from there to Tennessee and on to Shreveport, where Henry was supposed to pick up a car to drive to Los Angeles. But Henry got scared of the guy, Wade says, because "he thought he was

Mafia or something, and ran."

The McLennon County report says that Lucas went from Port Deposit to Wilmington, Delaware, where he laid carpet with Leland Crawford, one of his relatives, at a local carpet outlet. He returned to Port Deposit to live with Nora Crawford, another relative, over Christmas, 1977, and then left for Hinton, West Virginia, where he worked with Joe Crawford, another relative, at a carpet outlet in Beckley, West Virginia. It was there, according to records, that he met Rhonda Knuckles with whom he lived from January, 1978, until March, 1978, when he returned to Port Deposit.

In May, 1978, Henry helped Opal Jennings move her trailer to a new lot and helped her put up her canning later in the year. At about the same time, he moved in with his sister Almeda and her husband and worked in the wrecking yard. But in February, 1979, Almeda confronted Lucas with her granddaughter's bloodstained underpants. Lucas denied abusing the child or doing anything wrong, but he offered to leave. Almeda told him that he didn't have to leave unless he molested the child.

The next morning, however, Lucas left the house with Randy Kiser's pickup truck, supposedly to strip some cars over in the yard. Wade Kiser said that he didn't feel well and didn't go out. Wade told the investigators he became concerned, however, when Lucas didn't return home for coffee or lunch. Wade and one of his sons followed the truck's tire tracks out of the yard and onto the road. When Lucas failed to return to the house the next day, the Kisers reported the truck stolen along with tools that were inside. A day or two later, they were told by police that the truck had been recovered near Jacksonville, Florida, but that the tools in the truck were missing. The truck was inoperable, the Kisers were told, and not worth the trip to Florida to recover it, the report says.

Here, the records of Lucas' movements and his association with Ottis Toole become very vague. Lucas himself has told different stories to different people, as has Ottis Toole. However, according to the McLennon County report, Henry Lee Lucas arrived in Jacksonville, Florida, on February 11, 1979. Randy Kiser's pickup had quit running and Lucas had abandonded it. Lucas said that he was near a police station and told the officers that he was leaving the truck. The county police officers ran an NCIC check on the truck, which came back clear, and Lucas left the area. Henry himself says that he told the police the truck was stolen, but they let him walk anyway.

Henry hitchhiked into Jacksonville where he learned of a mission that provided food and a bunk. While waiting for the food line to open, he was approached by Ottis Toole and invited back to Toole's home in the Springfield section of the city. Living there at the time were Ottis' mother, Sarah Harley, her husband, Robert, Ottis's wife Novella, Ottis' ten-year-old nephew Frank Powell, Jr., and his eleven-year-old neice Frieda Lorraine Powell, whom

Henry called Becky. The report explains that Frank and Becky were cared for by Sarah Harley because the children's mother, Drucilla Arzetta Carr, was incable of caring for them.

According to his relatives, Ottis frequented the mission to pickup homosexual and bisexual lovers. Sarah Pierce, who had lived intermittently with the Tooles from time to time, told police that Ottis preferred bisexual lovers because in addition to his own relations with them, he liked to watch them have sex with her and occasionally with Becky Powell.

Ottis moved Henry into the upstairs bedroom he shared with his wife while his wife, Novella, moved out and went over to the neighbors. A few days later, Ottis got Henry a job at Southeast Colorcoat, a business owned by the Reeves family. The report says that Ottis had done this before for men he had picked up at the mission. Ottis had worked for the Reeves for seven or eight years, and the house he lived in was owned by the Reeves.

Lucas worked for about a month at Colorcoat. Then he went north with a companion who returned without him. Lucas himself had been hospitalized while up north because he had been attacked by Joe Kiser, one of his relatives. Another version of the story says that Lucas was beaten up by one of his brothers-in-law. After three days in the hospital, Lucas was transferred to a mission and from there he returned to Jacksonville and went back to work for Southeast Colorcoat.

In 1980, Ottis' mother Sarah bought a house on

Louise street and the whole "family," including Henry, moved. Henry had left Southeast Colorcoat at about this time and had gone into the junk sales and metal scrapping business full-time, dealing with local scrap metal companies in the Jacksonville area. Lucas sold cars, tin, cast iron, aluminum, aluminum cans, batteries, and radiators. He and Ottis used the house's backyard to store some of the junk and metal scrap, causing the neighbors to complain and Lucas and Toole to build a fence around the yard. At about this time as well, Becky began spending more and more time with Henry and accompanying him on junk-buying outings and trips to scrapyards. They continued living this way for the next year until Ottis' mother, Sarah, died on May 16, 1981. Lucas and Toole took Frank and Becky and headed west to California.

Henry, Ottis, Frank, Becky, and Becky's dog were gone from Jacksonville for about two to three weeks. They traveled through Houston, through Del Rio where they sold the truck, and to Tucson where Henry was ticketed for allowing Becky's dog loose in a city park. By the time they reached Arizona, the children had become homesick, so Henry and Ottis packed up their trip, hopped a slow-moving freight and rumbled back into Houston. From there they hitchhiked back to Jacksonville.

Once back in Jacksonville in June, Henry and Ottis helped Howard Toole get back his pickup that had been repossessed by the person who had sold it to him. Howard later reported to police that the pickup was stolen in July. It was recovered in Wilmington, Delaware, on July 8, 1981, where Ottis, Henry, Frank, and Becky had received Travelers Aid lodging and money. Lucas and Toole applied for food stamps in Wilmington on July 2. The Delaware State Police made NCIC inquiries on Lucas and Toole during July. Toole returned to Jacksonville toward the end of the month after having been hospitalized for illness in Virginia.

From Delaware, Lucas traveled to Maryland where he was arrested for the theft of Randy Kiser's pickup. This was the same charge that Hound Dog Conway would use to hold Lucas in a Texas jail prior to his confession to the murder of Becky Powell. He was held in jail from July 22 to October 6, where he was paroled to the Probation Department office in Elkton. His probation was later transferred to Jacksonville where Lucas had moved into an apartment occupied by Ottis and Novella Toole and a Betty Goodyear, who had let the Tooles and Lucas use the spare rooms in the apartment in exchange for work they performed for her. Becky and Frank had been remanded into their mother's custody in Auburndale.

In December, 1981, Drucilla Carr, Becky's and Frank's mother, committed suicide. Becky was sent to a Florida Department of Health and Rehabilitative Services Emergency Shelter in Bartow. She ran away from the shelter on January 3, 1982, and a "pickup" order was issued for her on January 5. The Jacksonville sheriff made inquiries about Lucas and Toole because he believed that Lucas had picked Becky up at the Bartow shelter and brought her back to Jacksonville. Lucas bought a vehicle on January 9, transferred the insurance on January 10, and left Jacksonville right about that time because he learned that the police were looking for Becky and him.

Ottis Toole, the McLennon County report says, continued living with his wife until the first part of May in 1982 when he and Novella left Jacksonville enroute to California. Novella told investigators that Ottis intended to find work in California, but while traveling across Texas, he picked up a hitchhiker named Kevin who was wearing a military uniform. The hitchhiker wrecked the car, causing Novella and Ottis to spend time in a hospital. After their release, Novella returned to Jacksonville while Ottis remained in Texas to work at a fence factory. He later hitchhiked back Jacksonville.

According to a different version of the story, beginning in 1979, Lucas drifted around committing burglaries here and there, knocking over convenience stores and gas stations, and even committing personal assaults and rapes until he wound up broke and hungry in a Jacksonville, Florida, soup kitchen where he met Ottis Toole. The two of them, according to this verdion of the story, became friends. Lucas told Toole that he had an electrician's license that he'd picked up in prison and that he was a mechanic. Toole took Lucas back to live with his family while Lucas helped support them through manual labor.

According to police sources, Ottis Toole confessed to a double homicide that he and Lucas allegedly perpetrated on November 5, 1978. The killing pair crossed paths with a young couple enroute to Georgetown, Texas, who had run out of gas on Texas I-35 just south of Round Rock. The couple—they were both teenagers—locked their car and started walking when Henry and Ottis pulled up in their car. Ottis pulled out a .22 handgun—Ottis always said that a .22 was his favorite weapon—and the victims froze. While Lucas forced the eighteen-year-old girl into the car, Toole pumped nine rounds into the young man's head and chest and rolled the bloody corpse into a ditch. With the girl still shaking from seeing her traveling companion murdered before her eyes, Lucas and Toole drove her away north toward Waco.

Ottis was driving when Henry raped the young woman the first time. He raped her repeatedly in the back seat while an angry Toole sat hunched over behind the wheel. Finally, just south of Waco, Toole stopped the car and ordered the girl out. In a fury that Henry was having intercourse with someone else, Toole fired six rounds into the girl and left her there on the northbound service road. Henry and Ottis drove off. Neither one has said what they talked about. All the records show is that Henry and Ottis returned to Jacksonville, Florida, in February, 1979 where Henry again took up residence with Toole's sister and became, in his words, the "guardian" of Toole's niece Frieda "Becky" Powell and his nephew Frank Powell.

In a third version of the story, which Henry Lee Lucas himself told after his conversion to fundamentalist Christianity in 1983 and wrote in a book entitled *The Hand of Death* that he co-authored with Max Call, Henry walked out on Betty Crawford and her children in Maryland in early 1977 because he could no longer support the entire family without any help. He was fed up with family life completely and drove west toward Pennsylvania's coal country where he quickly found a job running a loader at a mushroom farm outside of Carbondale. Another laborer at the farm was a taller, more powerfully built man named Ottis Toole who worked in the greenhouses. Ottis told Henry he'd been watching him for the better part of a week and invited him into town to go drinking.

The two men quickly struck up a friendship and spent their off hours drinking and cruising and eventually robbing small stores and gas stations along the township roads of western Pennsylvania, Ohio, Michigan, Indiana, Illinois, and Wisconsin. Henry said that he and Ottis began driving farther away from Pennsylvania with each junket and escalating the intensity and brutality of their crimes. If a store clerk resisted them in Georgia or a bank clerk didn't fork over the money quickly enough, Ottis would blow the victim away without saying another word. Lucas says he was more reasonable and would at least give a warning before doing any killing.

Lucas remembered one time in particular—and this was in a confession that he gave to the Georgia Bureau of Investigation—that he and Ottis robbed a convenience store in rural Georgia near the western border of the state. While Lucas pulled a .22 on the young woman standing behind the register and held it to her temple, Toole tied the struggling woman up and dragged her to the back. She started to scream and Lucas said, "Now you be quiet or I'm gonna have to shoot ya." She quieted down until Lucas and Toole had gone to the register when she started to resist again. Lucas returned to the back where he shot her through the temple. Toole had intercourse with her remains, and the two of them loaded cases of beer into the trunk of their car and drove off. Lucas told the story to the GBI agents as dispassionately as if he was reporting the news of someone else's crime. But he wanted to make it clear that he had at least given a warning.

Lucas has said that he and Ottis did not kill everywhere they went. If they were able to rob a store without resistance and without trouble, and if Toole wasn't particularly crazed, they would leave the scene without any vioience. However, hitch-hikers, vagrants, women with car trouble, strangers they picked up along the way were all potential victims, and most of them were killed by either Henry or Ottis. These were all crimes of opportunity, and none of them had any witnesses. In fact, years later when Henry and Ottis began mutually confessing to their murder sprees, the police were hard-pressed to find people who remembered the pair of drifters in the municipalities they talked about. Most of the people who might have testified against them were murdered.

Police said they were partly able to develop an itinerary for Henry Lee Lucas and Ottis Toole by tracking the registration numbers on the hulks of their cars that still littered some of the roadsides even years after they had abandoned them. Henry was a skilled mechanic and could extend the life of any car well past 100,000 miles, even if the car was barely working. He and Ottis would steal a vehicle and kill its driver, run the car or truck across three or four states, steal another car, hitchhike to a new location when that car died, and find another vehicle. Often the two lived out of their cars and ate at soup kitchens in church basements or at local storefront rescue missions and sold their blood for spending cash. They were always on the wrong side of the poverty line, even when they had the petty cash they had robbed from the convenience store registers. When they could find odd jobs, they worked as roofers, did construction, cleared fields, hauled trash, or cleaned up backyards.

Their crimes continued to escalate until the two of them were hired on as contract killers by an organization that had contacted Toole. Lucas said that he didn't question Ottis at all when he brought up "murders for hire." He only assumed that Ottis, in his words, "was in tight with people with a lot of money who wanted jobs done." Henry may not have understood much, he confessed to police years later, but he understood money in his pocket. After the second of the contract murders while the two of them were still in Texas, Toole said the two of them should split up for a while. Ottis said he would head back to Florida where Henry could reach him. Henry agreed and said that he would go back to Maryland and his half sister.

Henry's one sister, Opal, was still mad at him, he thought, because he had murdered his mother. Maybe his other sister, Almeda, would take him in despite his having walked out on his wife Betty, who was also Almeda's friend. But Almeda, according to this version of the story, was also mad at Lucas because she blamed him for the death of their mother. Shortly after Henry took up residence, Almeda turned on him. She accused Lucas of molesting her eight-year-old granddaughter and threatened to call the police if Henry didn't leave. Lucas says he didn't even argue. In his version of the events, he says his first thoughts were for the child who would find herself at the center of a sexual molestation controversy. He warned his sister, he told interviewers later, that by filing charges and forcing the little girl to corroborate a story that the mother was fabricating to get her half-brother out of the house, Almeda would be "ruining" the child's life. Lucas says he snatched up the keys to the family pickup he'd helped to resurrect and drove it south to Florida where he hooked up with Ottis again.

This time, Ottis invited Henry to come back with him to Jacksonville where he could live with the Powells. Within months, he and Ottis were on the road again, traveling between Maryland and California, Texas and Michigan, on a spree of robbing, mayhem, and murder.

Whichever version chroniclers believe to be true, all the records agree that by early 1979 Lucas and Toole were living in Jacksonville, Florida, with the Powells and that Henry had taken a fancy to Ottis' twelve-year-old niece Frieda. Her mother even told Henry that he should become her guardian because her real father "didn't give one good damn about either of his kids," and Becky and her brother Frank liked Henry more than their father anyway. How could Ottis' sister have known that in only three years, Henry would kill Becky with a knife, have sex with her remains, and mutilate her body.

Henry and Ottis took a quick trip to Michigan later in February of 1979 where they committed a string of robberies. In Lucas' confession, he remembered one brutal robbery of a small store in Rising Sun before heading back to Jacksonville in March, where he bought another pickup truck. This would be their transportation. Incapable of staying in one place for long, Lucas and Toole had planned another long circuit across the Interstates of the south and west where the two rootless vagrants could exercise their lust and aggression on unsuspecting victims. In their new used pickup, they set out, this time together with the children Frank and Becky Powell, on one of the most notorious crime sprees in American history.

On October 3, 1979, according to Lucas' confession, almost six months after Lucas and Toole had left Jacksonville with Becky and Frank, they pulled up behind a 34-year-old white woman who had developed car trouble along I-35 and William Cannon Blvd. in Austin, Texas. She was parked alongside the road. The four travellers had abandoned the pickup by this point and were driving a 1971 Chevy Malibu. Lucas saw the woman with car trouble and offered to help. He explained years later that women with car trouble along the road were free lunch.

"I'd offer to look under the hood," he once told an interviewer. "But even if I seen something wrong, I wouldn't fix it. I'd say, 'looks like this engine's had it,' and offer to drive her to a phone. But we'd never get to a phone. By the time she'd see the phone passin' by, she'd know she was a goner."

Maybe that's what happened to the young woman Henry, Ottis, Frank, and Becky encountered in Austin. Henry got out to look under the hood and pronounced the engine dead. Witnesses say they saw the Malibu parked behind the woman's car for hours. Later, witnesses say they noticed that the Malibu was gone and so was the woman. Her car remained there for days. On October 8th the woman's body was found in a field off I-35 in Travis

County. She was completely nude and had been stabbed 35 times in the upper chest, neck, upper arms, and back. There was also a wound just below her right breast and another just over her right forehead. Her attacker had made a long cut from her right wrist, along the inside of her arm to a center point on her chest, and from there straight down through the center line of her body to her pubic area. It was if she were a frog that had been dissected in a high school biology lab lesson. The tips of her nipples had been sliced off her breasts. Evidently, from the lack of garment threads in the wounds, the woman had been forced to undress prior to the stabbing. Her killers had taken her diamond watch, her diamond ring, and her credit cards.

Henry Lee Lucas confessed to the crime.

On October 31, Lucas murdered the young woman Boutwell named Orange Socks while he and she were parked along the shoulder of a Texas interstate. He dumped her body in a culvert alongside the road where she was discovered by a passerby. Her murder remained unsolved for years. But Lucas eventually confessed to the crime, was tried for the crime, was found guilty, and has been sentenced to death. The body is still unidentified.

Paradoxically, there is a work time sheet with Southeastern Roofing Company in Jacksonville, Florida which states that Henry Lee Lucas was working there part time from August 1, 1979 to December 26, 1979 and from January 2, 1980 to

January 9, 1980. Had Ottis gone back to Jacksonville and signed his time sheets in Henry's name? Had someone else used Henry's name? Yet, Lucas gave police information about Orange Socks that only someone who had been intimate with her would have known.

On March 19, 1980, work records show that Lucas was paid for 10 1/2 hours of labor with the Southeastern Roofing Company in Jacksonville. Two months later, he was charged with theft of a gun in Jacksonville. At that point, Lucas seems to disappear for almost a year, surfacing again in March of 1981 when he was alleged to have abducted a twenty-two-year-old woman from a phone booth outside a convenience store in east Texas at around 11:30 at night. Her body was found the next day between the railroad tracks and the Brazos River east of Richmond. She had been murdered, stabbed and cut 12 times with two different knives in the lower back and buttocks areas.

The fatal blow appeared to be a single stab wound in the right side of her neck. Police think she was probably sexually molested because she was menstruating at the time and the tampon she was wearing was forced as far as anatomically possible up into her cervix. Whatever had happened to her, police speculate, was unbelievably painful.

Just nine days later, Lucas is again alleged to have murdered a woman, this time a forty-six-year-old in her mobile home in Odessa, Texas. Lucas confessed to this crime, telling the police that this was the only victim he ever killed in a mobile home. He says that he stabbed her and raped her while Ottis killed her by strangling her with a telephone cord. Henry raped her again after she was dead and Ottis tore off most of her right breast with his teeth.

The following month, Henry, Ottis, and the kids were on their way back to Jacksonville when they stopped in Monroe, Louisiana, where they killed a clerk in a convenience store. Henry described it as a robbery in which Ottis killed the clerk with his .22 for the thrill of it and then "we had sex with the body." Frank and Becky were in the car during the robbery. The group then continued on toward Florida, reaching Jacksonville a couple of weeks later. They took up residence with Ottis' sister again while Henry worked at construction jobs to support the family. Medical records from the following month indicate that Lucas sold blood to the Alpha Blood Bank in Houston. Lucas himself describes this period as a time during which he and Ottis were back and forth across the south, never in one place for more than a few hours.

Perhaps the most horrific story Henry told police authorities concerned his travels through Georgia with Ottis and the two children. During a two-week rampage in 1980, Lucas and Toole circled around the entire state from the southern coastline just north of Jacksonville, to the Savannah coast, to Brunswick, and west to the Alabama border. Along the way, they robbed, raped, and killed. In 1984,

Lucas gave a chilling account of this murder spree to agents of the Georgia Bureau of Investigation.

First, he said, just over the Georgia state line he and Ottis abducted a sixteen-year-old girl from town and killed her, dumping her body along the shore of an artificially dredged lake. Further north in Brunswick, he and Ottis tried to rob a convenience store on a Sunday. Henry said that he and his companion got pissed off when they tried to buy beer on Sunday and were told by the man behind the counter that there was no beer for sale. "We went back there and Ottis shot him," Henry said. "He was mad because he wanted beer."

In Savannah, Henry recalled, "we picked up a blondish young girl at a truck stop and drove her south. We took her to a pond back in the woods and we killed her. After she was dead, Ottis mutilated the body and left her there." Near Heinzville Henry kidnapped a woman out of a parking lot at a YMCA. Henry stabbed her while Frank and Becky stood there and watched. "She was sort of a middle-aged white woman," Henry said to the Georgia investigators. Near Dublin, Georgia, Henry said they attempted an armed robbery and "Ottis killed an unarmed man inside the store, a convenience store." And just over the Alabama border in the south west corner of the state, Henry said "I personally killed a resident, a white female." Further away in Donaldsonville, "We went to a convenience store and Ottis and Becky went in and then Becky got back in the car. I drove the car down the road apiece and parked. It was a female that was killed in the bathroom in the store. Ottis killed her."

Outside of Albany, Georgia, Henry said that that was also a store where "I had gone looking for a place to rob, to break into. A white woman was inside and we tied the white woman up and I stabbed her in the back part of the store." And on the state line, Henry and Ottis stopped at what he calls a "Mom 'n Pop" store. Henry said that he went in and attempted to rob the store. He came upon a man who confronted him. Henry stabbed him and the man chased him outside the store where Henry turned on him and stabbed him until he died. In Douglasville, Henry and Ottis picked up a white young man in a bar and took him out in the country. Ottis was turned on and tried to force the young man to have sex with him. But the man said that Ottis was too dirty and wouldn't have sex with him until he cleaned up. Ottis became so frantic and furious that, Henry said, "Ottis just beat the man to death."

The entire story seemed like a cruel or crude joke. Why would these four people ride through the state of Georgia commiting upwards of ten to fifteen homicides, rapes, and robberies? Henry said that there was no reason for any of it, they were just plain evil. Ottis said that he did it for the thrill, the sheer thrill. He achieved sexual pleasure from watching the pain and suffering of others.

When their Georgia travels came to an end, Henry and Ottis brought the children back to Florida. Henry was off again, this time north to Delaware and Maryland where he was arrested for grand theft auto of Randy Kiser's pickup in Pikesville by the Maryland State police. He spent over three months in custody, from July to October, and when he was released, he headed back to Jacksonville. There he bought a car and worked at construction jobs until the need to travel came over him again.

It was December, 1981, and Ottis' sister was raising hell again about Henry and Ottis dragging the children all over the south. Finally, in December, the state of Florida intervened and remanded Becky Powell into juvenile detention for her own protection and placed in a juvenile home. Henry was disconsolate and Ottis could say or do nothing to cheer him up. Finally, the two of them hatched a plan to take Frank, break Becky out of the home, and drive across the country to California with the whole group. But Frank didn't want to come along, so Henry and Ottis waited until January when Henry bought another car. Then, in mid-January, they broke into the juvenile home and took Becky out. By the time the authorities realized what had happened, they had left the state and were on the road again. By January 20, 1982, they were in Houston, selling blood to the old faithful Alpha Blood Bank. The next day, they abandoned the car that Henry had bought outside of San Antonio along I-10 in a place called Kerrville.

Six days later they stole another car and picked

up a victim along Interstate 20 between Abilene and Colorado City, Texas. They bound and gagged her, strapping her hands behind her with her own bra, and drove her toward Plainview. Before they got there, they had raped her, stabbed her numerous times in her lower left chest, and cut off her head with a sharp instrument. Police surmised that Ottis must have had trouble with the decapitation because he had confessed to chopping her neck into three separate pieces before finally severing her head from her body. They dumped her body and the pieces of her neck on a country road a mile east out of Plainview. They then drove across Texas into Scottsdale, Arizona where they dumped her head in the desert. Henry said years later that he assumed it would simply blend in with the local landscape. The police have never identified the victim—they put her age at between 18 and 45—and they know that she was white. But all other details about her life were completely obliterated.

Henry and Ottis quarreled as they were leaving Texas. Ottis wanted them to head back to Florida and take Becky with them. But Lucas wanted to push west to California. Finally, Ottis left the two of them and went back to Florida. It was the last time, according to Lucas, that his friend and lover Ottis Toole would ever see his niece Becky Powell alive.

Chapter 5

The Hand of Death

"Who the hell got into that organization first?" Henry asked Ottis in the interrogation room of Sheriff Jim Boutwell's Williamson County jail in Georgetown. Local reporters and investigators who had been flooding the Henry Lee Lucas investigative Task Force with requests for interviews and access to the killer who was claiming he had killed upwards of three hundred victims were calling it "Lucas Central."

"I dunno, Henry," Ottis answers. "Seems like you and I got into it together."

"I know, I know." And there is general laughter off camera.

The cryptic nature of this conversation and the scores of interviews that followed it opened up a whole new field of inquiry into the Lucas/Toole spree murders across the south from 1979 through 1982. Henry Lee Lucas called it the work of The Hand of Death, and in interview after interview, after his religious conversion, he talked about the evil the cult preached and practiced. Henry talked about how he was recruited for the cult, and how the cult's bizarre rituals and demands resulted in a constant "flow" of murders as human sacrifices which showed devotion and dedication to the cult's sanctions of evil. Henry even wrote a book about his experiences in the cult and his subsequent conversion, entitled simply *The Hand of Death*.

As Henry described it throughout the months that they cruised across the south half of the United States, sometimes with Frank and Becky in the rear seat, Henry and Ottis behaved like the most devoted of practitioners to the bloody and demonic covenants of The Hand of Death. Upon Henry's self-professed conversion to Christianity, he renounced The Hand of Death as the influence that the evil he called Satan held over his soul. "They were all evil," Henry said, weeping over the murder of his beloved Becky Powell. "They were evil and their ways were evil. Now I got to confess in order to have any life after death."

Henry's story about The Hand of Death begins with a web of intrigue and conspiracy. He was first solicited to join the Hand of Death while he was on the road with Ottis, he once said, although the police reports said that he was driving with Wade Kiser. A man stopped the two of them by a drawbridge in Maryland and offered them what, under normal conditions, would have been the deal of a lifetime: delivering cars across the border to Mexico for $2000 a delivery. They'd have all their expenses paid, and the cars would be top-quality—none of the clunkers Henry bought out of junkyards and then repaired. There was only one hitch, Henry said. The cars were stolen. He had told Ottis "never drive with the evidence to convict you in plain sight." He knew that a stolen car was like a beacon to every cop on the road. Stolen cars were easy to identify, and it only took cops a few minutes to retrieve a stolen car report over the Teletype. If you were an ex-con, a stolen car was your ticket back to an eight-by-ten cell in the state penitentiary. If you crossed a state line, you'd be sent to a federal pen, which was even worse.

Henry said he was polite—Henry always described himself as polite—but he told the stranger that he wasn't interested in transporting stolen cars. "Stolen cars," he told the man, "were things you'd never see me deal in. You might as well carry the evidence right on your back like a flashing neon sign."

Oddly enough, Henry said about the conversation, the man not only appeared relieved to hear Lucas reject his offer so politely, the man offered Lucas an even better deal. "Killin'." Lucas remembered him saying. "Killin' for a group of people who'll pay you thousands of dollars for each contract of execution. You can make $5,000, $10,000 and maybe even more every time you kill for us. You will transport bodies for us, you'll kidnap for us, you'll do what we say."

The money sounded good and the killing part didn't bother Henry in the slightest bit. After all, he said to himself at the time, he was already killing, now he'd be getting paid for it.

"But there's something else," the stranger had told Henry. "You'll have to join our religion. It's different from other religions and once you're in, there's only one way out."

Lucas mused on that for a while, he remembered years later, but it didn't worry him at the time. After all, he thought to himself, he'd seen a lot of religions. "What type of religion?" He finally asked. He believed that the expression on the stranger's face meant that Lucas was supposed to ask what these people were supposed to worship.

"The religion is called The Hand of Death, and we worship the Devil," the stranger told him. "Satan gives us our power. We take you to a training camp and once you're a member, you're in it for life and for life after death."

If he decided to join this group, Henry told himself at the time, he'd be prepared for whatever they had in store for him, even if it meant that he had to join some cult. The money was good, and the organization — whatever it called itself — would give him the freedom to live the life he wanted to. He was a bitter man. He was mad about the hand of cards life had dealt him. He said he'd been stomped on by the world, and now he was ready to give the world back some of the stomping it had given him.

Henry and the stranger went their separate ways for the time being. Henry wasn't about to ride anywhere in a stolen car and figured he could hitchhike and bum his way south to Florida where he'd meet up with Ottis. Maybe he'd tell Ottis about The Hand of Death. Maybe they'd join up together. Maybe he wouldn't say a word until he'd scoped out the situation more carefully. Nonetheless, Henry remembers, he knew he had a family waiting for him down in Jacksonville that would put him up until he was ready to move on.

Henry also told another version of the story about his first introduction to the cult. In this different version, he says, he first learned about the cult in Florida when he met Ottis Toole in a Jacksonville Salvation Army storefront. "I was down in Jacksonville and met Ottis Toole one afternoon in a soup kitchen there," Lucas said. "He was a queer and he asked me to go home with him and meet his family, which I did, and I become a part of that family. We got to talking about our crimes and Ottis told me about a cult he was a member of. This reminded me of what my friends had told me in jail, and I told Ottis that I was interested in joining. This pleased Ottis very much and he grinned when I told him. He knew we could be together more and could become partners in crime."

In either version of the story, by 1979, Henry Lee Lucas was living with Ottis Toole and his family in Jacksonville and had made his decision to join the cult that he had heard about. Whether he had heard about it first from Ottis or from the stranger who stopped him on his way south, he remembers telling Ottis that he wanted to visit the cult and wanted Ottis to tell him how to get to the meeting place in Miami.

"I'll do better than that, Henry," Lucas remembers Toole saying. "I'll take you right down to Miami to meet up with this stranger and we'll go through all of it together." Ottis and Henry went down to Miami after Lucas had set himself up in Jacksonville with Ottis' sister to meet with the stranger and learn more about the mysterious group he called The Hand of Death.

They met the stranger in the middle of the night after they'd arrived in Miami. Ottis seemed to know exactly where the meeting place was, a fact not lost on Henry, he remembered years later. It was what looked from the street to be an abandoned warehouse on Miami's seedy waterfront. It was the type of location which in the 1980s would

91

be a setting for drug transactions and smuggling operations. But in 1978, Miami was still a depressed city struggling under double-digit inflation, an inflated dollar that had depressed the import/export market, and a collapsing real estate market that was keeping money out of the city. Even waterfront properties were abandoned and boarded up. This warehouse, outside of which Henry and Ottis were waiting with their car engine and headlights off, was just such a property.

The man they were supposed to meet was the stranger who had first proposed that Henry drive stolen cars for him. Henry had once given his name as Don Meteric, although he said later that he was not sure of his name. Meteric explained to Lucas that he already knew Ottis Toole and that Toole had been the facilitator.

"Ottis here's been doin' work for me for years," the man who Lucas said called himself Meteric revealed. "Why, I'm sure you know that Ottis'd up 'n disappear for a few weeks and come back with a pocket of cash. More'n enough dough for the two of you to go drinkin' 'n whorin' with. Not that you ever paid for what you got." And Meteric laughed until he began coughing so hard Lucas thought he was going to have a heart attack right then and there. Henry didn't get the man's private joke, but laughed along with him and Ottis. The big shock, Henry said years later, was finding out that Ottis already belonged to whatever this organization was supposed to be. Somehow, and Henry said to himself at the time that he would have a long talk with Ottis about it, he believed that Ottis had set this whole thing up from the very beginning to get Henry into this organization. After years of his mother, reform school, juvenile detention, Michigan prisons, and Ionia State Mental Hospital, Lucas had a particularly violent aversion to being manipulated. And he didn't like it now.

Months later, when they were on the road together, Henry asked Toole who he had set him up with Meteric and why he played dumb while Henry was talking about the deals Meteric had offered.

"Because you had to make your own choice," Toole purportedly told him. "There was only one way in and one way out of The Hand of Death. I couldn't get you to join just like I can't get you out. When I met you, I arranged for you to meet Meteric. If after that you decided all by your lonesome to join up, then welcome to The Hand of Death. You see'd the money I was makin'. You had to know that you could make some of it yourself." That satisfied Henry to the point where he didn't feel himself manipulated. By that time, it was too late anyway, because Henry had become an official member of The Hand of Death and had pledged his life and his life after death to darkness.

That night, however — the night that he was inducted into The Hand of Death amidst the dense swamps of the Florida Everglades — was a night that he would never forget. Lucas remembers that Meteric gave him his "standard speech" about dedicating one's life to the Devil and explained to him that he would obey orders unquestioningly or face the same fate as the people he would be ordered to torture and kill. Meteric described a "training camp" that Lucas would attend where he would learn about the sacrifices and rituals The Hand of Death expected its members to organize. "We're a close society, Henry," Meteric explained. "We take care of our own and the Master takes care of us all. But you'll learn about all that at camp. First you'll have to prove yourself by killing someone we tell you to kill. You'll ask no questions and just do exactly what you're told. If you do that, you're one of us." Henry simply nodded his assent — and with that they took off for the Everglades.

They took an airboat into the 'Glades — riding for what seemed like hours through indistinguishable swamps and yazoos. Finally they glided to a pier where Meteric exchanged greetings with a dock man and led Lucas and Toole to a small clearing. "Wait here," he said. And the two of them waited for another person to lead them to a tent where they were to be bunked. "We'll have your assignment for you shortly," Meteric said out of the darkness as Ottis and Henry waited for orders. "Very shortly." And he led them to a tent in the swampy wilderness where Ottis—he had been through this before—kept Lucas talking and waiting until they were summoned.

After what seemed like an hour or more of trying to make conversation with Toole and with two other strangers in the tent, Lucas remembered, Meteric came for them. Lucas had always been restless and not being allowed to talk to other people or to ask other questions, the way he'd go about getting information in bars and prison, made him edgy. Ottis kept telling him: "Don't ask no questions. Speak only when they says somethin' to ya. Don't start no conversations. You ain't here to pow-wow. You're here to join up and then we're on the road."

Normally, that would have been good enough for Henry, but he was already nervous because he felt that Ottis had set him up. He was in the right mood for a murder. "Your man is in the next tent," Meteric said. "You're to get him out of sight and cut his throat. Cut him clean because we'll be needing him later." Toole, Henry remembers, giggled like a little girl opening her presents on Christmas morning when Meteric said that they would have need for the body later.

Lucas and Toole made their way to the next tent. Toole had brought along a fifth of Jack Daniels to souse up their victim before the kill. "Adds spice to the taste," Toole said cryptically as they

95

crept along in the darkness. Henry didn't know what in the world he meant until much later that evening.

Evidently Toole knew the man, because after he'd cautioned Henry to wait outside, he walked right into the tent and struck up a conversation. The two mumbled in soft rumbling voices — Henry couldn't make out a word of their conversation — until Toole piped up in a voice that Henry could understand, "I got the Jack Daniels. Let's you and me head on down the beach for a nightcap. I got a new friend I want to join us. You'll want to get to know him. He's valuable." Lucas heard the victim say "O.K." and he followed Toole and the man down to the beach.

It was a good thing there was a bright full moon that night, he said to himself as he followed along behind at a safe distance, because without that light, he would have been lost in an instant. Then, just as if they'd walked through a door to the next room, they were standing on a beach that seemed to stretch all the way out to the horizon. Now he could see the distinct shadows of the two men on the beach as Ottis handed him the booze and the man put his head back to take a deep swallow. Ottis took the bottle from him and took a drink while Henry stole up behind him. Then, when the man took the bottle back from Ottis and put his head back for a long, smooth swallow, Lucas rose up and in one single movement grabbed the man's hair, snapped his head back, and cut his throat from ear to ear. Ottis caught the booze before it hit the sand.

There was a gurgling sound and the man staggered backward. Blood was spurting from his slit neck all over the ground. The victim dropped to both knees and Toole jerked him backwards so his eyes stared upward as the life oozed out of him. "You don't want to get sand in the wound," Ottis said to his friend. "Spoils the taste. You'll understand later." With a few deft strokes, Toole cut away the victim's clothing and then motioned Lucas to follow him back toward the camp where they met Meteric. Meteric seemed impressed, but he wanted to inspect the corpse himself. Yet, he had to admit it had taken less than ten minutes and the job was clean and silent. Lucas was an accomplished killer, just the type of person Meteric wanted in the group. And the wound was deadly accurate the first time. No multiple stab wounds on this job. It was a death blow from the start.

"We'll prepare him," Meteric told Toole. Then he turned to Lucas. "You've killed well tonight. There'll be many more. But tonight will be your introduction."

That night was Lucas' first experience with anything having to do with the cult of Devil worshippers. He'd never seen anything like it before. Lucas was made to swear that he would never reveal the secrets of The Hand of Death, that he would kill innocent victims wherever he found them, that he would deliver children upon command to the ceremonies of The Hand of Death, and that he would partake of whatever The Hand of Death offered him. As if to cement the pact that he had made with the "Master" of the organization, a man who spoke in deep stentorian tones that resonated through the swamps, he was told to eat chunks of flesh from the burned remains of the man he had killed. The man had been the used as a sacrifice in the cult's ceremony and was now consumed as a testament of devotion to the cult and to the membership. Henry took particular notice of the way Toole greedily drank the man's blood and ate every extra piece of the man's flesh he could get his hands on. Lucas ate some too; he had to, even though he didn't like it — too gamey for his palate. But the entire ceremony taught him that his fascination with the way Toole eagerly ate his victim's flesh was more than satisfied by what he saw at the ceremony. Toole, it seemed, had been taught to eat flesh by the celebrants at this kind of "Black Mass," as they called it.

For the next weeks, Lucas stayed at the camp and learned about arson, kidnapping, drug running, abducting children, preparing victims for ritualistic sacrifice, all types of murder, necrophilia, and practices with the dead. He learned how to stay undercover when police were looking for him, and how to camouflage his activities. The instruction reinforced what Lucas had read for himself in the prison library in Michigan: that once a person deviates from a set pattern, the police will follow the original pattern no matter how many blind alleys it leads them down. Lucas learned what he could do in Mexico and Canada while he was in hiding from police in the United States, and he learned that the Canadians and the Mexicans almost never exchange any information.

For Lucas, this was a crash course in Devil worship and his classroom was all of North America. After years of being the victim, he was told, he would now be the master. He was the perfect student. The Hand of Death training was an introduction to beliefs and practices he had only vaguely heard about in prison but had never witnessed firsthand. Most important, however, was the indoctrination. Lucas learned that by murdering in a relentless, cold-blooded manner, he would practice the exercise of personal power that had been given to him by what the cult leaders referred to as "the demonic force of the universe." Eventually, over the course of the many weeks he spent in indoctrination, Lucas said he actually came to believe in the power of the Devil and the power of the Devil over him.

"What I seen with my own eyes, nobody's ever seen before," Lucas said years later after his conversion to Christianity. "I seen the power of evil at work in the world and I felt it practiced through me. I came to believe that my own destiny was with the power of evil. It made me do things that today I wish I could undo, but I can't. I have to pay for what I done and confess what I done."

Lucas says that over the years he has returned again and again to cult ceremonies and gatherings. "We had many meetings. They were more or less party meetings. Sometimes we would go down to the beach somewhere or back in some deserted area. Everyone would be high on drugs. Sometimes a member would bring a victim, either alive or dead, or sometimes would only bring a head or another part of the victim's body. Each of us would testify about the destruction we had been part of since the last meeting. Sometimes we would use our own cult members, say, if someone was about to leave the cult, then they were as good as dead. If it were a girl, they would take a horn of a bull and ram it up into her. The high priest would come in with a hooded type cloak and could get people so worked up that they could walk through fire around the altar and not even feel it. We would get higher and higher on drugs. We would rub each other's bodies with the blood of the victim or of the animal and some members would drink each other's urine. During all of this, someone would be chanting and praying to the Devil. Towards the end the victim would be killed and each of us would drink blood and eat part of the body. Ottis like to eat part of the bodies, but I never could do that."

Then, Henry says, they would study the text of their dark, perverted religion. "There's a Satanic Bible with prayers and readings of the Devil. There's no place that ever spoke of Jesus Christ, but it speaks about the Devil and that Satan is the only king left here in this world. And I wasn't the only one who practiced this in our family. I killed with Ottis, with Becky and Frank Powell."

Over the course of seven weeks at their Everglades training site during Henry's first introduction to the Hand of Death, Lucas and Toole watched students succeed and fail. They watched as converts who couldn't understand what was expected of them were used as sacrificial bodies. They saw children, freshly delivered from the kidnappers' cars, processed for the dark ceremonies that took place almost every night. Some of these children were from upstanding families where they were loved and cared for until the moment a parent turned his or her back at a shopping mall or a department store. They were protected in their cribs except for the one afternoon when a stranger pulled up to a backyard and while an unwary parent was on the phone, checking on a roast, lighting a barbecue grill, or spraying a plant with insecticide snatched the child from a playpen or a blanket and screeched off down the street. By the time the car had rounded the corner, it was too late even for the police because, as Lucas learned, most kidnappers had two cars: one for the snatch and one for the get-away. The Hand of Death taught you how to never get caught.

Henry says that he and Ottis began their career for The Hand of Death by running kidnapped children from the United States into Mexico. There was an active market for American children off all ages, Henry told his interviewers. He was instructed to bring babies into Mexico for resale back to the US on the "grey market," young children for importation to European and Middle Eastern countries as sex slaves to wealthy business people and nobility, and fresh young pre-adolescent girls for parts in porno and snuff videos. As their "control" Don Meteric described it, the girls would be pampered and made up, primped and fondled for the one-time roles in movies that would have a wider audience than most Hollywood releases. Then the girls would be killed and their bodies dumped or used in rituals. According to Meteric, there were Hand of Death rituals in almost every state two or three times a year. And each ritual had to be supplied with fresh young children for the sacrifice. To Lucas' interviewers in 1983 and 1984, it was a gruesome description of a society turned deeply evil. But to Lucas, at the time, it was business and only business.

On their first trip, Lucas and Toole ran babies.

They were easy to find. Lucas had planned to make the first trip to Mexico empty-handed, a practice run to learn the route and learn what to expect from the border inspectors. He had been told that the Mexicans usually wouldn't check on children. Any kids coming into the country in a car that didn't look like it was running drugs wouldn't be at all suspect. He was warned in the strongest possible terms, however, not to try to run drugs back out of Mexico. "The Hand of Death will provide you with all the drugs you will ever need and can ever take," Meteric had once told them. "You're not to freelance." Henry realized that running drugs on their own was as dangerous as driving around in a stolen car. You might as well wear a neon sign for the police to see.

However, the Hand did provide them with heroin and morphine to inject into the children to subdue them properly on the long drive. Henry and Ottis made good use of it on their first trip. They found a baby all alone in a car in a San Antonio shopping center. The mother had evidently stepped away to get something and left her infant child in her unlocked car. Lucas and Toole were driving a station wagon provided to them by the Hand and they simply went from car to car in the first parking lot they came to, found the baby, checked that the car was unlocked, and helped themselves to the child. The baby, Henry remem-

103

bered years later, came complete with bottles, formula, and diapers. Ottis gave the child a shot of heroin which put him to sleep for the six-hour trip into Mexico. It was like taking fruit right off a tree. To make matters even better, the people at the ranch where the baby was delivered were overjoyed at the sight of a healthy white American child. "Relax," they told Henry, who had expressed just the slightest bit of concern over the child's future. "She'll grow up to be a debutante somewhere, far richer and far happier than with the person who left her in the car for you guys to find." And with that, Henry and Ottis were on the road again, looking for more babies in more unlocked cars in more unguarded parking lots in shopping centers throughout the South. Henry claimed to have abducted over a hundred babies during an eighteen month run while he was killing for money at the same time.

"When I first joined, I only did the kidnapping," he says about his experiences. "I only did the actual killings after a year of kidnappings and after training. Like I said before, I had killed in the past, but after I joined this cult, I started killing at many different levels. Instead of just robbing a store and killing the storekeeper, we would kidnap children, hitchhikers, prostitutes, or whoever and would slice people up and cut their heads off and take parts of their bodies to the cult meeting."

As a kidnapper for money, Lucas was one of

the most productive members of the cult. "I made over thirty-five trips into Mexico, each time taking three or four kids. And I can remember exactly where the house in Mexico is that we brought the kids. It's deep into Mexico and it's a big ranch type house, and we would take the children there. The bosses of the cult would tell us how many they wanted and the ones they would give me the best money for. These were usually small children between the ages of four and eleven. We would get a thousand dollars a load."

He and Ottis also called themselves "talent scouts" when they were looking for teenaged girls for the snuff videos distributed through The Hand of Death. Even in 1980, "snuff videos" were thought to be a myth by most people. There were rumors of people being killed on video tapes which were later sold through underground distributors, but even the police doubted their existence. Henry doubted their existence as well until he received orders from Meteric to snatch a couple of "starlets" off the street. "Let's make sure they're already dopers," Ottis had said. "That way we can take 'em with a shot of heroin or morphine. We'll tell'em there's more where that came from and by the time they're on camera it'll be too late."

"Get us a bright redhead, lots of freckles and big tits," Meteric had told them before their first trip to hunt for teenagers. "We want 'em to fuck like they know what they're doin', so keep a sharp lookout. We'll train 'em if we have to, but we want a fast turn-around."

To Henry that meant looking for young hookers, and he and Ottis knew where to find them. "You can look on any street in any city," Ottis had told Meteric. "Redheads, blondes, Asians, they're all there for the picking." And sure enough, Henry and Ottis headed northwest right out of Laredo and didn't stop until they reached Denver. They were far enough away from Texas so that whoever they snatched wouldn't be reported to any agency having even the remotest contact with the Texas Rangers. Even if they had to dump the body of a dead girl somewhere in Texas — because they'd overdosed her by accident — the county sheriff wouldn't be able to trace the corpse to Colorado. Henry and Ottis knew what they were doing and were operating as if they'd never get caught, Henry said to interviewers about the early 1980s.

There she was! Lucas and Toole were sitting in their Pontiac outside of a strip bar in Denver and saw the pretty redheaded girl working the street. "Hell," Ottis laughed between hacking cigarette coughs. "She couldn't be more than thirteen. Cunt ain't even growed a hole yet." They pulled up to the girl and Ottis lowered his window. "If you're lookin' for money," he said to her. "I got a deal you don't want to turn down. Rich cat we know is throwin' a party and wants some gals for his friends. The money's good, you're in the lap of luxury, and if you agree to be in his home movie, there's bonus cash and all the drugs you want."

"Count me in," the young prostitute said and slid into the car. "I could use a fix right now," Henry remembers her saying to Ottis. And that was just about the last thing she ever said. The shot of heroin nodded her right off and Ottis kept her drugged and smiling until they reached Mexico. Maybe she was aware of what was going on when the camera lights went on. Maybe she wasn't. Henry and Ottis didn't hang around to find out. They didn't even see her debut performance in the snuff video. But Henry says that it was a one-way trip for any teenagers they induced into their cars. "But they were whores anyway," Henry said years later. "And I got a cold chill whenever it came time to pack them in."

He and Ottis became so adept at picking up children, they were almost legendary in the Hand, Henry says. Lucas and Toole had it down to a science. As much as they knew about police procedures and when police walked away from an investigation, they knew even more about how to find the easiest kids to abduct. They traveled throughout fourteen states looking for children. They went to school playgrounds which were mostly unsupervised even in the middle of the day, municipal playgrounds where parents didn't know where their children were until it was too late, shopping centers where parents left children unattended in parked cars, and even nursery schools where Lucas said he and Toole could roam the halls almost at will. They scouted neighborhoods to see where the teenaged babysitters went after school and how late they stayed in people's houses at night. Sometimes they could pick up entire families of children along with their babysitters, drug them until they got to Mexico, and split them up according to their final destinations. They saw which families went to work with their kids, which kids went to school, where the busses let them off, and how far the kids had to walk on their own. "It's a great country," Toole would say to Lucas when they had their car full of sleeping children and were plowing straight for the border. Police would sometimes wave as they drove by; tollbooth operators would smile at the sleeping little angels strapped in nice and tight in the back seat, and nobody even asked to see a piece of ID, Lucas said about those months on the road. It was almost getting too easy.

"You know," Lucas said, remembering what happened to some of the children. "The Mexicans themselves wanted to raise some of the kids as their own. The pretty blue-eyed ones were actually sold to rich Mexican families, and these kids are living today. You can actually go down there and see blue-eyed blonde men with Mexican names, and chances are they'd be the kids me 'n Ottis snatched. Some of the other kids were sold into prostitution, some were used as sacrifices and were killed and cut up. Others were raised to be killers in the cult and are probably still out there killin' and snatchin' just like me and Ottis did."

Finally, Henry needed a rest and asked for a change. He and Ottis had been together constantly for over a year abducting children and running them to Mexico, Henry had told interviewers in the Hand-of-Death version of the story. And he was beginning to get tired of it. The money, although good, was quickly spent, and he missed the opportunity to spend time back in Jacksonville with Becky and Frank. He and Ottis were also killing regularly every month, as the Hand had told them to do, but Henry knew that there were other people in the cult who were getting paid very handsomely for their murders. Meteric had told the two of them over and over again that they were so good at what they were doing—kidnapping children of all ages—that the Hand himself, the master of the cult, Satan's minister on Earth, had wanted them to stay on their lucrative missions. But Meteric understood that even pack mules needed a break or else they would become stubborn. And Henry was getting ornery.

Ottis wanted a break as well. He was getting horny for some of his old boyfriends, Henry said. Henry wouldn't have sex with him, as much as

Ottis was pleading for it, and Ottis had lovers back in Florida whom he missed. Sure, Henry told interviewers, Ottis would have sexual intercourse with the children and the little boys they picked up. He'd have sexual intercourse with the remains of their murder victims and the hapless stragglers they'd pick up along the way, but he missed his friends. "Hell," Henry said. "Bein' on the road for so long'd make anybody turn mean."

Meteric knew when the rope was getting stretched too tight and ordered his prize kidnappers back to Jacksonville for a little vacation time. "We'll pay the freight," he told the boys. "We'll even throw in a bonus 'cause you made us a heap of money from your work." But on the side he told Henry that he'd look real carefully for some contract killings because he knew that Lucas wanted to graduate to bigger money. Toole, he said, would always be happy picking up kids, doping them into a stupor, and sodomizing them until he came all over the backseat of the car. That was his thrill, and he delivered the goods. Henry, he realized, was in store for bigger and better opportunities. "We'll set you up with a real important hit, Henry," Meteric assured him. "It'll bring in the kind of dough you'd be expectin'." But in the meantime, he told Henry to go back to Florida and wait for instructions from the Hand. "Mebbe see Becky," he told Lucas. "You'd be surprised to see how big she's gotten since you and Ottis were on the road last."

There was something in what Meteric said that made Henry long for Florida, the tropical sun, and the smell of the fruit. Texas was all desert, and the badlands were just chaparral and scrub. But Florida, Florida was like a paradise in his memory. Every time he'd been hurting and needed healing, he'd head south to Florida and Ottis and Becky.

To this day, Henry says, people have trouble with the cult story. He's told it hundreds of times, and later he said he'd retract it because he was afraid that the Hand would reach out to him even behind bars. "You have to believe that some group's out there organizing a lot of killing," Henry says, pointing to evidence. "Because the killings of kids are too similar to be the work of different people. No one wants to believe the cult story. The TV people cut it out of interviews. The writers don't write about it. But some of the law enforcement people in the different states are investigating it. It's the truth, even though it's tough to find evidence."

Lucas explains that anyone who studies how police work knows how to mix up the evidence to the point where the police don't regard it as evidence. "It's all there, they just don't know what to look for," he has told police who can't find physical evidence of his crimes. "It's the same with the cult," he says. "The cult members are just like me.

111

We were trained not to leave evidence. If it wasn't for me, they couldn't find out about me. I'm the one who's giving evidence about me. They ain't finding nothing about me until I tell them. But if you multiply me hundreds of times, you'd have a picture of the cult."

He says that there are thousands of people in the United States so filled with hatred that they would do anything to vent their rage on innocent people and seek personal power through the cult. The cult is a conspiracy, he says, with people in powerful jobs and in politically critical situations who make decisions based on what the cult tells them to do. "Sometimes I think it's an organization that wants to take over the government. They've already got their hands in a lot of mighty high places. Sometimes after a really good meeting we would all get together and talk about how there was going to be such a war and that we were going to wipe the country out. These are people that look just like you and me, too. They live in some of the best neighborhoods, or like me they travel and live on the road. They make their money by selling drugs and selling people. People with money will hire people like me to get them kids and kill their enemies. Some cult members just do it for the fun."

The last time a police went into the 'Glades to search for the cult training camp, Lucas says, "they went in with a helicopter, were shot at and now are going back in a land boat."

Even though people may dispute his claims, Lucas says that he can always recognize the mark of The Hand of Death. "I can tell because we were taught to leave a mark on the body or near the body. You can tell sometimes by the way a body is left. Each of the victims is a sacrifice to the Devil. You got different types of marks. You've got your blotches, you've got your stripe marks. You've got your pin marks and sometimes we would make a zig-zag with a ballpoint pen." Lucas says that another clear indication of a Hand of Death murder is an upside down cross carved into the victim's chest. "That mark is The Hand of Death," Lucas said.

But he tried to put it aside for the few weeks that he spent with Becky in Jacksonville. He didn't realize that she, too, would become a victim of The Hand of Death.

Chapter 6
Becky

"Becky was the sweetest, kindest young thing that ever happened to me." That's what Henry Lee Lucas would say about Frieda Lorraine Powell a year after she was dead, a year after he had killed her with his knife and he was confessing the misery of his soul to Sheriff Conway in his Denton County jail cell.

In 1980, when Lucas went back to Florida to see Becky, after his months on the road as The Hand of Death's most productive kidnapper, murdering Becky Powell was the last thing on his mind. All he wanted was some peace and respite from the months of kidnapping and killing. In his narrative about the Hand of Death, he wrote that he had told Don Meteric that he needed a rest and Meteric had readily agreed. He had even set up a contract killing for Lucas to perform in Texas for The Hand of Death to provide him with "pocket money" that would get him across the country.

Lucas had decided to pack Becky Powell up and take her to California where they would establish themselves as husband and wife. Becky would be away from her family, away from the Florida Welfare Department that kept nosing around trying to slap the fourteen-year-old girl back in reform school, and away from Uncle Ottis who was growing increasingly jealous of his niece's influence on Henry. Henry had always claimed that he was heterosexual first and bisexual second. But Henry loved Ottis like a brother and could talk to him more easily than any other living human being except for Becky. Now he was going to have Becky all to himself.

The transformation of Becky Powell from Henry's ward to his common-law wife is one of the most fascinating and lurid elements of the Lucas story.

When Henry met Becky Powell, according to some versions of the story, it was as early as 1976 and she was only nine years old. Her father had all but abandoned her and Frank, her younger brother, before Henry began staying off-and-on with the family. Becky's mother was a troubled woman who could not care for the children. They were raised by Ottis' mother, Sara Harley.

Henry would travel to Jacksonville, hook up with her Uncle Ottis, and the two of them would head off on killing and robbing sprees like a pair of good ol' boys off to the woods for a weekend of hunting and beer drinking. Gradually, as Henry began staying with the family on a regular basis, Ottis' mother began thinking of him as a member of the family. Reportedly, she once told Henry that he was always welcome in the family because the children's father never came around and Henry offered them the only fatherly care they had ever had.

Henry's influence was bad as well as good, Ottis' mother came to realize. While he claimed he really did care for the two children, he also put them in precarious situations by having them wait in the car while he and Ottis knocked over liquor stores and "Mom and Pop" convenience stores along old state routes in Florida and Georgia. Frank Powell has recently told police that he and his sister witnessed murders that Henry and Ottis perpetrated and might even know where some of the victims were buried. Eventually it was becoming clear to Ottis' mother that Frank and Becky were being badly influenced by Henry and his relationship with Ottis, even though Henry's presence always meant a steady influx of household money from his day-to-day construction work, his roofing jobs, and his robbery sprees. It was a trade-off, to be sure.

Henry was also an alcoholic, and by his own admission, rarely spent any time sober at all during his killing sprees with Ottis and the kids. He claimed he could hold his liquor well and was never even given a driving ticket during all his years on the road. However, he had been giving alcohol to the kids, and Frank was already showing signs of alcohol abuse.

Ottis' mother also objected to Henry's taking the children away from her for extended periods of time while he and Ottis were on the road. When they were traveling with Toole and Lucas it was impossible for the children to stay in school. The more the children were absent from school, the more excuses she would have to make. Gradually, the state social service departments were getting more and more involved in the children's extended absences. Ottis' mother found herself having to explain about Henry and Ottis to different people who wanted to know about the kinds of influence the two scruffy-looking men who always smelled from stale liquor were having on the children's upbringing. It was a situation that had started out as uncomfortable and was quickly becoming untenable. Eventually, Ottis' mother began saying, Henry would have to go. And if that meant that Ottis would have to leave as well, then she would have to live with that. Having the men leave, she believed, would be better than having Becky and Frank taken out of her care by the state and placed in reformatories, juvenile detention homes, or, worse, foster care.

Henry and Ottis had other plans. First, they claimed, they genuinely liked the children and liked having them around. Second, they felt the children provided them with good cover on their trips across country. People often took pity on the rag-tag band, especially on the little girl with the dirty face and big, hungry eyes. "She was like a little doll," one witness said about Becky. "When she looked at you, you'd give her anything." That's why when Henry and Ottis would take the children into a small convenience store, the clerks and owners would not worry about the strange behavior of the adults. Before they had a chance to reach for a gun under the register, Lucas or Toole would have a shotgun or a .22 pointed at their heads and would be leading them to the back of the store. Likely as not, either Henry or Ottis would kill them while the other partner would empty the register and the kids would take whatever they wanted from the shelves. Then the band would be on the road again, living out of their car and robbing another convenience store for their next meal.

Tensions at Ottis' house became worse with each planned road trip and, obviously, after each return. There were explanations to be made, work in school that had to be made up, interviews to be conducted by the different state agencies that suddenly turned up after the kids came back, and the endless worries about police cars turning up to arrest Henry or Ottis or the kids. If these fears weren't bad enough, the children themselves were becoming incorrigible.

At the same time that Ottis' mother was becoming worried about the criminal influence Henry had on her children, she was worried about Becky's development into a young woman. Henry was more like a father or uncle than anything else. But now she was turning fourteen. She was turning into a woman. You could see the way she was looking at Henry, the only man who had shown her any real attention or given her any encouragement. Henry supported her from time to time, and took her on the road with them. She was looking at Henry romantically, and that wasn't right.

As Ottis Toole's family situation in Jacksonville was building to a crisis, Henry returned with his permission from Don Meteric to change his metier from kidnapping to killing, with "time off" to relocate himself and Becky to the West Coast. He had also gotten his first murder-for-hire contract from the Hand and was now ready to head for Texas to complete the contract and collect the money. But right before Henry was set to pack up and go, Becky was picked up by a social worker and placed in an emergency shelter in Bartow, Florida. She would eventually be remanded to the custody of a detention home for juveniles because her mother had committed suicide.

Henry remembers that he didn't want to leave Florida on his assignments without Becky and enlisted Ottis' help in breaking her out of the shelter. It was as easy as breaking into a house, Henry said years later. He and Ottis simply drove onto the grounds of the juvenile center in Howard Toole's pickup truck, found where Becky was sleeping and walked her right out the door. Within the hour, they were on the road back to Jacksonville. The state issued a pickup order for Becky. Henry heard that the police were looking for him. He transferred his insurance on the truck and took Becky out of the state. They were free. Henry says that Ottis went along with them while Frank remained in Florida.

They drove into Georgia where they robbed their way across the southern border of the state, through Alabama and Mississippi where they also stopped for food and money at whatever Mom-and-Pop stores were along the state routes, and from there into Louisiana. Shortly before they reached Texas, Ottis split off and went his separate way. He knew that Henry had gotten a contract for a murder in Beaumont and knew the rules of The Hand of Death: only the person who gets the assignment carries it out. Everybody else must stay away. The job was Henry's and Becky was staying with him.

If there were warrants out on Becky and they were stopped along the road by a police officer in any state, then Henry could be charged with aiding and abetting the unlawful flight of a minor, endangering the welfare of a minor by removing her from her home, or, because Becky was an accessory and an accomplice to Henry's crimes, corrupting a minor. If the state authorities believed that Henry was having sexual relations with Becky, he could also be charged under federal statutes with illegally transporting a minor across state lines. Once charged with any of those offenses, Henry's probation and parole would be revoked and he would go back to prison to await trial. Indeed, Henry was taking an awful risk.

Henry recalls that after Ottis left them and they were traveling alone, Becky seemed to come alive as a woman. With her uncle in the car, she was still a child. She would whine when she wanted something and pout when she couldn't get it. But with Henry, she actually began to flirt, to entice him into doing things for her that he couldn't even think about with her uncle looking over her shoulder. As they stopped in motels along the way, Becky began to flirt seriously. She began to demand that Henry fondle her sexually.

Henry Lee Lucas was torn, he says, between feelings of passion and paternal devotion. His idea of sex was to rape and threaten a struggling victim until she succumbed to fear and violence.

After he'd raped her, he'd kill her and have sex with her corpse. That was sex to Henry Lee Lucas. But sex with someone he not only cared for but felt responsible to protect, that was a completely different experience. He was afraid of sex under those conditions because he didn't know what to expect.

Lucas also says that Becky continued her attempts to woo him night after night in motel after motel. There was not a single place they stayed together where Becky did not persistently demand that Henry satisfy her sexually. Eventually, he confesses, his own endurance began to wear and he was sorely tempted. "But I never made love to her," he says. "I always respected her on the road. She tempted me. She said that I wouldn't be a man unless I made love to her. But I didn't."

Becky was not to be so easily denied. Not only did she want Henry to make love to her, she wanted him to spend money on her, to treat her as if she were actually his wife, even though there was more than a quarter-century difference in their ages. Becky began to complain that she didn't have the right clothes to wear, that Henry was dressing her like a child when she wanted to dress like a woman. She complained that she wouldn't be quieted down unless Henry actually made love to her and taught her what it was like to be submissive to a man.

Henry says he steadfastly refused all of her demands for sex. He did, however, indulge her spending habits. He bought her sexy nightgowns and "baby-doll" pajamas. They shared the same bed at nights and he allowed her to fondle him sexually. After she was sound asleep, he said, he would leave the motel room, drive up the road until he came to a truck stop or a bar, pick up the first woman he saw and stab her to death while he raped her. Then he would get back to the motel where he cleaned the blood off and woke up the next morning with Becky as if nothing had happened.

One night Becky had been particularly difficult. She had challenged his masculinity in ways that she had never done in the past. She said she knew why he wasn't making love with her. "Because maybe you're like Uncle Ottis," she said. "Maybe you're a queer like Uncle Ottis and can only love men."

"Now you know that's not true, darlin'," he kept telling her over and over again. "You know that I love you more'n any man in 'is world's ev'r gonna love ya. But you're my sweet thing and I can never touch you like I touch them others. You know what Ottis 'n me does to those types of girls. I can't just touch you that way. Maybe soon, but not yet."

She wasn't satisfied, not by a long shot.

The next day, she was whining about beer. "We'll stop and get you a cold Dr. Pepper," Henry promised her, but it did no good.

"Daddy, I want a beer and I want it now," she whined.

Henry relented. He pulled off the interstate, bought a six-pack, and then spun back on again and headed off into the night. Becky sipped at her beer and snuggled up close to Henry, who easily navigated with one hand wrapped around her while a beer can hung off the end of it. She was small enough that he could hold her close and drink his beer with the same hand. He was careful though—Henry always was—and kept his speed exactly at 55 as if the car would explode if he went one mile an hour faster.

After a while, Lucas' rearview mirror suddenly burst into a display of Christmas lights. Reds, blues, and whites in a strobe-like array danced into his vision. It was a state police car. Henry checked his speed to make sure that he was doing a clear 55. Satisfied, he firmly pushed Becky away to the other end of the seat and shoved his beer can under the dash. He took her can away from her and shoved it down under her seat. Then he reached below his seat and cocked his sawed-off shotgun while Becky watched with her eyes as wide as baseballs. Henry gradually slowed his car to a stop as he closed his fingers around his weapon.

"If he takes but five steps towards the front of this car," Henry murmured with a low growl, "I'm gonna shoot his head off." There was no call for a cop to stop him when he was doing the limit. He was not going to get sent back to jail because some cop decided to get curious. He was going to blow him out of his shoes right then and there, pull the car into town, ditch it, steal another, and hightail it out of state before he could be tracked. He'd take the long way back to Florida and get the Hand to fake some work records for him to show that he was working at the time the cop was shot, if it ever came to his needing an alibi.

Henry put the car into park and let it sit. He lowered his window and while his engine was still idling, he counted the steps he could hear in the tarmac behind him. He watched the cop's movements very carefully in the sideview mirror as the officer stared at Lucas' license plate, took out his note pad, and flashed a narrow-beam flashlight along the rear of Lucas' car. Henry couldn't tell if the officer was writing anything down or not. Then the officer took his first step toward the driver. Lucas' hand tightened on the weapon. The officer took another step. Becky caught her breath. And then as the cop leaned forward for his final steps to the driver's window, a huge chrome Peterbilt swung around them without even slowing down for the trooper's lights and barreled off into the darkness.

"Your left taillight's out," the cop called out. "Get it fixed." And he spun on his heel, trotted back to his car, and took off down the highway after the roaring eighteen-wheeler.

"Oh Daddy, fuck," Becky squealed and giggled at the same time as she snatched her beer from the floor. "You were gonna kill that cop."

"Yes I was," Henry said. "But that didn't mean I wanted to. It only meant I was protectin' you."

Becky leaped across the seat at Henry and kissed him while she kept on squealing. "It was so exciting," she said. "Let's find us a place for tonight fast."

Even Henry had to laugh because he'd never killed in front of her before. But they drove down the interstate until they passed a sign for a motel and pulled off. Becky came on to him again later that night, rousing him from sleep and cooing in his ear that she wanted him to show her what it was like when a man loves a woman. But Henry wanted none of it. "Not yet, darlin'," he kept on saying as she ran his hands over his body.

The next day, Henry and Becky pulled into Beaumont, Texas, where he located the man he was supposed to kill, a lawyer who was about to confess to the police about an individual friendly with members of The Hand of Death. Henry had to make sure the victim would be found, had to make sure the corpse was mutilated enough to throw fear into the hearts of anyone else who thought to cross a friend of the Hand of Death, and he had to make sure that the Hand of Death knew it was one of their murders and not the work of somebody else.

Henry put Becky up in a motel and told her to stay put until after the victim was dead. No use having her running around distracting his attention when there was serious killing to be done. Then Henry followed his victim around town for as many days as it took him to figure out his schedule and when he'd be the easiest to kidnap and haul away. The man was private enough that Henry knew he'd be able to snatch him without having to set up a trap. And it helped that the man was a drinker. Henry knew how to lure a drinker into a quiet spot where no witnesses would see him cut his throat with a single swipe. And that's just what Henry did. He was sitting alongside his victim in the man's car, and as the man pulled his head back to take a long, deep drink, Henry swung his knife out and through the man's neck with a blow so neat, the man didn't know he was dead and was in the middle of a drink after his throat was cut clean through. "Likker run right out the bottom of his head," Henry would laugh to Ottis years later over cigarettes and coffee in the Georgetown jail.

Henry drove the victim's car out of town where he stashed the body in a shallow grave for safekeeping. Then he drove the man's car back to the bar, walked back to his own car, and headed for the motel where he picked up Becky. Together, they drove back to the grave where Henry and Becky dug the victim up, cut his head off, cut an upside down cross in his chest, and then reburied his parts. But they left the man's feet sticking up out of the ground and left his socks on. When the newspaper reports picked up that fact—and it was sure to be picked up because it was so odd— someone from The Hand of Death would relay the information to Don Meteric who would send his cash on the way. That was the way things were done.

Henry and Becky slept the sleep of the innocent, awoke before dawn, and silently stole out of Beaumont. They were headed west to California toward what would become the final adventure of their lives together.

Chapter 7
Ringgold, Texas

Henry and Becky arrived in California broke, hungry, and dirty after having been on the road for over three months. Whatever money he expected from the Hand for the execution in Texas had not caught up with them, and Becky was complaining that she wanted to go back to Florida where, as bad as it was, at least she got a square meal. Henry had begun to realize that as much as he thought he loved Becky, having her on the road with him wasn't the picnic he thought it would be when they had set out. First of all, they had no place to settle. Their truck had broken down and they abandoned it in Texas. From there they had hitched through New Mexico and into southern California, but were only drifting. Second, Henry said, there were no assignments from the cult, and Henry had to look for petty thefts or for odd jobs wherever he could just to keep them from starving.

In the absence of legitimate work and with the police looking over every drifter who wandered inside their jurisdictions, Henry and Becky had to stay extra careful. Henry was constantly mindful that Becky was a fugitive who, once identified, would turn into the kind of evidence that would get him in trouble. If caught, Henry would have been an accomplice to the flight of a fugitive, aiding and abetting a perpetrator in a federal crime, and endangering the welfare of a minor. It would have been worth at least fifteen years in a federal prison, and Henry wasn't anxious to walk into that kind of trap. Therefore, he and Becky kept low profiles despite Becky's desire to live close to the edge and knock off gas stations and liquor stores in broad daylight.

Henry claims he still had his responsibilities to the cult to fulfill. He remembers that the cult expected him to kill at least once or twice a month and to leave the bodies in locations where their discoveries would perplex the local police. Henry was good at that, but didn't want to mix responsibilities and his need to steal for a living. By robbing and murdering in the same jurisdiction, it would alert police automatically to look for all strangers. Henry knew that he and Becky stood

130

out like sore thumbs, so that he could not kill for the cult and rob for a living in the same place. As a result, he and Becky were often hungry.

Finally, in a 1985 prison interview, Henry says he and Becky headed north toward Oregon and Washington where the pickings might be easier. Henry claims that he and Becky robbed their way through the California hill country and into Oregon. He tells stories of stashing Becky in the shadows while he waited in the parking lots of roadside restaurants for single women to return to their cars. When they were alone, he would wait until they'd opened their cars, steal up behind them, cut their throats with a single swipe, and rob them of their money. He said he would drive their cars to a new location miles away to another restaurant to spend their money on his next meal where he would abandon the car and find another murder victim whose car he would steal. Henry said he knew exactly how the police operated. If there no reports of a stolen car, the car wasn't stolen. If the person was dead, the car wouldn't get reported. Henry would simply take the registration with him and say he was transporting the car for the owner. By the time the bodies would be discovered hours or days later, he and Becky would be long gone.

Henry said that because he wasn't making love to Becky, he still needed to kill in order to satisfy his lust. Prostitutes, he says, were his best bet, because he already hated them. Lucas still claims that there are scores of unsolved prostitute homicides in Oregon and northern California that fit this pattern that police have yet to trace to him and that he has yet to talk about.

According to their version, Lucas and Becky drifted further north into the State of Washington where Lucas claims he read about the stories of missing women in the rural counties south of Seattle. Lucas said he killed women according to the descriptions in the newspapers and left their bodies where police would discover them. "This is what The Hand of Death taught us to do," Lucas says. "They taught us to find cases where they was bodies turnin' up in graves and add to the pot. That way you'd up yer own count and get'em laid on somebody else. The police'd never find ya."

Lucas states that he murdered women in an area in Washington known as the Green River, but a check on the dates corpses were discovered and the dates of Lucas' confessed whereabouts conclusively proved that Lucas could not have committed those crimes. Other interviewers believe that Lucas might have fabricated the dates as well as the locations, especially since Lucas claims to have read about the crimes in newspapers. The first bodies in the Green River case were discov-

132

ered in July, 1982. However, in July, 1982, Lucas was at Ruben Moore's House of Prayer in Texas where he stayed off and on until August. In late January, 1982, local Hemet, California, businessman Jack Smart spotted Henry and Becky through his windshield as he drove home at night. He said to interviewers years later that he took pity on the pair of stragglers who looked like they were at the end of their endurance. He stopped the car, picked them up, and gave them a ride back to his place.

Their last junk car that Henry had picked up along the way had broken down and had to be abandoned. They had just gotten a free meal at a local community assistance storefront and they were slugging their way west on foot during California's rainy season along one of the rural roads off Interstate 10 where it intersects with 79.

Jack and his wife ran an antique shop in the area, and were always in need of people to do odd jobs and construction work around the place. Antique stores require a high degree of physical overhead because there's always refinishing to do and repair of the items that are constantly coming in and going out. Jack's shop also needed work, especially up on the roof which was leaking during southern California's rainy season. Henry had worked in the auto repair shop and the chair factory during his years in the Michigan penitentiary

133

and knew how to make repairs to just about anything. He had also spent years as a roofer in Florida and had worked in the paint factory also.

Jack was struck by the neediness of his two passengers, but he didn't realize in the darkness at first just how young Becky looked. Even his wife remarked that she was only a child. And her one-eyed companion looked more a mutant than a threat. They were both filthy, wet, and as raggedy as any two human beings could have ever been. The Smarts said they took pity on Lucas and Becky and gave them the first hot meal the two said they'd eaten in weeks. During the after-dinner conversation, Lucas said that Becky was his wife and that he was a carpenter of sorts, a man who could do odd jobs around the house as well as repair roofs. He told Jack that he was just plumb out of money and was looking for any kind of construction or cleanup work. Becky was a good worker, too, Lucas said, and knew how to clean and cook.

Jack offered to let Henry work at his antique shop for free rent and board at a small apartment he provided for them. He even offered to let Henry hire himself out to other local residents so that he could buy clothes and other necessities for himself and Becky. The Smarts took a liking to Henry and Becky. They didn't see his dark side, only a harmless drifter and a little waif who tagged along after him wherever he want. And Henry Lee was a hard worker. He'd finish his jobs, do what you told him you wanted, and settle back with his beer. He didn't eat very much either. "Jes' set out my pot o' coffee an' a ashtray an' I'm fine," he'd say in a backwoodsy twang that the Smarts found to be homey and harmless.

At dinner, Henry would often talk about his boyhood in the Appalachian coal-mining counties of Virginia. He would talk about his tough up-bringing. Henry regaled them with stories of life in the three-room, dirt-floor cabin in the woods where Henry would live with pigs, goats, chickens, and a mule.

Sometimes Henry would disappear for a day or two and would return without telling anyone where he'd been. No one asked, not even Becky, and Henry would drop back into his daily routine as if nothing were any different. If stories about missing women or the mutilated bodies of drifters and hitchhikers sometimes circulated around the general store, the post office, or the short teller lines at the local bank, no one paid them any heed. And certainly no one, no one at all, even thought about associating stories of mutilated hitchhikers with the humble Henry Lee and his pie-eyed teenage companion.

Henry sure was good with his hands. He spread more tar patch on more roofs during the rainy season than local residents had ever seen. And he laid more shingles on more roofs faster than any other roofing people had ever seen. Despite the frequent trips to the coffee pot during the day and the ever-present beer can in the afternoon, Henry was a worker you could rely on. He also cleaned out yards, hauled trash, rewired your fuse box, and cleaned out your gas heater better than the other local contractors who passed through. In the four months that Henry was in residence in, he was a valued laborer. But the Smarts had another idea.

Mrs. Smart had been getting phone calls from her relatives over in rural Ringgold, Texas, about the declining health of her elderly mother Kate "Granny" Rich. Old Kate Rich was a spry and feisty widow who was living on her dead husband's retirement checks and social security. She wanted to maintain her independence as long as possible and not be forced to move in with relatives in Oklahoma, but at the same time she realized that she was growing weaker and might soon need people to do the household chores, the shopping, and the cooking. Also, her cousins joked to Mrs. Smart, her mother's house was in such a state of disrepair that if someone didn't hire a contractor soon to shore it up, it would simply fall down around her ears.

The Smarts had an idea: why not invite Henry

Lee and Becky to move in with Granny Rich to repair the entire house and serve as help around the house? Becky could cook and clean, they reasoned, and Henry Lee could begin repairs on whatever needed fixing. Just their presence in the house, the Smarts suggested to their family up in Wichita Falls, Texas, might make everyone feel more comfortable about Granny's decision to maintain her independent residence. But the idea had to be sold to Granny Rich herself, who wasn't likely to do something purely on the advice of her grandchildren and great-grandchildren. She didn't like people telling her what to do. And she didn't like charity.

Why not let Granny Rich take the couple in as a couple of dependents, the Smarts suggested to their Texas cousins. Let Granny be the magnanimous widow who was willing to give two drifters a roof over their heads, albeit leaky, in exchange for household chores and a sense of protection. But the offer would have to come from Granny herself, not from the relatives, and not from the Smarts who didn't want anyone to feel they were offering charity in the old widow's name. The Smarts also had to convince Lucas and Becky to move to Texas and give up their apartment behind the antique store in exchange for sharing a house with their mother, an old widow. Would they do it? Would they leave for Texas? Jack Smart believed he could do it because the prospect of a house gave them greater freedom to move about, and they would have Granny Rich's car to use, which Henry was more than capable of fixing whenever it broke down. It was a perfect fit, and all that needed was for the deal to be sold.

Kate Rich's grandchildren met in Texas to tell the old woman the story of how Jack Smart had seen Henry and Becky trudging along the shoulder of a lonely road on a chilly, rainy, California night in January after just eating their first meal in days out of a paper bag. They said that he had stopped for them out of sheer pity and had been struck by the sadness in the little girl's eyes. He had sheltered and fed them on the first night and the next morning, when he heard their tale of trying to reach California in a junk car that had broken down somewhere in Texas, he gave them a place to stay behind the store for a few days where they could dry off and look for work. It turned out, the relatives told the old woman, that the man was a roofer, electrician, and general handyman who could fix anything. The little girl was his fourteen-year-old wife who cooked and cleaned and sorely needed an education and some old-fashioned religion in her life. The Smarts let Henry and the little girl stay with them since the end of January. How sad can a story be, the relatives wondered aloud.

Kate was intrigued. Her family's story had caught her attention. "Just walking along the road?" she asked, reportedly. The assembled family nodded slowly but affirmatively, masking their attitudes of bemusement with a collective demeanor of concern.

"Fourteen years old, you say?" Another nod, this time with even greater concern.

"Christians?"

"The little girl should be," one of the nieces piped up. "But right now she's living in that small apartment behind the antique store. Girl sorely needs an upbringing, but her husband, he's about thirty years older than she is, and he's been down on his luck so long he doesn't know what to do."

The assembled relatives described how hard the man's life had been, how he grew up in the Virginia coal-mining hills, how his father had no legs and died in a snowbank, how his brother had knocked his eye out, and how he'd day-labored most of his life. "Darn good fixer-upper, though," one of the nephews said as Kate Rich looked hopelessly around the room, her eyes registering the sagging roof beams, crumbling plaster, leaking pipes, and buckling floor. Then an idea began to resolve itself somewhere in old Kate Rich's mind.

"I could raise this little girl to be a Christian like I did all of you," the old woman said. "I'm giving a little child a chance to get some book learnin' and a man a chance to work for his meals. It's fair deal."

"If you think so, Granny," another nephew began.

"And if you'd come up with the idea yerself, we'd 'a done it sooner," Granny continued. "Instead of that poor girl's havin' to near starve on the road." With that, Granny made the decision to invite Henry Lee Lucas and Becky Powell to Ringgold, Texas, to live with her, take care of the house and chores, and, for Becky, to receive a proper education.

The family called the Smarts to tell them that Granny had invited Lucas to come to Texas, and Mrs. Smart and her husband broached the idea to Henry and Becky.

"It's just like we'll have our own place," Henry reportedly told Becky who had wanted to stay in California with the "Smarts. She was afraid of going on the road again and being with someone she didn't know. Becky was starting to change. She felt she had set down some roots and had taken a liking to the Smarts. Now, just when she was getting used to the situation and to working in the store with Mrs. Smart and minding her own home with Henry, she was being asked to move again. She wanted to put her foot down and say no, but the Smarts were insistent that they talk about it because, they said, not only was it a good idea for them, it was good for Granny Rich. In the end, Henry and Becky agreed, and the Smarts drove them to the bus stop in Hemet and paid for tickets for the trip to Ringgold and their meeting with Granny Rich.

They arrived in Ringgold in May. At first, he and Becky were quickly befriended by most of the townspeople. Ringgold was rural. It had a post office, a general store of sorts, a bar and package store, and a small cluster of widely spaced houses. Its residents knew one another by their first names.

Eighty-year-old Kate Rich welcomed the bedraggled couple when they got off the bus with absolutely no possessions whatsoever. She warmed quickly to Becky Powell, showering the fourteen-year-old with more affection than Becky had received from anyone in a long time. Granny Rich could clearly see that Becky had been hurt and was still hurting. She was old before her years, the widow Rich reportedly told her friends, but still more of a child than she should have been at fifteen.

Mrs. Rich wanted to turn as much responsibility over to Henry and his companion as quickly as possible. Some of her relatives have suggested that that might have been a mistake. Because Mrs. Rich warmed to Becky, she believed that Becky had warmed to her. Henry was no different. Henry, even to this day, according to people who have interviewed him over extended periods of time, has a charm about him that makes strangers want to like him. He counts his jailers and the police officers who supervise his task force among the closest friends he's ever had. And they, in turn, find him likeable despite his occasional cantankerousness and mood swings. Mrs. Rich found Henry charming as well. He asked nothing from her except for the many pots of coffee that he consumed throughout the day and pack after pack of cigarettes. He also drank a prodigious amount of beer, but, "Hell," she was wont to say, "this is Texas. And if a man in Texas can't drink his beer after an honest day's work tarring roofs in the hot sun, then there was no point in getting up the next day."

After a few weeks, Lucas and Becky became part of the local landscape. Henry would routinely show up at the general store in the mornings with orders for Granny. He would be responsible for her mail, and he was supposedly making repairs on the house. Granny, at least for a while, seemed to drop out of sight. Now that she had Henry and Becky, there was no need for her to run her own errands or even to leave the house much. Mrs. Rich was, in fact, a semi-invalid and, by her own description, "near blind." All she seemed to want was companionship.

Mrs. Rich's kindness toward Becky grew with each passing week. At first she pitied the girl because she didn't seem to have any of the basic family skills that Kate Rich was used to seeing in fourteen-year-olds. The child lacked an identity of her self and seemed totally dependent on whoever else was around. Becky didn't talk much about Henry or what she and Henry did on the road, but Mrs. Rich seemed to have had an inkling that it wasn't pleasant because Becky seemed ashamed of it. Kate Rich was comfortable with Henry, though, because of the ease with which he was able to talk to her. In fact, Kate got to be so trusting in her attitude toward Henry Lee that she gave him money so Lucas could buy groceries for the little family.

After Henry had become a familiar person in town, people remarked that after the first few weeks of his residence in town, the money he was spending wasn't for household supplies. At first, the people at the general store minded their own business. But Henry and Becky were always so dirty, and he spoke in a backwoods way that sounded strange and menacing. His one eye spooked the people in Ringgold as well. But it was also becoming more and more obvious that Lucas wasn't buying food for Kate and Becky, he was just buying beer and other items. The locals became suspicious of the goings on at Granny

Rich's house, and it was as if a general alert had been sounded through the town.

"He was buying cartons of cigarettes and cases of beer," a store clerk had told the Montague County sheriff's department in the investigation that unfolded years later. "And the checks had been made out by him and signed 'Katy Rich.' Granny never signed her checks that way."

The store clerk was also concerned over the amount of items charged to Kate Rich's store account. He kept an accurate record because he realized that these were items that Mrs. Rich would never purchase herself. Calls had also been placed by Becky which requested deliveries in large quantities of items that Kate Rich herself had barely used when she lived alone. The charge account was paid for with another check signed "Katy" Rich.

Finally, the store clerk had had enough. He was concerned about Mrs. Rich, worried over the amounts of goods being charged and paid for with questionable checks, and downright nervous about the one-eyed man and the little girl living in the house with the old widow. He notified the group of Mrs. Rich's relatives that lived just over the state line in Oklahoma and reminded them that Mrs. Rich had a very strange drifter and his teen-age wife living with her. The family didn't react immediately, but waited to see if the situation

144

changed in any way. When it didn't, the family decided to act.

The Rich family traveled from Oklahoma and descended upon the Kate Rich household in the early hours of the morning. They had seen from the list of charged items and deliveries that Granny Rich herself couldn't have consumed these items and therefore wouldn't have ordered them. They wondered whether anything had happened to her and decided to act that very day. When they arrived at Mrs. Rich's house, they found the old woman sitting at a kitchen table amidst weeks of accumulated filth and debris. Nothing had been cleaned. Rock-hardened food was splattered all over the stove and the wall. Utensils had piled up in the kitchen sink to the point where the sink itself was barely visible. Mud had been tracked in through the kitchen and not cleaned up, and the windows had been left closed so that the entire household smelled foul from human sweat, stale cigarette smoke that was still hanging in the air, and from rancid or spoiled food.

The family members looked around the house and found Lucas and Becky sound asleep on the living room couches, obviously snoring off a drunk. There were deep cigarette burns in the couch cushions and the rugs were scorched where cigarette ashes had fallen, begun to smoulder, and had been stomped out. The house was a filthy pit and a firetrap just waiting to go up.

Without even bothering to call the sheriff, the family evicted Lucas and Becky on the spot, driving them to the center of Ringgold and offering them money for bus fare. Anywhere, they told Lucas and Becky, they would send them anywhere just so long as it was far, far away from Granny Rich and Montague County. Lucas was still hanging on the edge of a drunk, and he was vastly outnumbered by the relatives surrounding him. He didn't put up a fight. Becky even seemed traumatized by the events of the morning, and Granny Rich had lapsed into a state bordering on shock and disbelief. The family's sudden appearance was like a splash of cold water.

Lucas agreed to go quietly along with whatever the family wanted. He accepted the money and told the family he wouldn't come back because he was catching the next bus to Wichita Falls. They left him and Becky at the town's center, the Ringgold general store which served as the rural bus stop for the area, and went back to the Rich household. But Henry and Becky didn't get on the next bus. Instead, Henry folded the money into his pocket and told Becky that they would hitch a ride back to Wichita Falls, where he was still expecting a bank money order from the Smarts from whom he'd requested money in order buy supplies for repairs to Granny Rich's house. Actually,

Henry was planning to return to California and the Smarts to complain about the way he and Becky were treated. At least they would have money to help them along the way, Henry believed.

As they marched dejectedly along the rural state route, Henry and Becky must have looked almost as forlorn and hapless as they were months earlier when Jack Smart spied them through his windshield. This time, however, a jocular man in an old, worn-out, pickup truck passed them, stopped, and asked them where they were going.

"Out to Wichita Falls," Henry said. "I need to pick up some wages."

"Well hop in, friend," the driver said. "I'm going in that direction and you can come along."

He drove them to the post office in Wichita Falls and waited for Lucas to come back out while Becky waited with him in the truck. But when Lucas reappeared in the doorway, he was wearing a look of gloom. The check hadn't arrived, and he and Becky were clean out of money.

"Well, you folks can stay down at my place for a couple of weeks," he said. "I'm a preacher." He stuck out his heavily calloused hand. "I'm Ruben Moore, and I have a small religious community just outside Ringgold in a town called Stoneburg. I call my place The House of Prayer. You can stay there."

147

"Be obliged," Henry said, and he and Becky rode with the Reverend Moore to his community while Henry plotted their next move and tried to figure out how he could best get back on the road again, because the urge to kill was once more coming over him.

Chapter 8

The House of Prayer

In July, 1982, The House of Prayer was a long chicken coop sitting on an old ranch in Stoneburg, about ten miles south of Ringgold. The Reverend Ruben Moore explained that it was a little religious community, a small group of "Christian believers" who read the gospel together and shared their revelations, lived on the same plot of land in little shacks, shared their food in a community kitchen, raised their children, and helped maintain the upkeep of the grounds. There was little Henry Lee Lucas could do to contribute to the group, he told Rev. Moore. He didn't profess to being a practicing Christian, although Becky said she had some instruction in the faith, but he did have mechanical skills.

149

"I have my own roofing business," the Reverend Moore told Lucas. "And I'm always looking for honest labor."

"Well, I'm a roofer, by trade," Lucas reportedly said.

"We can feed you," Moore told Lucas and Becky. "We can help you get set up. You can work for me as a day laborer, if you want, and do work around the camp to earn your keep. There's a lot of fixing up to do, more than I can handle. The rest of it is up to you all to figure out. If you want to work for me, you can. 'Course, you'll have to attend church meetings every Sunday. That's the only thing we ask."

Henry accepted a temporary offer of lodging at the House of Prayer while he figured out what he would do next. He says that he didn't want to accept any charity from the commune, but Moore's offer of honest work in exchange for food and lodging was something he did like. Henry signed on as a commune worker even before the trio bounced into the commune. Moore also gave him a standing offer to help him in the construction company and earn whatever spending money he could. By the end of the day, Becky and Henry had been assigned a small shack amidst the other group members.

Henry and Becky quickly settled in. Henry says the camp was in a state of disrepair. The roofs were leaking and peeling back on the small shacks and there was a lot of carpentry work to be done. He began hammering, scraping, and tarring within the first twenty-four hours. In a few days, he had begun making gradual repairs to the shacks throughout the commune. He and Becky began attending regular Sunday meetings as well and became practicing members of the little religious colony.

Henry didn't mind at first. He thought it would be interesting, a change of pace, something different for Becky. He planned to sit through the services because it was required. He didn't plan to do any believing or any praying. He had told interviewers that in The Hand of Death he had already pledged his life and soul. He had been told, moreover, that there was no way out of the cult. He said he accepted that.

Becky, on the other hand, had never experienced regular church meetings before and began to change right before Henry's eyes. First, she began to make new friends in the community within the first few days. Members of the group would stop at their shack while Henry was patching the roofs of other structures and talk with Becky as if she were a regular, upstanding citizen. Becky discovered she wanted friends. It was as if she had found a new family. And people were attracted to her warmth and her naivete. One older woman

151

actually called her a "lamb" who had been sent into their community to provide them with an example of true innocence.

Henry couldn't complain, however. Within a couple of weeks, Ruben Moore had put him on a work crew and he was beginning to earn "credits" and even a little spending money. He and Becky had most of the food they needed provided for them by the community in exchange for Henry's labor. The House of Prayer also provided Henry with a perfect cover for the times he would pick up unwary victims. He said that he was free to roam at will, robbing, raping, killing over the state line in Oklahoma where he believed he was not likely to be traced back to Texas. He made sure to keep his crimes out of Montague County where Stoneburg and Ringgold were located so that the local sheriff would have no reason to come calling. And he always killed strangers because there was never any connection between him and his victim. It was all working perfectly until Becky got religion.

Henry should have noticed the signs. He should have noticed how Becky's circle of friends grew and grew among the women in the community. This was a fundamentalist sect, after all, and they were quick to trust and to open up to anyone who professed to seek knowledge of the gospel. Henry, of course, didn't profess anything except his pot of

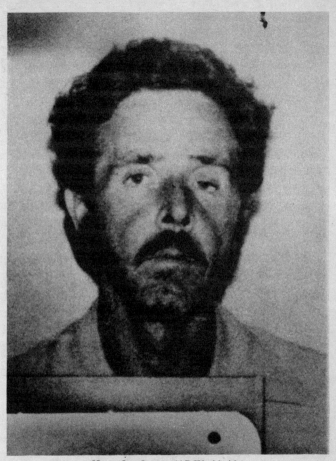
Henry Lee Lucas. (AP/Worldwide)

Henry Lee Lucas walking out of the Montague County courthouse
after his bail was set at one million dollars on June 24, 1983.
(UPI/Bettman)

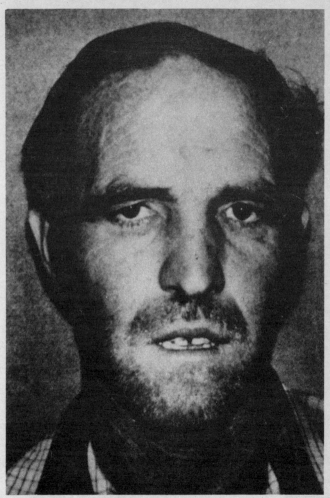
Ottis Elwood Toole. (AP/Worldwide)

Frieda Lorraine "Becky" Powell.

"Becky" Powell and her brother Frank Powell in Florida.

"Orange Socks," the unidentified female victim found in a culvert
along I-35 in Williamson County, Texas.

"Orange Socks" as found by law officers in November, 1979. She is wearing the pair of socks for which she was named.

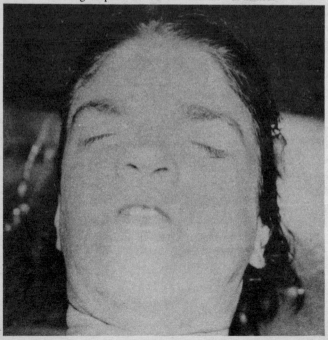

Face of "Orange Socks" on the autopsy table.

Henry Lee Lucas indicates location where he claims to have buried Granny Kate Rich's clothing on the west side of U.S. 81, approximately three miles north of Stonesburg, Texas. (Courtesy of the District Attorney's Office, Montague County, Texas)

Law enforcement officers digging in the old chicken house for the buried remains of Kate Rich at The House of Prayer community. (Courtesy of the District Attorney's Office, Montague County, Texas)

Wood-burning stove in which Henry Lee Lucas burned the butchered body of Kate Rich. (Courtesy of the District Attorney's Office, Montague County, Texas)

Williamson County Jail, Georgetown, Texas. (Courtesy of Nan Cuba)

Henry Lee Lucas in his cell at Williamson County Jail. (Courtesy of Nan Cuba)

Henry Lee Lucas in his "office" looking at photographs of seven of his alleged victims. Law officers Captain Bob Prince (l.) and Sheriff Jim Boutwell (r.) are present. (Courtesy of Nan Cuba)

Henry Lee Lucas accompanied by Sheriff Jim Boutwell and Captain
Bob Prince near the site where "Orange Socks" was found.
(Courtesy of Nan Cuba)

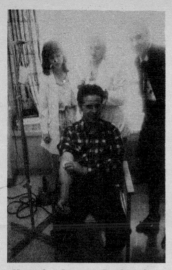

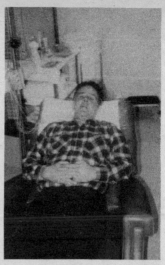

Henry Lee Lucas at Presbyterian Hospital, Dallas, Texas after his blood was drawn for analysis. (Courtesy of Nan Cuba)

Henry Lee Lucas undergoing an EKG test at Presbyterian Hospital. (Courtesy of Nan Cuba)

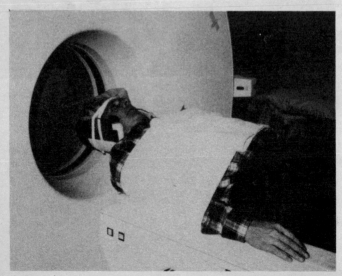

Henry Lee Lucas just before his Magnetic Resonance Image (MRI) test at Baylor Hospital, Dallas, Texas. (Courtesy of Nan Cuba)

Henry Lee Lucas's freehand sketch of one of his
alleged victims.

The following three photos are examples of the paintings by Henry
Lee Lucas stored in Sister Clemmie's home. (Courtesy of Nan Cuba)

Henry Lee Lucas confessing to the murder of two females at the crime site in San Luis Obispo County, California. (AP/Worldwide)

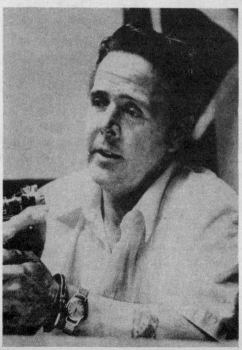

Henry Lee Lucas at Pulaski County Circuit Court in Little Rock, Arkansas, confessing to the murder of a convenience store clerk there. (AP/ Worldwide)

Henry Lee Lucas on Death Row in Huntsville, Texas recanting his
previous confessions. (AP/Worldwide)

coffee, his packs of cigarettes, and his cans of beer. He cut down on beer, however, because he could see that members of the community didn't approve of his drinking. He didn't want to leave the community, though, because he was becoming strangely satisfied in the stable living arrangements that he had finally managed to provide for himself and Becky.

Henry was always guarded to people, he says, and quick to anger. He says that he kept muttering or whispering threats under his breath whenever people stared at him too long or whenever he felt that things weren't going his way. "When I'm around people," he said, "I feel tense, nervous. I guess it's because I haven't been around people. Most of the life I've lived has been alone."

The sect members said that they were wary of him not because he was continually nervous, but because he seemed menacing. "It was that look in his one good eye," one of the members reportedly said. Lucas seemed to have a threatening manner toward Becky that became more and more obvious as she more deeply involved with the church's meetings.

Becky found meaning in the group's religious practices even more quickly than Henry could have imagined. She attended prayer services and other meetings, enjoyed the communal atmosphere of the encampment, and even visited Kate Rich, who lived only ten miles away. Despite the problems with their living arrangements, Becky had become close to Granny Rich during her short stay there, and the widow Rich had come to look upon the child as partly her own. She still thought of Becky as her little "waif," and was pleased that she was settled so close to Ringgold. And as Henry grew increasingly hostile to Becky and to her new-found religion, Becky grew increasingly closer to Kate Rich. She soon started practicing fingering out tunes on the rickety old church piano.

Between the anger she was feeling from Henry, the encouragement she was receiving from Kate Rich, and the strength she was deriving from the worship services at the House of Prayer, Becky slowly began formulating a decision in her own mind. She talked about it with Kate Rich, although Lucas would not know about it until weeks later. Becky knew that as long as she stayed with Henry at the House of Prayer, she would forever be a fugitive. She was happy in Stoneburg, to be sure, but she was always afraid of the sheriff or the Texas Rangers. She was afraid of the flashing lights of any passing police car because she knew that just as sure as she was learning how to cook and take care of Henry, one day those flashing lights would be coming for her.

She was a fugitive who had crossed state lines

in order to escape from her reform school. She believed she had committed a federal crime and was only implicating Henry in a federal crime every day she stayed with him. But she believed that if she voluntarily returned to Florida and gave herself up, she might even get off with a reduced sentence because she would have proven herself to have been rehabilitated. She finally reached her decision. She would not wait any longer. She would tell Henry that she was going back to Florida and take charge of the rest of her life. If Henry fought her on it, she would go back alone or call her Uncle Ottis to take her back home.

She waited until she saw Henry laughing a lot. He'd had his beer on the job, made a little money under the table, and was feeling pretty flush. That's when she let him have it. She was so full of joy, she said. She was full of forgiveness. She was full of the need to get her life back instead of living in fear of the police. She wasn't angry, just ready to start living again. It was surprising for Henry to hear her talk like that and he wasn't prepared for it. He put up a fight. He said that he just wasn't going to give up the life he had to go back to Florida where he'd just have to lose her. He cut the argument off and crawled onto the bed. There was no talking to him now, she thought to herself. But she had planned to be relentless, and relentless was exactly what she was going to become.

Over the next few weeks, members of the commune could hear Henry and Becky arguing through the window. They could hear her cry when Henry turned sullen and wouldn't answer her, and they could hear the rising menace in his voice when he was crossed. "Nobody would have put up with what I have," people heard her complain to him during one of their arguments. And they heard him growl, "You didn't think it was so bad when you lit out with me from that home." And Becky would be silent because the fight would be over for that night. It would pick up during the week, when their voices again would float over the encampment on the hot Texas nights as midsummer approached.

On one particular night in early August, the sounds of fighting coming out of the Lucas shack had become particularly intense. Becky started crying and she threatened that if Henry wasn't ready to take her back home right away, she would call her Uncle Ottis and tell him to get her. "And if Uncle Ottis doesn't come for me, then I'm hitching back on my own." Then there was a long silence. People thought they might have heard Henry muttering something, but they couldn't tell. Fight's over, they thought to themselves.

But Henry said he had kept on talking, trying

to reason with Becky as best he could. But he could see in her eyes that she meant business. He didn't like it, but he prepared himself for the inevitable and told her that he would make plans to get them both back to Florida. Becky promised Henry that when she got out of the reform school, she would return to him and the two of them would pick up right where they left off, except that Becky would have served her sentence and would have a clear conscience knowing that she was no longer a fugitive. That was the best Henry was going to get out of her that night. He acquiesced and made his plans to tell Ruben Moore.

There is another version of this same part of the story which is chilling in its implication. According to this version, Henry told interviewers Becky told him that she had been born again and had seen the revelation. She was entitled to whatever she wanted to think, he told her, but that he was serving another power which she knew he had pledged himself to. "There's no way out of The Hand of Death," he told her. "No way out if you want to stay alive. Remember that." But he said that Becky told him that she had been saved and that she would confess her sins. And they included the things she knew about Henry Lee and Ottis Toole.

But Becky remained adamant and told Henry that not only did she want to begin a new life, but that she wanted Henry to confess his sins as well and join the spiritual congregation. Henry agreed to participate at the meetings on Sunday instead of just showing up and sneaking out after they were halfway through. Moore was allowing him to do that because he knew that Henry wasn't really a practicing Christian. He was too good a worker to lose, however, and as long as he just showed up, the Reverend Moore was content with that. Maybe someday it would stick and Henry would actually come to join the service. That's why Ruben Moore was surprised when Henry didn't sneak out the doorway midway through the next prayer reading.

Becky was pleased that Henry was staying at the meetings. But it quickly became not enough. Now, Becky told him, her mission was to convert him. Before the entire community, Henry would confess his sins—really confess, she said, just like she'd confessed.

"Jes' like you confessed?" Henry snarled.

What did she mean and to whom did she confess her sins? Just how much had the girl told?

"Nuthin' about you and Uncle Ottis," she said. "Jes' how ah been a sinner."

But Henry was worried. He knew that his hard work was paying for what Becky ate. They got to sleep in dry beds at night because of Henry's climbing up on roofs in 120° heat and smearing

158

hot tar over the worn spots. The tar burned his hands and the sun fried him. But it was work, and Henry liked it. He just didn't like having Becky tell him that he was a sinner after he had reroofed the meeting house. He also had to get to the bottom of this confession thing, and fast. If Becky had begun to talk, she was not only incriminating herself and revealing that she was a fugitive, she was incriminating Henry, Ottis Toole, and possibly The Hand of Death as well. He himself would have to pay for whatever Becky revealed, as would she. Henry could take care of himself, he always believed, but Becky was putting herself in jeopardy. It was at that point that he came to a decision. As much as he liked living at the House of Prayer, they would have to leave, if only to protect their mutual secrets.

Henry knew that he wasn't going to intimidate Becky into shutting up. He had to make her feel responsible for bringing potential danger to him and her uncle, to make her feel guilty for incriminating them if that's what she was doing. He also had to find a way out of what was becoming an increasingly difficult situation. Becky actually made it easy for him when she demanded that they return to Florida where she would go back to the reform school to serve the remainder of her sentence.

Henry didn't realize at first how easy she was

making it for him. He only saw that a lifestyle he had grown accustomed to and that had provided him with a perfect camouflage had become increasingly endangered by Becky's flirtation with religion. When she told him that it was time for her to head home, he burst into rage. But as she described to him her feelings about the group and her need to keep on confessing her sins, he realized that it would be easier to get her out of the community now and get back after she was in Florida. If she turned herself in voluntarily, he might not have to wait for her for very long, and she might even have outgrown this religious stuff by the time she got released. Henry didn't like going back, but he knew that he was going to learn to live with it. Then he asked Becky his chilling question: "Answer me directly, darlin'—did you tell anyone here anything 'bout you know what, me 'n yer Uncle Ottis."

"No, Daddy, I didn't tell 'em nothin'," she said. He believed her.

Henry promised to begin making the arrangements the next day. It would be like saying goodbye to family, Becky told herself, but for her own good it had to be done. Henry and Becky stopped fighting. They had come to an understanding. Henry would make the arrangements, and Becky would come up with a story about her having to see her family in Florida.

In August, the arrangements were made and Henry shook hands with Ruben Moore for what they both assumed would be the last time.

It was August, 1982, and Henry and Becky walked out of camp early the next morning to begin their trek east. They were on the road again like two drifters hitchhiking, looking for rides along the interstates that would eventually take them back to Florida where, Henry knew, he'd be saying goodbye to Becky for a long time to come. The thought of it was making him angry, but there was little he could do about it except try to coax her into changing her mind and her way of thinking.

A day or two later, Henry and Becky had reached Denton County and found it impossible to get a ride. Truckers would slow down as they passed them, leer out their windows at Becky then spot Henry shuffling alongside, and speed on by, leaving the two stragglers choking on diesel fumes. They were finding it impossible to get a ride from anyone. Henry and Becky soon realized that it was going to be a long, long trip. Maybe the times had changed. Maybe the news of dead bodies piling up in unmarked shallow graves along I-35 and other Texas thoroughfares had made local drivers more wary. Nobody seemed to be stopping to pick them up.

Eventually, after a long day of dragging through

the hot Texas sun, they decided to find a motel where Becky could shower and Henry could fall facedown on a bed. But there were no rooms at any of the local motels around the area. The sky was threatening as dusk pushed toward night, and occasionally heat lightning would explode behind the low-hanging clouds, but there was no rain. Becky finally suggested they simply lay out their bedrolls and sleep in an open field. Henry was too tired to argue. He wanted to get to his beer and fall asleep.

The two spread their blankets out and Henry started drinking heavily. He began complaining. He hadn't been this miserable in a long time. He thought these days were long gone, he said. They had a home at the House of Prayer until Becky up and went crazy on him with religion. He had a job. They were making money and she was even still seeing her old friend Granny Rich. There was no reason for this foolishness. What was the point of going back after all? She'd only have to serve time in a reformatory. They would have to be separated. And wasn't the reason she had escaped in the first place to be with Henry? Why go back now? It no sense.

What if she got back to the reformatory and they sent her to a foster home? Becky couldn't answer that question. "Then we'd really be separated," Henry growled. "I'd never find you and I'd never get to see you again." Then he reminded her that there was probably a warrant out for him because of her escape. He would have to be punished, and Becky was bringing him right back to the law and to prison. Likely as not, he reminded her, there were burglary and murder warrants out for him as well. Did Becky really want to see him back in jail, quite possibly for the rest of his life? And what if they charged Becky with being an accomplice? She'd spend the better part of her life behind bars as well.

"Nope, too risky," Henry said. They were better off staying at the House of Prayer where people liked them and he could make some money. He'd thought it all over. She could even believe what she wanted to as long as she didn't incriminate Henry.

But Becky wouldn't stop fighting, and Henry couldn't figure out why. She was complaining that they had to sleep outside. She was mad that for all the work Henry'd done, he couldn't get them a car they could drive back to Florida. They were both so tired at this point that neither of them could think straight, but still Becky kept pushing.

"It all started because I wanted to go back to the House of Prayer," he says, remembering each moment in the smallest detail. "We argued for a long time and it was sort of hot. Heat, you know, and stuff. I took my clothes off and laid down upon the blanket and Becky took her clothes off except her bra and panties. And we kept arguin', cussin' each other. Finally I just told her that we were going back the next morning and she just hauled off and hit me upside the head and that was it. I just stabbed her with the knife. I just picked it up and brought it around and hit her right in the chest with it. She sort of set there for a little bit and then dropped on over."

Henry remembers that he was almost in a state of shock at first. This was a person he had loved. He had truly cared for her, he said, and in a single instant it was all over. He had destroyed someone he loved. He remembers that all he could do was try to make love with her dead and bloody corpse. "I took her panties and bra off and had sex with her. That's one of those things I guess that got to be a part of my life — having sexual intercourse with the dead."

Then he took her ring from her finger and began to dispose of the body. Whatever he had thought about what he had just done, whatever shock he was in, he still didn't want to get caught, he says. After he had intercourse with her corpse, he remembers, "I cut her up in little tiny pieces and stuffed it in three pillows that we had. I dumped the stuffin' out of the pillows and stuffed all of her in there except her legs and, I guess you'd say, her thighs. Then I put all that in there.

I got up and walked down the field a piece."

Henry remembers he wandered around for hours realizing that something was terribly wrong with him. He'd killed before, hundreds of times before, he said, but it was never like this. He couldn't get the living Becky out of his mind. He couldn't get her face, her voice, her demeanor, or her spirit out of his consciousness. She was a presence that was staying with him. His other victims had been like pieces of rock or clumps of sand, inanimate objects who were never really there. But Becky was indeed different. It was unsettling to him — a radical feeling. Henry had never had real feelings for another human being in his life. Now that he had killed Becky, he recognized that he indeed had feelings for the dead girl, and they were feelings he couldn't do anything about because she was dead by his own hand. Henry was experiencing remorse.

Chapter 9

Granny Rich

Henry wanted to run away, he remembers, to go as far away from the killing site as he possibly could. But then another voice began playing in his brain. He remembers that it told him that he still had to account for Becky's disappearance because people had last seen them together. He had learned that one of the quickest way to remove suspicion from yourself was to provide a plausible explanation for your whereabouts immediately. Witnesses and police had a funny way of taking your explanation, if it was made quickly enough, as part of the truth. The crime needed to become something that happened *after* your version of the truth was accepted as reality. That was how you got away with it. And Henry had become an accomplished master at creating an alternate truth to explain his whereabouts whenever police questioned him. He was adept at avoiding police interrogations because, he said, he always knew what they were looking for and he always knew how to turn suspicion away from himself.

Therefore, Henry realized, he had to return to the House of Prayer to explain that Becky had left him and to beg them to allow him to return. In that way, he told himself, if Becky were ever missed, it would be presumed that she had run into trouble after Henry returned to the commune and not while they were together. He would bury Becky later when he could face her again. He left the pillowcases and Becky's legs under desert scrub by a small tree. And for the rest of the night, before he attempted to return to the House of Prayer, he spoke to Becky as if she were still alive.

"I wanted her spirit to forgive me," Henry said. "I knew it was still there and that it wouldn't give me any peace."

Two days later, he walked into the House of Prayer encampment and broke down in tears at the first sight of the Reverend Moore.

"She drove away with another man," he told Moore. "Drove away in his eighteen-wheeler and left me standing by the side of the road."

Moore tried as best he could to console the weeping Henry Lee Lucas, but even he believed at the time that Becky was better off without him. Lucas might have been a good worker, but he was mean and Moore sorely feared for that little girl the whole while she was in Lucas' shack. Now that she was gone and Henry was back, Moore felt, maybe he'd have a good influence on Henry. Moore could not have even guessed at the truth.

As Henry cried and told Moore that until he could figure out where his future was taking him, he simply had nowhere to go. "Maybe I could just work for you for a spell until I figure out why my darlin' drove away from me."

Moore believed that he could have told Lucas straight out why Becky left him, thereby saving Henry a lot of trouble. But Moore said nothing because he believed that a man should have the time to work out his own difficulties. Besides, Moore believed, this was clearly a message to him that he had the opportunity to turn Henry's life around. Maybe he could make a difference and give Henry Lee Lucas hope for a better life to come. Thus, the Reverend Moore took pity on Henry Lee Lucas. He saw him as a penitent sinner who had returned to be pointed in a new direction. Moore asked the other members of his congregation to take pity on Henry as well and, as Henry sat in his shack that evening, he believed that he had convinced everyone he had spoken to that Becky had left him. It didn't ease his pain at having killed Becky and at having to face the rest of his life without her, but at least, he told himself, he would not have to go jail for killing her.

Henry let himself drift back into the daily flow of the community while he looked for a way to put his murder of Becky behind him and, more importantly, to break the news to Ottis. He figured he could handle Ottis, but killing Becky still hurt him more than he realized. Maybe, he said to himself, formally burying the girl would help. "Two weeks later I came back to bury Becky," Henry said. "I went over and buried one bag of her remains and they were buried there at the tree. And I wanted to bury the rest of her but I just couldn't do it. Left the body right where it was."

He later admitted to returning to the site many times during the two weeks. He tried, as best he could, to talk to her spirit, to ask for forgiveness, and, he says "to tell her that I was sorry for having killed her." Henry made a promise, he told interviewers the following year. "I told her that someday I would join her, wherever she was, if I could ever figure out a way to get there." His remorse over a reflex murder seemed to have thrown a switch somewhere in his psyche. He was no longer interested in covering his tracks with the same cunning as before.

169

"It broke for me," he said months later while in jail. "Nothin' was the same after that. It was like I was walkin' through shadows." From that moment on, his criminal career began to unravel. Now Becky's voice, he claimed, was among the voices searing through his brain. Only her voice was telling him to confess, he said, to find an end to misery now that he had killed the only person he had ever loved.

Kate Rich had been calling him ever since word spread through the tiny little communities of Stoneburg and Ringgold that the one-eyed drifter had returned without his girlfriend. People were curious and strangely stirred to pity when they heard—third, fourth, and fifth hand—that the angel-faced little girl with the big dark eyes had left him for a truck driver out on the interstate. Kate had asked about him and Henry offered to drive her to church one Sunday evening in September, a little less than a month after he'd killed Becky.

It was a warm night when Henry pulled up in Ruben Moore's old car, and they were very early. Lucas said he wanted to drive into Oklahoma with her to pick up some beer before the service. But the drive took longer than they expected and Henry began drinking the beer before he even got back into the car. He began to drive erratically, as if his mind were somewhere else.

Lucas started complaining about Becky when

Kate asked him why she left him. He told her how Becky had deceived him, how she had led him on, how she had tricked him into taking her away from The House of Prayer so that she could run off with the first person who picked them up.

"That doesn't sound like my little Becky," Granny Rich said.

"There's much you don't know about your little Becky," Henry answered, now clearly getting mad that Kate wasn't sympathizing with him and blaming Becky for running off.

Maybe in Henry's mind he had actually come to believe the alibi he'd created to explain Becky's disappearance, and was living in his own denial. Then he explained that they had fought right before they saw the truck driver, and that Becky had slapped him because he wanted to bring her back to The House of Prayer. That was more than he was going to take from a spoiled fifteen-year-old, he explained.

Kate Rich became even more suspicious and started asking him exactly where Becky was. By now it was already too late for church, and Lucas, clearly angry at being asked so many questions and at being late for the one thing he had planned to do with Kate Rich, told Granny that he would drive her home. But, as Lucas confessed months later, Granny persisted with her questioning. She wouldn't let up. On the way back into

Ringgold, Lucas suddenly realized that he'd had enough. He spun the wheel without warning and turned the car sharply off the highway and onto a dirt road leading to a remote old pumped-out oil patch where he stopped the car and slammed it into park.

Had Kate Rich asked one too many questions about Becky? Had she challenged Henry's story in ways he couldn't answer? Had she threatened him? Not even Lucas is sure about what triggered him to kill her, but he did. He turned upon her with his knife as she sat next to him in the car. He plunged the knife deep into her left side with savage violence. Kate Rich slumped against the door of the car and as she slid down, Lucas reached across her, opened the door, and pushed her dead body out of the vehicle.

He dragged her away from the car and with the tip of his knife cut an upside down cross between the old woman's breasts, had sexual intercourse with her corpse, and dragged her into a culvert where he lodged her in nice and tight with a two-by-four from the oil construction site. Then he shoved her clothing down a nearby drain pipe and drove back to The House of Prayer where Ruben Moore was waiting for him. Moore wanted to know how the service had been because he was pleased that Kate Rich had convinced Henry to go to church. But Lucas explained that old Kate was sick and couldn't go. He wanted to go back to her later that night, he said. In reality, however, Lucas needed to collect garbage bags from the mission because he wanted to bring Granny's remains back.

Later that night, Lucas returned to where he had lodged Kate Rich's remains and pulled them out of the culvert. He cut them into small chunks which he put in the bags and drove back to The House of Prayer. He worked through the night as furiously as he could, burning each little piece in the wood stove in the communal kitchen until all that was left of Granny Rich was bone chips and ashes. The job was finally completed shortly before dawn and at 5 AM, Henry took the car and pulled out of Stoneburg. No one saw him go.

While Kate Rich's relatives began calling her as early as the following Monday, Lucas was already in a frenzied panic as he tried to escape from murders where he had a direct connection to the victims. He realized eventually that Ruben Moore would tell whoever would soon be investigating Kate Rich's disappearance that Lucas had been possibly the last person to see the old woman alive. Any way he looked at it, Henry realized, his days of anonymity were coming to an end. His only hope was to accumulate as much money as possible and disappear.

First, Henry drove north, looping into Oklahoma, where he broke into a store and stole a number of television sets. Then he drove back into Amarillo, where he quickly sold off those sets for cash, and on into California where he'd planned to look for work. Eventually Henry headed for the Smarts to beg for a job, lodging, and food while accumulating cash through robberies for a trip back east until things cooled down.

Meanwhile, Granny Rich's relatives drove to Ringgold to search physically for the woman when she wouldn't answer her phone. When they realized she had disappeared, they filed a missing person's report with the county sheriff, Bill "Hound Dog" Conway. They told Conway about Lucas and about Kate Rich's continued association with the drifter whom they suspected of stealing her money and placing her in dire jeopardy. They gave Conway Lucas' address at The House of Prayer. Sheriff Conway asked the Reverend Moore about Lucas and Moore confirmed that as far as he knew, Lucas had driven to see Kate Rich on that past Sunday for church. But Lucas, Moore told the sheriff, said that Kate Rich was sick and they never went to church. Mrs. Rich's relatives confirmed that they had been calling Kate without an answer since Monday morning.

Hound Dog Conway's suspicions were aroused. Who was this one-eyed drifter who suddenly seemed to disappear after having allegedly seen

Kate Rich the night before? Conway checked Lucas' name against NCIC records and got an eyeful back over his teletype. He discovered that Lucas had served maximum security time for a previous homicide in a Michigan penitentiary, he received records of Lucas' previous convictions in Michigan for parole violations and the attempted rape and kidnapping of a teenaged girl, and he received current information about outstanding warrants for Lucas for violation of his parole. But without information from Lucas, Conway had no direct link to the missing Kate Rich. Moreover, because Lucas had left his jurisdiction, Sheriff Conway could only wait until he returned in order to question him.

Henry Lee Lucas drove into Needles, California, in late September, but the car broke down before he could reach Hemet. He abandoned it and hitched to the Smarts' antique store. He was desperate and hungry. His cash had run out and he was almost crippled by his growing remorse over having killed Becky. Lucas remembers that he was quite fearful, because it seemed as if a web were closing tighter around him. He was no longer the invisible killer. He was driving a car that wasn't his, and he knew that Kate Rich's relatives would start making phone calls to the police when they realized she wasn't in the house. Would Katy's grandchildren call Jack Smart and his wife about him in advance as well.

He had to chance it. But by the time he had reached the Smarts, his luck had already run out. Indeed, according to Lucas' version of the story, Granny Rich's Oklahoma family had phoned ahead to the Smarts, telling them about the old woman's disappearance and asking them to alert them if Lucas ever showed up. When Henry arrived, the Smarts welcomed him as if they suspected nothing, but they telephoned their relatives in Oklahoma that evening, who immediately notified Sheriff Conway that Lucas was living behind the Smart's store in California.

"Can you keep him there?" the Smarts were asked. They relayed the message to the Smarts who answered that they had sheltered Lucas and Becky before, and they knew how to keep his suspicions from being aroused. They just didn't want to keep him under their roof for too long if he really was implicated in the disappearance of Kate Rich.

But in the meantime, Sheriff Conway had not been idle. His trace on Lucas was paying off and the records search on the car that Henry had taken from The House of Prayer had turned up a vehicle registration that had not been properly transferred. Conway found the name of the original owner of the car in Wichita Falls. The original owner had died. He was an old man, but his relatives claimed they had just received a letter from the California Highway Patrol about a car that had been abandoned in Needles which the police said was still registered to the dead man. Conway immediately called the California Highway patrol and asked them to impound the car. When the CHP told the sheriff that there were bloodstains all over the front seat, Conway asked the Highway Patrol to pick up Henry Lee Lucas at the Smarts' antique store in Hemet as a material witness in the murder of a Texas resident. If the blood on the car seat matched Kate Rich's, Conway would have gotten his man.

The CHP surrounded the Smarts' residence later that day and took Lucas into custody. They told him that they had received an impound order from Texas regarding the car that Lucas was said to have abandoned in Needles. They also told him they had a search warrant for the car and that they intended to run tests on bloodstains that were found in the front seat. They asked him to make a statement. But Lucas was cagey.

"That's my own blood," Lucas told the CHP about the stains. "Cut myself a while back."

The CHP reported Lucas' answers to their questions about the bloodstains to Conway, who asked Kate Rich's relatives for the old woman's medical records. Because Kate Rich herself had not been found, there were no actual blood samples to go on, only the record of her blood type from her medical history. Kate had type A blood. According to Lucas, the CHP asked him for a blood sample to type against the stain. Lucas knew from his studies of police procedure in the prison library all the way back in Michigan that most dried blood becomes type O. He himself was a type O. He gambled that the blood types would match.

"It's a funny thing about bloodstains," Lucas said years later when he remembered the incident. "In that dry, desert heat, blood dries out pretty quick. Most of the blood tests police use are for fresh stains. Takes a doctor to run tests on old blood. These officers only had a blood type to go on. They told me that if my blood type was the same as the stain, I could go. I figgered the odds were in my favor."

He was right. Even though the blood from Kate Rich was originally a type A, it had dried and could not be matched against any actual blood from Kate Rich because her body was still missing. Lucas' sample tested type O, the same as the stains in the car, and the police went no further. Without a sample to match the stain against, without a match to the purported missing person, and without a California warrant or an extradition order for Lucas, they had to let him go.

Henry had slipped out of Sheriff Conway's grasp and out of custody. By the end of September, he had left California altogether, hitchhiking his way east and north, still in remorse over having murdered Becky, but desperately seeking to escape the police. But he also put too much hope in the events in California. If they hadn't caught him on the bloodstain, he thought to himself at the time, *they hadn't found old Kate's remains*. Likely as not they hadn't found Becky either. Without physical evidence, Lucas knew, there was no evidence to hold him on. He believed that he could remain free if he stayed out of the area for a few months and sought work elsewhere. That's just what he intended to do.

Chapter 10
The Final Spree

Lucas didn't waste any time in California once the Highway Patrol released him. He says he hitched out of Hemet that day to New Mexico and turned straight north. He intended to go as far away from Texas as possible because he knew that Conway was after him for information about Kate and Becky. It didn't matter that the bloodstains on the car seat didn't match. He'd have to spend more than few months on the road before it was safe to cross the Texas border.

In a final spree, he first spent time in Oklahoma, robbing convenience stores and killing the victims to eliminate any witnesses. Then he went through Missouri, Indiana, and Illinois. He claimed he was looking for work, looking for money, and trying to run away at the same time.

He was morose without Becky and couldn't return to Florida. He simply had no destination in mind. He flirted with the idea of catching a ride back to Maryland to his sister or to his ex-wife to ask for money, but he abandoned it. He remembered that there might have been an outstanding Maryland warrant for him and didn't want to run right back into police charges.

October 1, 1982, found Henry in Decatur, Illinois, where he had tried to find work on a construction crew but was turned down because he had no state identification. That gave him an idea, and he applied for welfare. At the very least, he thought, applying for public assistance not only would provide him with money, it might also open up some new leads to jobs. There were certainly plenty of jobs listed on the bulletin board of the welfare office. But he found out that waiting for the welfare application would take a few days, and he was out of money. "I'll be back in a few days," he told the welfare applications clerk and left the office for good. His application remained open for weeks after that.

He hitched a ride just off a state route south of Decatur after nightfall to a truck stop in Missouri where he spied a young woman in an old station wagon waiting for gas at one of the pumps. The gas station was almost empty except for a few eighteen-wheelers parked in a lot some distance off from the diesel fuel pump. Most of the drivers were probably sleeping, he told himself. She was a perfect target. He waited while she parked her car, got coffee from a nearby machine, and went back to her car to unlock the door, still balancing the coffee in her other hand. Lucas slid up behind her and pushed the blade between her ribs.

"Unlock the door and don't say nothin'," he hissed. "No one here can see a thing. I just need a ride and don't want no trouble."

The woman was in her thirties and scared about traveling alone, Lucas remembers. She didn't even put up a fight. She turned the key in the lock, stood back while he opened the door, and slid to the right side of the front bench seat of the wagon while Lucas climbed in behind the wheel. He pulled out of the station and onto the roadway while the woman slowly sipped her coffee in silence.

"We didn't say nothin' to each other," Lucas remembers. "I just drove south, figurin' on headin' into Texas by the next day. Then I was feelin' this chill come over me and I knew that she was goin' to die."

Eventually the woman nodded off and as Henry drove, he remembers, he could feel powerful urges coming over him. He wasn't interested in terror at all when he turned off the road and stopped the car shortly before dawn. If he was going to kill her, he was going to do it now before the truck traffic started to build. The woman awoke with a start when the car jerked to a halt. With one quick stroke, Lucas brought the knife up from his side and sliced her across the neck. She grabbed her throat and then Lucas plunged the knife directly into her neck again and the woman fell back across the seat. Lucas reached across her, opened her door, and pushed her out onto the gravel. Then he got out, cut off all her clothing and had sexual intercourse with her until the cold chills that he was feeling were all gone.

Lucas didn't even bother to hide the body. He dragged her off to a nearby grove of pine trees where he took her money, her wallet, all her identification, and her jewelry and drove the car further south into Texas until he abandoned it just south of Fredericksburg. The homicide of the young woman who was found in Magnolia and the abandoned Ford station wagon would remain mysteries for the Texas Rangers and the Montgomery County sheriff until Lucas confessed to the crimes in 1983 after he was charged with the murders of Becky Powell and Kate Rich.

Following a familiar pattern, Lucas didn't stay in Texas for long. He had pocket money now and hitched a ride with a trucker back north into Indiana where he figured he would bum around until his cash ran out. Then, he said, he hoped to find work and hide out until it was safe to go back.

Sheriff Conway hadn't given up hope of getting Lucas back into custody. With a Maryland warrant for possession of a stolen vehicle that Conway had pulled off the NCIC, he had a way of keeping Lucas in jail while he investigated the disappearance of Kate Rich. He still had no information about Becky Powell. The only thing Florida authorities could tell him was that a Frieda Powell had escaped from a juvenile detention home back in 1981 and hadn't been seen or heard from since. They asked him to contact them if he arrested her but doubted that they would press for a formal extradition. She was out of the state and no longer their problem until she returned to Florida.

Lucas, meanwhile, had been unable to find work since the trucker had dropped him off in Indiana stone country south of the college town of Bloomington. He recalls bumming around the IU campus for a while—it was football season and there were plenty of coeds—but the town was much too crowded and Lucas was sticking out like a sore thumb. Finally, in desperation, he placed a phone call to Ruben Moore, told him that he was plumb out of money, and begged him for a place to stay.

"I been lookin' for Becky," he told Moore in the collect telephone call. " 'Cause the trucker said they might be headin' north. But I couldn't find her."

Ruben Moore knew that Conway wanted to talk to Lucas in connection with Mrs. Rich's disappearance even though he didn't know that Hound Dog already had a warrant for Lucas' arrest. At first he told Lucas that he couldn't help him but then decided to talk to the sheriff. He told Lucas to call him back again in a couple of days. Meanwhile, Moore called the sheriff and told him that Lucas had called and said he was desperately out of money, hungry, miserable, and wanted to come back to Stoneburg. Conway drove out to The House of Prayer and told Moore that Lucas was wanted in connection with Kate Rich's disappearance. He also told him that Becky Powell had not contacted her family in Jacksonville or, to anyone's knowledge, returned to Florida. Conway asked Moore to get Lucas back to Stoneburg.

When Lucas called two days later, Moore had apparently relented. He told Henry that he would send him $100 and that he was welcome back at The House of Prayer. He didn't tell him, of course, that Conway had an arrest warrant waiting for him or that he wanted to interrogate him regarding Kate Rich. By the end of that week, Lucas was on his way back to Stoneburg with the cash in his pocket.

Henry walked into the commune on a Sunday, according to his recollection, and saw the Reverend Moore at the afternoon church service. Moore called Hound Dog Conway that evening and by the following morning, the sheriff's car pulled into the camp and Lucas was in custody. The sheriff told Henry that he had a Maryland warrant for car theft.

"That ain't nothin'," Lucas reportedly said to the

sheriff, but it nonetheless gave Conway all the legal reason he needed to put Henry in his Montague County jailhouse while he figured out how to get the information that he needed out of him.

What Bill Conway didn't immediately know was that he had Lucas at more of a disadvantage than he realized. Lucas was a chain smoker, going through two or three packs of cigarettes a day. He also, apparently, lived on his coffee. "I'm used to drinkin' 'bout fifty cups a day," Lucas said. "They jes' set a pot in front of me and I drink it 'til it's gone, then they set another pot up and I drink that."

Without his coffee and cigarettes, Lucas quickly began to lose control of his faculties and became very agitated in his cell.

"Get the heat on in here," he called out at night. But the jailers were told not to respond.

"Just act like you don't hear him," they were told, and the more Lucas asked for heat, the more they pretended they were deaf.

Conway could also see that the lack of coffee and cigarettes was having an effect on his prisoner. Maybe he'd talk in return for a pot of fresh, strong coffee in the morning, especially if it came on the heels of an especially long night without any cigarettes. But Lucas was also able to wait out whatever was coming his way. He had been trained, he said, by the doctors at Ionia to endure all kinds of hardships without breaking.

But Bill Conway had more tricks up his sleeve. It was getting on toward the end of October, over a year since Lucas had killed Becky Powell and Kate Rich, and a desert chill was settling over this part of Texas. But Conway kept the air conditioning turned up and kept the lights on in Lucas' cell. While waiting for word on the Maryland warrant, he figured he might make it as uncomfortable for his prisoner as possible. Thus, a waiting game ensued until Bill Conway thought that his prisoner had had enough.

"Henry, we want to ask you about Kate Rich," he said to Lucas after a couple of days without coffee or cigarettes.

"I didn't know old Katy Rich that well," Henry told the sheriff. "Me 'n Becky done some work for her over in Ringgold, but Becky was closer to 'er."

"Now, we want you to help us as much as you can, Henry," Conway told him. "Because we want to get to the bottom of this and we think you have information that can get us the answers."

"I'll help anyway I can," Lucas remembers he told the sheriff. "But I really don't know nothin' 'cause the last time I saw Katy Rich she was sick and couldn't go to church like we'd planned."

"You think you can help us out with some information about Becky?" Conway reportedly asked.

"All's I know is that Becky and I were hitchin' 'n a trucker pulled up 'n give us both a ride," Henry said. "We headed north, towards Indiana, I think, and the trucker stopped and he 'n Becky told me to get out of the cab or they was gonna blow my head off. The trucker had a gun and Becky was glad to go with him. Like to have broke my heart, sheriff, 'cause I loved that little girl."

This was no help at all and the sheriff knew it. He had a feeling—in fact he could even smell it—that Lucas was lying like a practiced felon. The sheriff knew that Henry had served time in a state penitentiary for murder and that he'd been in and out of jails since he was a teenager. He also know that Lucas had been in a Michigan mental hospital and that prison records had confirmed that he'd attempted suicide. The sheriff took a chance and asked Henry if he'd agree to a lie detector test.

"If you think that'll help, sheriff," Lucas reportedly said. "But you'll only find out what I already been sayin's true."

"That's all we want, Henry," the sheriff said. "We just want to know the truth."

Lucas said that he had been trained in the art of lying. In prison in Michigan, where he said he defended himself against the psychiatrists who would try to "tie you up with your own stories . . . If you asked me a question," he said. "Whatever answer I give, that would be the truth. There'd be no way you'd know that I was makin' anything up. That's how I fooled the sheriff in Montague County."

Lucas knew that the trick in taking a lie detector test was to not to turn actual lies into actual truths but to turn actual truths into actual lies. That way, he said, they'd never know which was the truth or which was the lie. "If it's all the same," he told interviewers, "even they'd know you was lyin', they wouldn't know which was the lie."

The polygraph operator reportedly was as confused as confused could be by the results of the first lie detector test. He tried to force Lucas into an obvious lie to get his benchmark readings, but Lucas said that he told himself that whatever he was saying was the truth. Then, he said, he made himself restless and agitated when he was asked questions to truthful statements because he hadn't had his coffee. "Thinkin' 'bout how much I want coffee and a cigarette always makes me edgy."

It worked. The polygraph operator told Hound Dog that he could tell from Lucas' readings that he was holding something back, but he couldn't get a definitive answer on where he was lying. Conway confronted Lucas about his answers as well.

"I know you're holdin' some things back on me Henry, and I got to know the truth," he said.

But he told him that the lie detector test did not reveal that Henry was lying about what happened to Kate Rich, even though the story had changed from the last time he had made a statement to the sheriff. He informed Lucas, however, that he would continue to hold him on the Maryland warrant until the state decided whether to extradite him or not. This was a legal arrest and Lucas would remain in jail. Unfortunately for Conway, Maryland's response was quicker than he expected. The state attorney informed the sheriff that the state was not about to file for extradition. Conway had no reason to hold Lucas in custody any longer. He had kept him in jail for just over two weeks. Before he let him go, however, he asked him to help him with any new information he might remember about Kate Rich or Becky Powell, and he also asked Ruben Moore to keep an eye on Lucas.

Henry was driven back to The House of Prayer where Moore made good on his promise to report anything that Lucas did or said to the sheriff. However, Henry worked hard for the contractor, making repairs to the camp and helping him on his construction jobs. Moore had no complaints, but when he noticed that some tools were missing from a box—a hatchet and a long knife—the contractor became worried. In one version of the story, the Reverend Moore reportedly kept a pistol with him at night just in case Lucas decided to attack anybody. But Lucas acted as though he were glad to be back and worked as hard as he could to pay Moore back the $100 he had sent him and to work off his room and board.

Toward the middle of November, a hunter found an old purse in a dry stream bed just outside of Ringgold. Conway asked around about it and Kate Rich's relatives confirmed that it had belonged to her. But stories and rumors ran wild through The

House of Prayer that the sheriff had found articles that belonged to the missing widow. A few weeks later, Kate Rich's house mysteriously burned to the ground and Lucas was one of Conway's prime suspects, although he never formally filed charges against him.

With the Rich investigation still on his mind and Lucas a suspect in the suspicious fire, Conway and a Texas Ranger went to Needles, California, to examine the bloodstains in the car that the Highway Patrol had impounded. They searched the car and took samples of the seat covering back with them for testing, but nothing they found in the year-old stain was conclusive. Without Kate Rich's body there was nothing they were going to prove. They didn't know, of course, that Lucas had already incinerated the body in the wood stove in the communal kitchen of The House of Prayer and that there was almost nothing of Kate's remains left in the world.

Conway still wanted to examine Lucas again and drove to The House of Prayer to ask him to take another lie detector test. "This time it'll be different, Henry," he told him. "This time I want you to go to Fort Worth with me where we want to ask you more about Frieda Powell and Kate Rich."

Lucas agreed. He still believed he could fool any polygraph operator, but the lie detector test was never given. Once the operator learned from Lucas' records that he had been an inmate in Ionia State

Mental hospital and that he was diagnosed as a schizophrenic, he refused to administer the test. He told the sheriff that whatever he might discover would be inadmissible anyway not only because lie detector tests couldn't be used in court, but that even evidence gained with the knowledge of a subject's responses to a lie detector test were inadmissible if the subject had been diagnosed as psychotic. It was simply a waste of time and the operator wouldn't be a part of the investigation.

Hound Dog wouldn't give up and found another operator who agreed to perform the test. This time Lucas was picked up again and was driven all the way down to Forth Worth. The lie detector examination began, as it had before, with questions designed to get a baseline response for Lucas' reactions. Again, Lucas was able to move all over the board, creating falsehoods where there should have been truths and truths where there should have been falsehoods. But Conway also had a strategy he thought might just trip up the drifter. He was prepared with a surprise. After having lulled Lucas into a rhythm with the same types of questions he was asked back in the Montague jail, Conway suddenly unfolded a large roadmap in front of him. Lucas seemed visibly surprised. Then Conway pointed to the spot where Mrs. Rich's purse was found. He told Lucas that they found old Granny Rich's purse right there and was that where Lucas hid the body?

The trick worked, but not well enough. Lucas successfully lied through the test, but his reaction to the map was such that Conway searched the area with his own wife after they had brought Lucas back to The House of Prayer commune. While Lucas worked throughout the week, Conway searched the area, but he and his wife could find nothing. They didn't know that Lucas had long since returned to the area where he had buried Granny Rich on that first night, retrieved her body, cut it up into burnable chunks, and fed it to the fires in a stove. They didn't know that all that was left of Granny Rich was safely mixed with the potash pile Reverend Moore kept behind the kitchen.

Right about this same time, Lucas found another murder victim. He confessed years later to hitching a ride with a teenage girl who was shorter than he was and forcing her at knife point to drive into a remote wooded area in Montgomery County. "She was a real nervous type," Lucas said. "She had these chewed-up fingernails and she was bitin' them the whole time I was holdin' her. I thought she'd eat her own fingers clear down to the bone. She was a strangle."

Lucas said that he made her get out of the car and strangled the life right out of her before she knew what was happening. Then after he strangled her, he took off her clothes and cut a jagged scar in her left breast. Then he had sex with her body, he says, and he tried to set fire to her. He claimed that he was again following the training he had received from the Hand of Death by varying the M.O. and leaving strange marks on the victim. "That way," he told an interviewer, "when the newspapers reported a body and said it had a strange mark or was burned or had a cross carved on it, you could claim it as your own by the mark you'd left."

The following month, Lucas spotted a seventeen-year-old girl, by his own identification, hitchhiking along the road and gave her a ride in a car he had borrowed. He didn't even wait to drive her to a wooded area. He stopped the car, strangled her, and then drove her to another desolate area where he had sex with her body repeatedly and then tried to burn her. "I put gasoline on the body," Lucas said. "And she caught a few times, but she wouldn't go up. Then I didn't want no one to spot the fire and call the police so I left her sort of charred up in the woods and drove away."

He returned to The House of Prayer and worked "quietly" for the next month when he left to go over to Bowie to take his Texas driving test. He stayed there for a couple of days taking the examinations, but returned to camp before anyone became overly suspicious about his whereabouts. Finally, toward the end of May, Lucas began announcing that he was restless and was thinking about going back on the road. He had his driver's license now and had, for all intents and purposes, again gotten away with two murders. Now he wanted to get moving again. And, strangely enough, he even trusted the Reverend Moore to hold one of his possessions.

Lucas told Ruben Moore that he would be leaving camp and asked the reverend if he would lock up a .22 caliber handgun that Lucas had been keeping. Lucas put the weapon in a brown paper bag along with some rounds of ammunition and handed it over to Moore. "I'll be back," he told Moore, and the contractor locked the weapon up in a safe in his office. Lucas drove out of camp and spent the next four days on the road, arriving at Deming, New Mexico, on June 8 and in San Jon the next day.

Moore called Sheriff Conway the day Lucas left on June 5 and reported that Lucas had handed him a .22 with a few rounds for safekeeping. That's all Conway needed to know. Possession of a firearm was a Texas felony for a convicted felon and Lucas was going to spend some heavy time in Conway's jail. This time, he felt, he had him and he wasn't going to let him get away. Lucas called Moore on June 10 and said that his car had broken down in San Jon. He thought, Lucas told Moore, that he was going to find information about Becky and Kate Rich, but that nothing had worked out and that he needed a ride. Moore notified the sheriff and drove out to pick up Lucas.

They arrived back in Stoneburg on June 10 where Moore, without Henry's knowledge, turned over the gun to the sheriff.

On June 11, Henry was drinking coffee in the commune's kitchen when Sheriff Conway walked in and looked right at Lucas.

"How you doin'?" Conway asked Lucas as he walked in the door.

"Well, it don't look like I'm doin' too good," Henry answered as Conway showed him the warrant for his arrest, slapped the cuffs on, slid him into his police car, and drove him down to the county jail.

As Hound Dog Conway ushered Henry into his cell and slammed the bars behind him, he heard Lucas whisper to him, "Sheriff, you sure know how to put a man down."

That was the last day in his life that Henry Lee Lucas could claim he was a free man.

Chapter 11
Blinded by the Light

Henry Lee Lucas huddled in the darkness of his cell in Hound Dog Conway's Montague County jailhouse. He knew the sheriff would do whatever was necessary to get him to confess, but he wasn't going to give him the pleasure. Henry prided himself on thinking that nobody could break him, that nobody could get information out of him that he didn't want to give.

"They tried to break me at the mental hospital," Lucas said. "But I outsmarted all of 'em. They beat me, they put electric shocks on me. But I did what they said and I got out."

But here it was different, Henry remembers. Conway was making it harder for him by depriving him of his cigarettes and his coffee again. His four-pack-a-day habit had begun to wear him down quickly and his need for coffee was also eating at him. Henry lived on cigarettes and coffee, as anyone who's ever interviewed him has come to see, and without the nicotine and caffeine, he loses control of himself very quickly. He'd endured Hound Dog's jail before, he consoled himself, when they had him in on that Maryland warrant and set him up for those lie detector tests. But this time, they had him on something that would stick.

After a short time, Henry was in the pit of misery when he tried to hang himself with a pair of stockings, but it didn't work right away so he slashed his wrists with one of the razors they had given him to shave with. His jailer, Joe Don Weaver, came running into his cell when he saw Lucas hanging in the corner, blood running down his wrists, and he cut him down. Sheriff Conway called the ambulance and with a deputy riding shotgun over him while he was in handcuffs and strapped to the gurney, Lucas was transported to the hospital in Bowie where doctors sutured up his wounds and kept him on a respirator until he was stabilized. He was kept on oxygen for the night and then transferred within a day or two to the jail at Wichita Falls, Texas. He stayed in the Wichita Falls jail for about a week before Hound Dog brought him back to the jail cell in Montague County.

It was cold, Lucas remembers. He was shivering. It was damp. He was miserable. He stared up at that lone light bulb in a fury. He would have done anything for one cigarette butt. When he remembers it, he says that after all he had pledged to The Hand of Death, he felt he had been abandoned by the power of the cult. But he wasn't about to break. In a moment of anger, he broke the single light bulb in his cell and he was plunged into darkness. But yet it wasn't darkness. Something was wrong here, very wrong.

"I hated everything. I took and destroyed everything I'd ever known or loved," Henry says, thinking about that night in the darkness of his cell. He was as disconsolate as any human being had ever been, he says about that night.

"I was sitting there, and I began to notice a real small light over in the corner of my cell," he remembers. At first he was transfixed by it because he didn't know what it was. He thought it was another light bulb and he figured he'd break that too. But it wasn't a light bulb. And it didn't go away when he walked over to it. "And I kept watchin' it and it was jus' like it was suspended there in the air, you know. So I kept watchin' it. And it kept getting bigger, and it kept on. Then I heard somethin'. I heard somethin', a voice maybe, somethin' say 'If you follow me, I will forgive you.' And it shocked me in a way because I didn't know who it was. I didn't know what it was, and so I called in an officer, one of the jailers."

Joe Don Weaver came running down the hall when Henry called out to him. "I seen me something terrible," Henry said, but Joe Don said that Henry was only having a delusion. It was brought on, he told him, by Henry's injury and maybe he was still in shock. Joe Don left Henry to his thoughts and Henry turned his attention back to the light.

"He came to my cell again," Henry says about Joe Don Weaver after he'd called him back a second time. "And I asked him, I said, 'What are you tryin' to do, bug my cell?' And he says, 'What do you mean?' And I says there's a light in here and somebody keeps on talkin' but I can't understand, you know?' And I watched the officer walk around everywhere he could in that cell. He never walked through the light, the light would never block him out. You could always see the light. And him, too. And he walked all around that light, and all up to next to where it was at and everything else. And he never seen it. I don't know why he didn't see it, but he didn't. He come back to me and says, 'There's nothin' here. You're just havin' hallucinations.' And I said, 'It's not hallucinations. I see it.' And he says, 'There ain't nothing here. They's jus' nothin' here.' And so he

200

goes out and locks the door."

Henry was left alone again and again he began to think about the light that would not leave his cell.

"So I go back and sit down in the corner in my cell and the light keeps getting closer to me. The prettier the light'd get, the closer it'd get. It kept gettin' prettier and prettier, prettier, prettier. And directly I could see sort of a shape inside the light. And I don't want people to get me wrong that I heard a voice. I mean as far as the voice was, I don't know whether I actually heard it, whether I felt it, whether it was some way of sensin' I heard it, or what, I don't know. I heard it ask me to confess my sins to man. It said that if I confess 'em to man that He would forgive me, and He would take over my life. And I couldn't accept it, you know, at first. I didn't know what to say. I didn't know what to do. So I just spoke out."

Lucas says that he called out in the darkness of his cell to the strange light that seemed only to illuminate itself and nothing else. Even though he was calling out, no one seemed to hear him except the voice deep inside his brain. His jailer never even came down the hall even though Lucas was calling out. The whole thing was eerie, Lucas remembers.

"I said 'I can't. I can't help it. I don't know

201

where these people's at. I don't know how to show nobody anything. I don't know how to go back to anybody.' He says, 'If you'll confess your sins to man I will show you.' And I jus' knew there was some kind of feelin' of bein' empty, in other words. And so I told Him then, I said, 'I will accept You if You'll help me.' So the light got closer to me and when it did I felt the pressure of a hand on my shoulder. I couldn't see the hand, but I could feel it. And He said, 'I will forgive you.'"

Lucas said that in that single moment, for the first time in his life, he felt peace. "And so from that day on, I started confessing my sins to man. I didn't ask man's forgiveness. I didn't ask anybody's forgiveness because God Himself forgave me 'cause I was confessin' to man. And the only way that I can confess my sins to man is by what I'm doin'. And so He has taken me and He's shown me."

Lucas called out to his jailer again, this time louder than before with an urgency that seemed to penetrate the darkness. And Joe Don came running down the hall because somehow he knew that something was up.

"Joe Don," Henry said to the jailer who stared at him in disbelief. Maybe Lucas even looked different. "Joe Don, I done me some terrible things." And Lucas went on to describe the essence of the light in his cell and the power of the light and the voice of the light. And Lucas said to Weaver that the light had asked him to confess his sins so that he could be forgiven and Lucas said that was exactly what he was intending to do.

Whatever Henry said, whether it made sense or not, Weaver reportedly believed that Henry might be ready to talk. However, in the years following this incident, Weaver has denied that it ever took place. Nevertheless, Lucas says that he did call Weaver and Weaver did walk through the light and tell Henry that he couldn't see anything there.

Tears were blinding Henry as he begged Weaver to let him write a note to the sheriff. "Just give me some paper and a pencil," Henry asked.

"I'll be right back, Henry," Weaver said. "I'll get you something to write with." He told the sheriff what he was doing and suggested that he come as quickly as he could because old Henry was about to pipe up. He brought Lucas his pencil and paper and Henry scrawled a quick note to Sheriff Conway telling him that he'd killed Becky Powell and Kate Rich. But Lucas didn't sign the note. It was not a real confession. He said that he wanted to see the sheriff personally. Joe Don came back and told Henry that he would take him to the office.

"You'll get some coffee, Henry," Weaver said. "And maybe we'll scare up a pack of cigarettes for you, too."

Lucas sat back in the warm office, not feeling cold for the first time in weeks, and savored his coffee. It warmed him up even further on the inside and made him feel like he belonged to the human race. He took a deep drag on his cigarette and felt his lungs fill with smoke. He waited for the nicotine to hit. He waited for the floating sensation that made him feel that he could go on living for a few minutes.

"Henry, I have this note here," Hound Dog said, waiting for Henry to feel real good about the coffee and cigarette and not wanting anything in the world to take that feeling away. "I have a note that says you want to tell me something about Becky Powell and Kate Rich."

Lucas began confessing almost at once, he remembers. "I was told that I must confess my sins to man," he told the sheriff. "And that's what I aim to do."

He began by confessing to the murder of Granny Rich. He described to the sheriff the ride to the "beer joint" in Oklahoma, their arguing in the car, Kate's probing about Becky's whereabouts and the church service they missed. He told Conway about the sudden stabbing, the sex, the mutilation, and the culvert. He described his fear at being caught, and how in order to cover up the crime he brought the body back and painstakingly carved it into little pieces that he fed to the flames

204

of the kitchen stove. "There's nothing left of Katy Rich," Lucas told Conway. "I put her ashes out with the rest of the potash where she's no different than anything else in the pile."

The sheriff was a patient man. He had waited this long for a confession to the Kate Rich disappearance; he was inclined to let this take him as far as it would go. Part of the sheriff wanted to get on out that potash pile and see if he could find any of Kate's remains, but the careful law enforcement officer knew that once a murderer begins to confess, you go with that confession, take careful notes and ask all the right kinds of corroborating questions, and search for the evidence later.

Henry told the sheriff that the voice in his cell told him not to stop, not to hold anything back. "If you confess your sins to man," Henry kept repeating to the sheriff, "then I will forgive you." Henry said that he wanted forgiveness and he wanted it from the moment he killed Becky Powell. He described his last night with Becky. He said that they had fought, that he felt she had been saved by the "Christian Katy Rich" and rejected him. He told the sheriff how he demanded they return to The House of Prayer the next day and how when she slapped him he killed her. Then he told the sheriff how he cut her up into smaller pieces so he could stuff them into the pillows they were carrying in their bedrolls. He told Conway how he kept returning to the site where he had left her, how over the course of two weeks he had come back again and again and talked with her spirit. "I kept asking for forgiveness," Henry reiterated. He said that he talked with her spirit about his new life and how he would meet her again someday after he had been forgiven of his sins. It was the light, he claimed, through which he would be able to return to Becky. Pity had been taken on him and now there was a way for him to confess, to pay the penalty, and to return to Becky. He explained that talking to Becky was a "more or less general, what you'd say, man-and-wife conversation."

Then Henry explained that for the first time in his life, he felt remorse for the crimes that he'd committed. It may have seemed strange to anyone listening to him at the time, but Henry cried and said that he knew that what he'd done had hurt people. He couldn't escape that hurt now, even though some of the crimes he'd committed were perpetrated months or even years before.

"I did feel a change in me," Lucas said. "I could feel people. I could feel their hurts where I couldn't before. I could feel real sorrow where I couldn't feel before. I could feel their expressions, which I couldn't before."

Without pause, and in the same monotone he

began the conversation in — after he had cried briefly over Becky — he resumed his confessions. He asked for a paper and pencil. Then he startled the sheriff and his deputy by drawing some of the women he was now confessing to having killed. He made about forty confessions in all, and he drew pictures of their faces. Their eyes were uniformly large, their lashes were uniformly long, but Lucas included sketches of the jewelry he remembers them wearing. These were the first pictures he had ever drawn, but he seemed fascinated by attempting to show shading and highlights with his pencil by coloring in shadows in their cheekbones and illustrating depth. He even used cigarette ash to achieve tone and contour around the necks and chins of his portraits. It was like nothing the sheriff and his deputy had ever seen before.

Next to the pictures, Lucas scrawled seven pages of notes, his initial attempts to recall some of the crimes:

"One killed in New York," he wrote. "Light brown hair, blue eyes, 5-6, 135 lb. Buffalo, would have been strangled with white cord, gold ear pins. Had dress on, light blue, inside apartment. Joanie, white pretty teeth with gap in front top teeth. Blue eyes, small pin ear. Hair below shoulders. Threw over bridge with head and fingers missing."

Henry couldn't stop confessing. He spoke through the night and Conway stayed with him, realizing that he would soon have to confirm as many of these missing persons cases as possible that were outside of his jurisdiction. He was immediately concerned with closing the Becky Powell and Kate Rich cases, but wanted to get as many other Texas and regional cases closed as well.

As the confessions multiplied, Conway called in other law enforcement authorities to begin the process of checking the claims. But he also refused to be distracted and continued to press to clear the two cases he had started with. Conway knew that confessions could be suppressed and recanted. He knew that Lucas could say that it was the cold of the cell or the deprivation of coffee and cigarettes that caused him to break down and confess to crimes he didn't really commit. He knew that Lucas had taken drugs and could easily say that he was withdrawing from narcotics. And Conway also knew that he was talking to an individual who had been diagnosed a paranoid schizophrenic, who had received shock treatments during an extended stay in a state mental hospital, and who had just claimed to have experienced what could only be described rationally as a delusional experience or a hallucination. Conway wasn't one to doubt the faith of revelation or the sincerity of a confession borne out of remorse of conscience, but he was also dealing with a diagnosed psychotic.

Hound Dog Conway ordered a complete search of the two murder sites Lucas had described in his confessions. Lucas was taken to each of the sites—he directed the sheriff to the precise spots, he says—where he made videotaped confessions to the crimes. At the site of Becky's murder, sheriff's deputies found the remains of a teenage girl exactly where Lucas said they would be after he led them to the tree where he said he had buried the pillow. Then over at The House of Prayer, Lucas led them to the kitchen stove and the pile of ashes where deputies found animal or human remains that were charred but unburned and unmistakable human remains and bone chips.

Conway had his corroborating evidence and proceeded to trial where Henry repeated the accounts of his murders to the Texas judge. He told about the fighting he and Becky were doing on the night of the murder and her desire to force him to give up his life of crime and get a normal job. He repeated Becky's quotes that "no one should ever have to put up with what I've had to put up with," and "I'm not going to live like this anymore. You're going to settle down like a real man."

Lucas claimed that he had a deep chill within him at the time he killed Becky and Kate—the same chill he had once said overcame him at the time of each murder. That chill has since become the study of psychologists, neurologists, and criminologists for years since Lucas first talked about it. Simple physical phenomena has also been observed in other serial murder cases, especially those involving men who claim they had been abused by their mothers who are subsequently charged with the rape and murder of women. It is a phenomenon that those who have made these confessions and who have claimed to have been victims of abuse say is unmistakable and inevitably preceded each of their homicides.

Then Lucas dropped his biggest bombshell right there in the Texas courtroom. According to accounts of the hearing, the judge asked him whether he understood that he was confessing to homicide and that he would likely spend the rest of his life behind bars. Lucas said that he understood the nature of the crimes he was confessing to. He said that there were over a hundred crimes that he would have to clear in order to set the record straight. The judge was shocked and asked Lucas—he knew that the defendant had been diagnosed a psychotic—whether he himself believed that he was sane. Lucas said that he felt he was sane, but his hundred or so victims, girls he killed for sex, might have thought differently. The judge ordered a complete investigation into the crimes that Lucas said he had committed as well as tests to be performed to determine his defendant's competency.

Over the next several months, between June and November, Lucas began confessing to hundreds of crimes. Dozens of law enforcement officials beat a path Conway's door to continue investigations into unsolved murders, child kidnappings, missing persons, rapes, executions, and straight-out robberies. Before too long, the news of Lucas' confessions had begun to spread out of Texas and into other areas of the country. Vague snippets of descriptions to police about someone who may have been a one-eyed man prowling in the vicinity of a crime before a body was discovered or a convenience store had burned down caused state and county prosecutors to request Sheriff Conway to set up interviews with Lucas. As obliging as Sheriff Conway wanted to be, he realized that he could well have a tiger by the tail.

The press also began to catch a whiff of the blood that Lucas was talking about. It was 1983 and the country had been fascinated by the ongoing "Ted" murders in Washington State, the Atlanta Child Murders in Georgia, the Gacy murders in Chicago, and, of course, the Manson murders in Los Angeles. The country was going "serial killer crazy" as one lurid magazine article described it. With serial killers apparently running wild over the country and headline-breaking cases emerging every few months, the stories about a one-eyed drifter in Texas who had already served time for killing his mother, and who was now claiming over a hundred murders around the country began to draw reporters from every state as well as from foreign countries. Everyone wanted to know more, and stories about Lucas made evening news broadcasts and *Life* magazine.

Lucas was not a stupid man. By his own admission, he understood how the police operated and what they gave in return for what they got.

From the very beginning, some observers have noted, Lucas established a pattern of toying with law enforcement authorities. He confessed to obtain favorable treatment in jail. He also appeared to enjoy being the center of a "show," and he seemed to like changing his story so as to manipulate the lawyers and investigators interrogating him. He enjoyed playing hot and cold. As he once told Ottis Toole, "if they act like they treat you like you ain't good enough fer 'em, I just clam up and tell 'em I got nothin' to say. They either treat me like a man or they don't get nothin'."

Henry was treated humanely by most of the authorities charged with the disposition of his cases. He won concessions through that humane treatment but he did give better than he got, and evidence was actually uncovered in more than one case which seemed to corroborate that a crime had been committed. But Henry was probably treated with no greater deference than any other infamous killer. He took more polygraph examinations over the course of the ensuing months of 1983 and 1984 and was found not to be responding accurately. However, polygraph operators claimed Lucas was a poor polygraph subject, they said. It was best to find other ways of testing the accuracy of his confessions. But Lucas also said that he wanted to test the people around him. He was openly trying to manipulate his jailers and interrogators to show how he could influence the system. Criminologists have said that many prisoners who have no hope of ever seeing the outside again exert control in the only way they know how: tricking the system to show that they can influence their environment. Psychologists call this a natural reaction to captivity.

Part of Lucas' attempts at manipulation consisted of confessing to crimes that he could never have committed. He embellished the tales of his own life history.

"There were some things that I doubted, but it soon became apparent that he was no novice at murder," said Texas Ranger Phil Ryan, who was one of the early participants in the Lucas story and who had helped Hound Dog Conway and Jim Boutwell with their investigations of the Rich and Powell disappearances. "Then later," Ryan said.

"Henry's attitude sort of changed. The numbers became overwhelming. I doubted a lot of it."

At one point early in the investigation he claimed to have murdered his Virginia school-teacher, Miss Annie Hall, when he was thirteen. He had once described Annie Hall, as having been one of the "kindest people I ever knew." This was an astounding claim and authorities began a search for Annie Hall that resulted in discovering the eighty-five-year old retired teacher living in Austin with relatives. Newspapers had a field day, pointing to how Lucas had confounded the police and set them jumping off after a completely false and outlandish murder confession. But Lucas said that he was simply "testing" the officers interrogating him the same way he toyed with his victims. He wanted to see if they'd follow his leads.

Henry Lee Lucas was convicted of murdering Kate Rich on October 1, 1983 and received a seventy-five-year sentence. He was transferred to Denton County almost immediately afterward and put on trial for the murder of Becky Powell. Henry's lawyer asked the court for a verdict of voluntary manslaughter and offered Henry's tears as the evidence for the more lenient judgment. Henry sobbed during the closing remarks, but the jury found him guilty as charged and he was sentenced to life imprisonment. It was November, 1983.

Now that he was convicted of the two murders,

Lucas' confessions had some credibility even if some of them were more "confabulated" than actually real. Sheriff Conway knew that he really had his hands full. He and other law enforcement authorities who visited Stoneburg knew Lucas was lying about many things. They knew his growing accounts could not be trusted. He changed and embellished at will. But there was enough detail and corroborating evidence at some of the crime scenes to lend credence to many of his claims. And Lucas demonstrated an uncanny ability to lead police and investigators directly to crime scenes and describe events it seemed that only he could have witnessed. He made drawings of his claimed victims, some of which proved to be remarkably accurate representations. Thus, the long process of sorting the facts from the growing fiction about Henry Lee Lucas had begun in earnest.

By November of 1983, Conway had successfully taken Lucas through two separate murder convictions and had played host to dozens of prosecutors and investigators, psychiatrists, and bereaved individuals seeking lost children. Conway himself had transported Lucas hundreds of miles for questioning in other locations and jurisdictions. Now the strain on him was beginning to show. This was an expensive process and Montague County was not a wealthy jurisdiction. Some of its citizens were beginning to grumble at the expense of maintaining Lucas. He was convicted. Pack him off to jail. Let the state pay for it and be done with it, many of them said.

Bill Conway knew another sheriff, Jim Boutwell, who might be able to handle the traffic and who had unsolved homicides Lucas could help him with. Boutwell had all those murders over on the interstate that he had to solve and with Lucas confessing to crimes all over the place, only a fool would discount the possibility that at least one of Jim's cases might be a Lucas murder.

There were other advantages to getting the Williamson County sheriff involved in the growing investigation. Jim Boutwell ran a relatively well-funded courthouse and jail. He was in the shadow of the state capital, in the central part of the state, and he had money to spend on investigations. Hound Dog also knew that Jim Boutwell was a popular sheriff, a straight-shooter who had built powerful relationships with highers-up in the Texas Department of Safety. Boutwell believed that jurisdictions should cooperate with one another on solving crimes that take place across county and municipal lines. He was among a growing cadre of police officers who saw the danger in criminals like Lucas who could lead different police departments on wild goose chases before disappearing off the official radar. Boutwell had also interviewed

Henry in the past and had established a relationship with him that was built on trust.

On November 25, 1983, Hound Dog Conway officially transferred custody of Henry Lee Lucas to Sheriff Jim Boutwell of Williamson County. As Conway expected, Boutwell used his contacts with the state to obtain the formation of a task force of Texas Rangers who could help Williamson County with the expensive process of coordinating Lucas' contacts with other law enforcement agencies throughout the country. The task force that eventually became the center of so much controversy was born the day of Lucas' arrival in Georgetown.

Lucas passed out of Conway's hands, but not out of his life. During the months that Lucas had spent in Stoneburg, he had become a national figure. It was an unpleasant experience for the county and an expensive set of events for which someone would have to be called to account. The following April, Bill Conway was defeated for re-election. The massive amount of money he had spent in prosecuting Lucas and then babysitting him while other lawmen investigated his whereabouts in relationship to their unsolved crimes had become a major issue in local politics. It cost Conway the election.

Hound Dog was the first of Lucas' "shadow victims." These are the victims who have had to deal with Lucas and have found their reputations smeared, their professionalism questioned, and their lives torn apart by the whirlwind that accompanies not only Henry Lee Lucas but other notorious and headline-making serial killers as well. Even though Conway was named "Texas Lawman of the Year" by the Texas Sheriffs' Association, it was only a bittersweet victory because he had lost the job that had put him in contact with Lucas in the first place.

From Montague County, the focus on Henry Lee Lucas shifted to Williamson County and the Georgetown jail where Lucas would hold court for Huntsville and then years until he was transferred to Florida for a new set of sensational trials.

Chapter 12

Georgetown and Controversy

The Williamson County Jail, Henry Lee Lucas's new home, is a deceptive building even to this day. Judged only by its exterior, it is an old stone structure that sits alone and grim atop a small hill like an old frontier fortress. It is a forbidding, cold, antique structure that has housed more than its share of pain and death. The jailhouse has been in continuous use for over a hundred years and is reminiscent of countless of other old jails around the country that were built long before people realized that jails were more than human pits. Many of these antiquated structures are dank, depressing places of chipping lead paint and splintered wood that enclose dark cells with fetid holes smelling of decades-old urine and feces. They reek of human waste and wasted lives. Many such county jails in

Texas at that time were barely maintained by frugal local governments who lacked the resources to do much better.

But the interior of the Williamson County Jail was in stark contrast to its exterior. There had been some serious remodeling done before Lucas was signed in as a permanent resident. There was no pitted, chipping paint or crumbling wood. Instead, it was a well-maintained facility, freshly painted and alive with the beeping and flashing of a technologically advanced local law enforcement communications center. The hallways are narrow and the rooms are small, but the corridors are well lit and lead to offices with computers and communications terminals, video equipment, and high-speed printers. Williamson County Sheriff Jim Boutwell's office is on the second floor, up a narrow flight of stairs that, though worn, are certainly not forbidding.

The prison section of the jailhouse is newer. It had been rebuilt and is as well maintained as the sheriff's department. Although it isn't plush it is clean, well-lit, and run humanely and efficiently. Prisoners are allowed televisions in their cells and certain personal effects if they provide them at their own expense. The jail even has cable, but only for those prisoners who can pay for it.

There are approximately one hundred permanent prisoners serving time in the Georgetown jail, mostly for local offenses. Along with them, there is a shifting population of transients being held for trial or for transfer to state and federal institutions. For the most part, these are inmates in jail for more serious offenses, including violent felonies. Thus, Sheriff Boutwell must preside over a mix of prisoners with different security requirements. But his experience in business as well as in law enforcement has seemed to qualify him for this kind of difficult managerial role.

Boutwell is a celebrated Texas lawman who is not only a study in contrasts to Hound Dog Conway, but is also a person who came out of commercial enterprise and international service for the United States government. Boutwell is a licensed pilot, has flown as a test pilot, has sold airplanes, and had even developed and built an airport. He was a Texas Ranger and worked as a United States government agent in 1959 just after the Communist takeover of Cuba. He was instrumental in assisting several prominent Cubans to defect to the United States, in a dangerous cloak-and-dagger game, while representing an aircraft manufacturer.

Before he took custody of Lucas from Conway, Boutwell had already achieved considerable notoriety in another famous Texas murder: the University of Texas tower sniper. During the tense showdown when law enforcement sharpshooters and special weapons teams had deployed around the tower, Boutwell flew the airplane that distracted Whitman long enough for the assault officers to break through the barricades and reach the killer. Boutwell had been sheriff of Williamson County since 1978.

When Boutwell took custody of Lucas, not only was he looking for an answer to the Orange Socks Murder, he also stepped into the middle of an ongoing interstate investigation involving 875 agencies from 40 different states and Canada. Ostensibly, each agency was responsible for its own case, but the coordination required was enormous. And Henry Lee Lucas was becoming a media figure around the nation and especially in the jurisdictions where he was being investigated for unsolved homicides. Sheriff Boutwell helped coordinate the gargantuan task of administering the Lucas material, through an official Texas Ranger task force.

The entire Lucas task force was swamped with requests for case clearances from jurisdictions around the country. Henry's statements that he had abducted and killed people around the country, and his stories about a mysterious demonic society that was responsible for thousands of child abductions prompted wild speculation about a national conspiracy. Lucas fed this speculation with his accounts of secret ceremonies in the Florida Everglades and his runs to Mexico with Ottis Toole and a clutch of drugged children.

Boutwell and the Texas Ranger task force, however, were not charged with "investigating" any of Lucas' claims beyond the immediate cases under

Boutwell's jurisdiction. In fact, the Texas Rangers were never authorized to conduct investigations, but were asked only to coordinate the information flooding the Texas Department of Public Safety regarding their prisoner, make him available wherever possible to visiting investigators, and to use their best efforts to obtain information to assist outside agencies in clearing "Lucas cases." Boutwell and the Texas Rangers understood the important distinction between "coordination" and "investigation" and when charges were levelled against them in the press that they had bungled an investigation or had failed to follow through on an investigation, they repeated that they were never charged with the responsibility of conducting an investigation outside of Williamson County to begin with.

The Lucas task force was assigned to a small office on the first floor of the Williamson county sheriff's office and jail. Next door down the hall was a small interrogation room which had a work table, a filing cabinet, and several straight-backed chairs. That room later became Lucas' office, in which over an eighteen-month period, he held interviews and confessed to over a thousand crimes. Those people who participated in many of those sessions have reported that over the course of the eighteen-months, Lucas' fantastic stories often became the routine of the day. Participants described a kind of symbiosis that developed between Lucas and his interviewers.

Henry was a highly skilled player at the real-life game of "institutionalization." He clearly knew his regular limits, knew how far he could exceed those regular limits and when to stay well within bounds. The task force members also learned when they could rely upon Lucas' cooperation in the interviews and when they could not. There was plenty of give and take and a reciprocity of awareness on both sides about what the task force members and Lucas could expect from one another. As direct as the meetings between Lucas and the task force were, the task force members knew how to play Lucas' moods. However, Lucas never appeared to the participants to have been pampered or bribed for his cooperation. He lived in a small cell that was slightly set apart from the main cellblock and conducted meetings in his "office."

"When we first brought him here, we put him in a cell in the back with the rest of the population," Sheriff Boutwell said. "But the other prisoners gave him a lot of trouble—they had heard about some of the killings he had admitted to, so we had to move him."

In cellblocks, inmates who are associated with child murders or molestations are typically called "short eyes," and Lucas, because of his confessions, was threatened by the other inmates. Prisoners also tend to turn their hostility on inmates who confess to or are convicted of savage sexual crimes against the victims. As a confessed sex killer and child kidnapper, Lucas was a prime target of inmate hostility.

Boutwell moved Lucas to a more private cell which was smaller than the cells in the main population, but it provided a greater security for his prisoner. The cell was about eight feet by four feet with a small "catwalk" in the cell about three feet wide. Lucas had a wall-mounted sink and a bed. He later began adding his own paintings, a picture of Becky Powell, a color television connected to the county-wide cable—which someone else provided for him—and other articles. Lucas was also provided with a "bottomless" pot of coffee and cigarettes. Boutwell knew that keeping Lucas in caffeine and nicotine was one sure way of keeping him cooperative during the arduous interviews that lay ahead of him.

Boutwell also treated Lucas with respect, and this was an important factor in his prisoner's later dealings with the task force. He allowed Lucas to dress in street clothing, providing him at least with a pretense that he was somewhat different from the other inmates in the system. Boutwell also allowed Lucas to carry a pocket comb because he was conscious about his appearance during his "office hours", and an empty wallet for him to keep in his back pocket. In other words, Boutwell went out of his way to provide Lucas with all of the trappings of normality that he seemed to need in order to conduct his "business" with investigators from around the country.

Boutwell also allowed Lucas to receive visits from Sister Clementine, a self-professed Catholic lay minister, who, Boutwell realized, helped keep Lucas calm and cooperative. Lucas was encouraged to visit with Sister Clemmie as much as either he or she wanted, and the two of them formed a relationship in jail.

Lucas' staggering confessions had received national attention in the media by late 1984. Everybody wanted to know more about the Lucas crime spree. Sheriff Boutwell and the Rangers obliged and let it be known through normal police channels that the task force existed to implement investigation of any of Lucas' claims that any jurisdiction wished to examine. As a consequence, the telephone was busy constantly. The Texas Department of Public Safety installed extra phone lines at its own expense to facilitate the frantic communication between the Rangers and investigators from other jurisdictions as the news about the task force spread and other police departments looked toward them to clear their missing and murdered "unknown victim" cases.

The Texas Rangers began keeping two lists. One, which Lucas came to call his "social calendar," was a list of investigators who wanted to interview Lucas regarding unsolved crimes. The other, a more critical list, was a collection of brief summaries, usually a paragraph or less, of the crimes to which

Lucas had admitted during interviews with visiting officers. The Rangers wrote a synopsis and included on the list only those confessions that visiting officers felt might be valid. In other words, if the visiting officers said they believed that Lucas was guilty in their particular cases, the paragraphs summarizing his admissions were written up. This "Synopsis of Cases" was periodically duplicated by the Rangers and sent to law enforcement agencies around the country that requested information about Lucas.

"We frequently found conflicts," said Texas Ranger sergeant Bob Prince who headed the Ranger side of the task force. "When that would happen, we would note it on the log. If two different agencies claimed they believed Lucas had committed crimes in their areas on the same day, and they were too far apart for that to be possible, we would notify both agencies. Then it was their responsibility to resolve the conflict."

Bob Prince made it as clear as possible publicly that the task force was not just taking Henry Lee Lucas at his word. They had established a *pro forma* procedure for dealing with Lucas' claims, even the most fantastic claims, verifying each one of them against his known whereabouts at the time, cross-checking claims from different agencies against one another to eliminate as much as possible the conflicts between agencies, and summarizing only those admissions that had impressed officers as possibly true. The task force members understood that part of their jobs as coordinators was to establish a credible paper trail involving the Lucas admissions. They had to keep the kinds of records that established a legal framework for any subsequent prosecutions that might arise. Consequently, the task force was procedure-oriented with regard to the way it processed the Lucas information.

The movements of both Henry Lee Lucas and his partner Ottis Toole were entered on the log because each frequently implicated the other in a crime. By tracking the movements of each of them separately, as well as the two of them jointly, the task force members could keep records of whether it was even possible for them to have been traveling together. The Lucas/Toole entries also made it possible for the task force members to cross check against earlier admissions and evidence that might have turned up in other jurisdictions. On the log sheet, an (L) entry indicated a Lucas "event" while a (T) entry indicated a Toole "event." Typical entries were:

9-4-77 thru 9-10-77 (T) Supposedly working in Pontiac, Mich.

9-4-77 (L) Claims to have murdered ELIZA-BETH MARY WOLF in Davis, Calif. Occurred at apartment. Stabbed numerous times in front and back.

9-7-77 (L) Admitted the murder of GLENDA BETH GOFF, WF-18 in Houston Tex. Kidnapped from college and shot one time in head with .22 caliber. Body found in Bellville, Tex. on 9-13-77.

9-17-77 thru 9-31-77 (T) In Jacksonville. Fla. jail. Received 45 days in jail. NCIC inquiry made by Jacksonville SO on 9-18-77.

10-1-77 thru 10-30-77 (T) In Jacksonville, Fla. jail.

10-22-77 (L) Admitted murder of GLEN D. PARKS, WM-47 at his residence in Bellmead, McLennan County, Tex. Victim tied with strips of sheet and shot with .38 caliber in back and head.

10-30-77 (L & T) Confirmed murder of TINA MARIE WILLIAMS, WF-17 in Oklahoma City, Okla. Vehicle had broken down — picked up and resisted rape. Shot 2 times and pushed from vehicle.

11-1-77 (L & T) Confirmed murder of LILY PEARL DARTY, BF-18 in Harrison County, Tex. Shot twice in head with .32 caliber weapon.

12-19-77 (T) Cleared the murder of JOHN CARTER SWINT, WM-66 in Houston, Tex. Shotgun blast to back of neck.

1-4-78 (T) Inaccurate work records show working in Jacksonville, Fla.

1-9-78 (T) Payroll check cashed in Jacksonville, Fla.

Work records and payroll checks would later become subject to controversy because of conflicting stories regarding who cashed them, who they were actually issued to, and who had actually performed the work credited to Toole. As task force members were coming to find out, in a serial killer investigation the killer often leads police to the right clues indirectly. What might turn out to be an alibi for one jurisdiction actually turns out to be evidence in another jurisdiction. This was a process of trial and error, and as task force members became aware of conflicts in evidence, especially in work records and cashed checks, they found reasons to discount them.

Lucas and Toole, it later turned out, had claimed they had a "deal" with the employer in Florida who, for a cut of their salaries, faked the records as needed for the two men. One employee of the company later served jail time for fraud and for forging payroll records. The Rangers and Boutwell did not consider the records completely reliable, but felt they were duty bound to report them on the logs. Thus, because of their own integrity and honesty with respect to the procedures they had established, Boutwell and the Rangers found themselves challenged when a claim by Lucas or Toole was later found to conflict with a work record. But because the procedures of logging Lucas and Toole events proved so valuable for the coordination of the agency information flooding Georgetown, the task force saw no reason to change the rules when the rules bumped into a local county *investigation* of a Lucas homicide claim.

Once the paper trail, meticulously recorded by Bob Prince, in particular, was established, the days of task force work and Lucas "meetings" became routine and even somewhat humdrum. "We would set appointments as we could schedule them," Prince recalls. "Sometimes we had him booked as much as three months in advance."

Lucas' social calendar became so heavy at times that people who showed up for "stand-by" appointments or even for scheduled appointments had to be kept waiting while the backlog was processed. There were a few hurt feelings, a few distraught individuals whose questions were not answered as quickly as they might have liked, and individuals who, because they had somehow offended Lucas, were treated to his cold shoulder. The task force members tried as best they could to accommodate the needs of visiting prosecutors and investigators, but the traffic was intense.

"A typical case would involve a telephone call from a jurisdiction, say in Virginia," Sergeant Prince remembers. "The sheriff or an investigator of some kind in that area would tell us that he had a crime of some kind, usually a murder, and ask if Lucas knew anything about it. We would take just enough information to check with Henry, such as the general location, city or county—Henry was good about remembering counties—and the approximate date."

In fact, medical specialists would later determine, Lucas had a condition which many serial killers share, called "hypermnesia," or overmemorizing. In this condition, hypermnesiacs recall very specific details about an event. Sometimes they will key on names, sometimes on locations, sometimes on smells or colors. They may confuse an event with an event, but their recollection of the tiniest details is often astounding to interrogators. In Lucas' case, he was able to remember facial shapes and skin tones. He was able to talk about items of clothing and specific pieces of jewelry the victims were wearing, as if the inanimate object had a greater validity than the human being he had attacked.

Lucas' hypermnesia allowed him to provide police with details they hadn't even realized existed until they went back to the crime files. But Lucas' memory had to be jogged with a place name, usually a county. And this memory jogging was the subject of a later inquiry in Texas in which the task force members were accused of feeding Lucas information in advance of the interviews so that he would appear knowledgeable. By spiking the information in advance, detractors said, the task force members were enhancing their own roles at the expense of the cases they were assigned to clear.

But task force members said they had a specific procedure in dealing with new information being fed to Lucas. After providing Lucas with a general location or a county name, Prince recalls, "we would ask Henry if he had any 'cases,' as he called them, in that area. If he said he did remember one, we would call the officer back and tell him. We also would tell him he was welcome to come down and interview Henry himself. If he wanted an appointment, we put it on Henry's 'social calendar.' "

And come they did, hundreds at a time—sheriffs, chiefs of police, detectives, prosecuting attorneys, investigators, and many others.

"When they arrived," Jim Boutwell explains. "One of us, usually Bob or Clayton, would give them a briefing. We would tell them that Henry was generally cooperative, but liked to be treated with a certain amount of respect. He was cooperating voluntarily, and if they abused him verbally or berated him, he would shut up and tell them nothing."

This important *caveat* also raised eyebrows in official circles. Just who was this one-eyed criminal who demanded so much respect? He was an inmate, a prisoner who'd been sentenced to life for murder. Police interrogators and prosecutors routinely didn't treat people like Lucas with respect. Rather, they demanded information from them in order to get them to confess. But Lucas presented them with a new experience. He wanted to be sympathized with. He wanted to be thanked for helping them clear their cases. He believed he was actually in charge of the case. Sheriff Boutwell understood this. He also agreed that for Lucas to assume responsibility for the crime, it was critical for him to assume some form of management of the case.

Boutwell also made it clear that Lucas would lie to investigators as often as he was motivated to tell them the truth. He tested his interrogators, played games with them, and liked nothing better than to send a pompous prosecutor off on a wild goose chase.

"We also warned them," Boutwell reminds people who ask him about the task force procedures, "that Henry told about as many lies as he did the truth and that they should take nothing he said as the truth unless they could independently verify it."

Although this is a standard police procedure—to verify everything independently just in case the confession doesn't hold up—many investigators, in their excitement to close a case, sometimes don't realize that their line of interrogation gives too much away to the person being interviewed. Boutwell was clear in his admonition that Lucas was an especially dangerous person to reveal information to because he was inclined to use it. Lucas was practiced at being interrogated, he knew all the ins and outs of dodging questions or giving police false answers. Now that he was supposed to be behind bars for the rest of his life in a situation where he had no control, the only control he was capable of exercising was control of the investigations that came his way.

"We also warned each of them not to give their case away," Boutwell says about the briefings. "Henry was good at picking up on clues and then claiming them as his own memory. We told them to ask questions, but tell him nothing beyond what was absolutely necessary to establish a starting point for discussion."

That having been said, Boutwell explains, he advised interrogators to establish some sort of rapport with Lucas. By setting up a relationship in advance, by letting Lucas know that they saw him as a human being, investigators would have an easier time with him. Some lawyers asked Boutwell how they were to establish a relationship with a confessed sex killer.

"We told them to just chat quietly with Henry,

and listen to what he said," Boutwell says he told them. "We could furnish a video tape and an operator if they wanted one. We asked, if they decided Henry was their man, that they replace the tape and take it with them. If they decided he wasn't, then we kept the tape and erased it."

Finally, Boutwell says, the task force wanted investigators to "commemorate" the interview if they believed that Lucas could really be guilty of the crimes he was admitting to.

"We asked that when their interview was over, if they thought Henry was their man, they give us a brief synopsis of the case for the log," Boutwell says.

It was this procedure that was called into question months later when other prosecutors in Texas challenged what the task force was doing. They claimed that the task force had, in fact, prepped Lucas and prepped visiting investigators separately. In so doing, they were suggesting that visiting investigators feed Lucas information if they wanted their cases cleared. However, other observers who have reviewed the thousands of pages of cases and synopses, the hours and hours of video tapes, and have reviewed the eyewitness testimony of dozens of participants, dispute any charges that the Texas Rangers or the task force rigged anything. But the controversy over the Lucas confessions continues, and probably will continue for years to come.

Chapter 13

Sister Clemmie

Henry Lee Lucas once described Sister Clementine, "Sister Clemmie," as a very devout Roman Catholic, a gentle woman who had raised three children, an artist, and a musician. Even before Henry arrived in the Georgetown jail, Sister Clementine had begun visiting the prisoners in Sheriff Boutwell's jailhouse. Henry said that part of what she bestowed on the inmates she visited was a sense of dignity. She gave them small personal items such as bars of soap, toothpaste, and toothbrushes, and she distributed cigarettes and candy. She also contacted inmates' relatives and passed messages back and forth between family members who were separated by prison bars. She handwrote letters for those prisoners who could not write and, Lucas says, she prayed with those who were in need.

Henry says she was also a teacher of the gospel. Sister Clemmie had established something of a lay ministry in the Georgetown jail as early as 1981, in which she held Bible lessons and conducted religious instruction for those inmates who wanted it. For other inmates, Henry says, Clemmie only listened to their stories and waited until they asked her for help. Merely having someone listen to them, Lucas explained, was something more than most inmates had ever experienced in their lives.

Clementine's sister had heard of Henry Lee Lucas' story from the local Dallas newspapers, which had covered the dramatic events unfolding in Montague County. The newspapers described Lucas' self-professed conversion, his story about the white light in his cell, his report of the voice which he said told him that if he confessed, he would be forgiven, and his subsequent confessions to hundreds of homicides throughout Texas and the rest of the country. The woman reportedly told her sister Clementine that she was impressed by what she sensed was Lucas' fervor in his revelation and complained that, typically, the news media had never reported it. They, she explained, were focused on the lurid nature of Lucas' crimes and not on what she interpreted to be his desire to confess. She told Clemmie that Lucas needed someone to believe in him and to show him what road he had chosen to take.

Clementine was interested and was, in Lucas' words, "stunned" when her sister asked her to pray that Henry would be ultimately remanded to Georgetown where Clementine would have the ability to meet him and minister to him. At first she doubted that she would ever get to him in jail. Then she doubted whether a woman was the appropriate minister. Her sister told her that during a mass, she had uttered Henry Lee Lucas' name and had received a revelation that a woman's understanding would be the strongest ministry for him. "It will be your understanding," Clemmie's sister reportedly told her, "that will teach Henry."

Sister Clementine is a strange blend of evangelist and strict Catholic. She has been described by people who've met her as so fervent, she seems more like a fundamentalist Christian than a Catholic. She is an attractive, middle-aged brunette who speaks with a squeaky twang. She is married to a music professor at Southwestern University, has raised three children, and spends time with her sister's family as well. Her sister, who is also active in the Roman Catholic Church, is also married to a college professor. He teaches at Southern Methodist. Clemmie gives piano lessons to children in the area, counsels, sings, and prays with inmates at institutions besides the Georgetown jail. In her prison ministry, people have said, Clemmie has become a confidante of inmates who have told her stories of prisoner death threats, violence behind bars, and drug transactions that take inside the world that most people never see.

Henry says that during the period he was in Hound Dog Conway's custody, Clemmie and her sister were praying for him to come to Georgetown. Of course, he knew none of this until Clemmie confided it to him after he arrived. He says that passages from the Bible were revealed to them as an enlightenment to show them that Henry was destined to cross Sister Clementine's path. Then one day in August when Clemmie was unloading her car beside the prison, taking out bags of presents she was going to distribute to some of the prisoners, one of the trusties broke the news to her.

"Sheriff Boutwell brought in Henry Lee Lucas, the serial killer, last night," the trusty reportedly said.

Henry says that Clemmie at first felt excited and then anxious. She was being given the opportunity to minister to the most notorious serial killer in the nation who only a year before had borne testimony to his conversion. The entire situation seemed impossible at first, but, Henry says, she believed it was her task to perform the impossible. Henry says that Sister Clementine believed her destiny had finally been laid out for her, and she didn't want to fail.

Clemmie's first obstacle was placed in her path

240

by "Hutch," one of the jail administrators who ordered her not to go near Lucas under any circumstances. Henry says that the sheriff's officer ushered Clemmie into his office and warned her about Lucas' reputation. He said that Lucas was a woman killer, a woman hater, a serial killer whose hands were considered deadly weapons. Hutch told Clemmie that because he'd been in jail for all these months, he hadn't had the opportunity of chasing down women and killing them. The sheriff didn't want Sister Clementine to be his first victim.

Clemmie asked whether she could leave books and "things" for him with one of the jailers. But the sheriff's officer was adamant. According to Lucas, Hutch told Clemmie that if she left anything for the prisoner, he would be naturally curious. He would start to ask where these mysterious presents came from. He would eventually want to see Clementine, and that's where the problems would start. The prison had made a decision not to allow Clemmie to see Henry Lee Lucas for her own safety. There was no way they could guarantee that he wouldn't kill her and cause a bigger problem for all of them than if she simply stopped coming. Therefore, he said as sternly as possible, she would have to promise not to see Henry Lee Lucas. If she made any attempt to contact Lucas, she would be barred from the prison and her ministry would end. He asked her to give her word right on the spot that she would refrain from seeing Lucas. Unless he had her word, he told her, he would have her removed from the prison and never allowed back in. Reluctantly, Sister Clementine said she would try her hardest to respect the officer's wishes. But under no circumstances, she pleaded, should she be banned from the jail.

During the next two to three months other prisoners to whom she was ministering asked about Lucas and about whether she'd visited with him. Henry says that Clemmie told one prisoner about the warning she'd received from the sheriff's officer never to speak to Lucas. She told the inmate that the sheriff had threatened to end her jail ministry if she were ever to make any contact with Lucas. When she told the prisoner that the sheriff's officers were afraid that Lucas would kill her, the prisoner said that he himself would kill Lucas if he ever touched her. Henry explains that in that moment, Clemmie came to understand the disruptive effects her contact with Lucas could have had on the rest of the inmate population. Clemmie realized that for the good of the other prisoners, as well as Lucas, it was better for her to keep a wide distance even though she did very much want to speak to him.

Through October, each and every day, Clemmie would take the elevator up to the second floor of the jail to the library where she would meet other inmates and teach her Bible studies class. In order to get from the elevator to the library, she would have to pass the maximum security cells with their thick steel doors and their closed food slots. Henry says that Clemmie often paused at the door to his cell, knowing he was inside but fearing to venture close to the door for fear of violating the officer's prohibitions. Did he know that she was outside, she would ask herself. Was Henry aware that there was someone in the prison who was very much interested in his plight?

In fact, as Clemmie was soon to find out, Henry Lee Lucas did learn about Clemmie. He says that he could hear her high heels clicking along the cellblock floor every day. He wondered at first whose they were. What woman was walking past his cell everyday? His curiosity began to eat at him. Then Henry says that he overheard other prisoners talking about a "Sister Clemmie" who taught the gospel and visited prisoners in their cells. She never came to see him. Whoever she was and whatever she was doing, Henry thought in those early days in Georgetown, this Sister Clemmie was not going to be one of his visitors. He was going to remain alone in his maximum security cell, kept away from other people except police, prosecutors, and investigators from other states. He says that for the first time in his life he experienced a feeling of loneliness that went beyond his missing Becky Powell.

Henry says that Sister Clemmie was also feeling

more than curious about the mysterious inmate she was forbidden to see. She kept her promise to the prison administrator and did not attempt to make contact with him, but on days when he was out of the prison in other jurisdictions or being interviewed in one of the interrogation rooms, she ventured a peek into his cell through the food slot. She told him, he now says, that she could see inside the narrow cubicle and was overcome with a feeling of remorse and loneliness. She says that she could sense his feeling of deprivation and loss, and felt pity.

Finally, as Christmas approached, Clemmie said, she said a prayer just outside Henry's cell. He says that she knelt down by the closed food slot when she was certain that no one was going to walk by and prayed that she and Henry would have occasion to meet and that, in Henry's words, "the breach between them would be closed."

On Christmas Eve, Henry says, Clemmie returned to the jail with a box full of Bibles for the prisoners. She'd also wrapped gifts of cookies and candy and, along with her youngest daughter, distributed her gifts through the cell block. That night, Henry remembers, the security checks in the prison had Christmas carols playing on their radios and the atmosphere was as festive as anyone could expect for a prison on Christmas. But nevertheless, Sister Clementine was trying to make her rounds so as to get back home in time for dinner and midnight mass. After Clemmie had handed out her Bibles and gifts, she noticed that there was one more Bible in the bottom of the box. She'd counted them out carefully before they left, she told herself, and she thought she had the exact amount. Why would there be an extra Bible? She asked her daughter whether they'd packed an extra just in case, but her daughter shook her head. She'd been standing right next to her mother when she counted them out. Nope! The extra Bible just seemed to turn up.

Clemmie believes that that in itself was a miracle. As she looked down at the Bible, Henry explains, she had an inspiration to deliver that Bible directly to Lucas' cell. She knew, he says, that in so doing she would be breaking her promise to the jailhouse administrator and to Jim Boutwell, but she also knew that she had been scrupulous in counting out the number of Bibles exactly. She wanted to make sure, Henry says, that each prisoner in her ministry received a Bible. If there was an extra Bible in the box, then there had to be an extra prisoner in her ministry. And that prisoner, Henry says, had to be him.

Clemmie and her daughter were already on the front porch of the jail when they made their way back into the cellblock and up on the elevator to the second floor where Henry lived. At first, Henry says, Clemmie was tempted to leave the extra Bible on the library shelf and go home. But she screwed up her will and stood outside Lucas' cell. She called out to him by name and asked him if he was on the other side of the door. He answered with more of a grunt than an acknowledgement. She told him who she was and said that she had a Bible for him. Then she lifted the food slot. But she said that she wouldn't give him the Bible unless he said that he really wanted it, would read it, and wouldn't deface it or destroy the pages.

Henry remembers that he knelt down by the food slot so that he could see her and take the Bible. He promised her that he would read it and, in his words, "respect it." Then he looked out at her through the slot and she at him. Lucas said that Clemmie remembered that when she saw him the first time, she saw that his droopy glass eye made him look more like a pirate than anything else because it seemed so squinted, but his good eye was teary. She pushed the Bible through the food slot and their fingers touched. Then she pulled back and introduced him to her daughter.

Henry says that he was polite and respectful toward the two women. He said hello to her daughter, thanked the women for the Bible, promised to take good care of it and read it every day, and wished them a Merry Christmas in return for their Christmas greeting. Finally, before they left, Henry said that he had heard about her and confessed to wondering whether he would ever get the

246

chance to meet her. He referred to her as "the famous Sister Clemmie" and said that he had heard her singing to the other prisoners. Clemmie said she was moved by what Henry said, but said that she had to go before one of the jailers saw her talking to him. And with that she withdrew and walked down the corridor. In her own heart, Henry says she told him afterwards, she felt that she had fulfilled her mission. She had delivered a Bible and made contact with Henry Lee Lucas.

Clemmie had no further contact with Lucas until the end of the following month when she stood again before the door of his maximum security cell, waited until the corridor was empty, and spoke to him through the food slot. She asked him first if he was inside. When he answered, he remembers that he recognized her voice and told her that he was reading his Bible every day as he had promised. After a pause, Henry asked Clemmie what happens during a baptism, what it meant, and why people considered it important in the Bible. With a sudden inspiration, Clemmie asked Henry if he had ever been baptized, and, when she heard that he had not, asked him whether he wanted to be.

When Henry asked how he could be baptized, Clemmie asked him for a cup of water from inside his cell. He brought it back to the food slot and she told him to hand her the cup through the slot and to kneel as close to the slot as possible so that she could reach him with her hands. Henry says that he believed that Clemmie must have been filled with a mixture of happiness and trepidation because even though she was baptizing—something very important to her—she was also in direct violation of the prohibition the sheriff had laid down. Yet, he says, Clemmie persisted.

Henry says she prayed silently at first and then acknowledged that she was only the instrument of his baptism. She then dipped her finger in the water and marked him with the sign of the cross, then a second time, then a third for each member of the Trinity. When she had marked him, she asked him to put the cup of water by his knees and together they recited a *Pater Noster*. As they finished the prayer, one of the jailers came around the corner and saw Clemmie with her arms extended through the food slot of Henry's cell.

He stormed up to her, Henry says, and glared down at her—both in fear for her safety and anger that she was breaking the rules—and asked whether Henry had hurt her. Finally, when he was satisfied that Lucas was not trying to grab her through the food slot, he demanded to know what was going on. Clemmie explained that she was baptizing Lucas, and the jailer simply looked at her. From his expression she understood that he knew she was breaking the rules but that he wasn't about to do anything official as long as he knew that *she* understood that he knew she was breaking the rules. It was all done without words, and Clemmie walked away and kept her distance for part of the next week.

Each time she passed Lucas' cell, while she was keeping her distance, she would tiptoe by the door so that any guards would see her abiding by the sheriff's rules. However she also made at least some small noise, Henry says, to let him know that she was outside. On the third day, however, Lucas says he called out to her from inside his cell and asked if the high-heels passing outside belonged to her. When she answered, he asked why she hadn't spoken to him for the past two days. Clemmie whispered back that because the jailer caught her, she was afraid that the next time she spoke to Lucas, her ministry would be terminated at the Georgetown jail. Henry protested and said the whole thing was ridiculous. He says he complained to her that he wanted to learn about the gospel. But Clemmie persisted and told him flatly that if she broke the rules, Jim Boutwell would bar her from the jail. And as she walked away from Lucas' cell, Henry remembers, he began calling out for Boutwell louder and louder. Clemmie scurried away down the hall, not wanting to be around if Henry and Boutwell got into an argument.

Clemmie stayed away from jail the following Monday. She figured, Henry said, that if he and Jim Boutwell had talked about Sister Clementine's ministry, it would be best if she didn't show up at the jail until she'd spoken to the sheriff. She also figured that it was better for her to sit it out for a while to let tempers cool down. She was not the kind of person, Henry says, who wanted to stir up a hornet's nest among the sheriff's officers and wind up losing the Georgetown ministry she'd worked so hard to build.

She didn't have to wait for long. Jim Boutwell called her late in the morning to tell her that he had moved Lucas out of the maximum security wing to a slightly larger cell with a "catwalk" between the bars of the cell and the window. That way, Sheriff Boutwell said, Lucas could have a visitor who could stand on the catwalk and talk to Henry in privacy. Clemmie asked why Boutwell was telling her all of this. He replied by asking her to minister to Lucas and to continue talking to him. But he made it clear that he didn't want her to get near the bars or to come into physical contact with Lucas in any way.

Jim Boutwell explained that Clemmie would have to be alone with Henry. She would be the only one on the catwalk and the security door to the area would be locked. A guard would come for her if she needed it, the sheriff explained, but Henry had given him personal assurances that he trusted her and liked her and that there would be no problems. He allowed her to sit on a chair in a small space on the catwalk between the prison wall and the bars to Henry's cell, then he locked them both behind a steel door. Sheriff Boutwell said he believed that Clemmie would be O.K., and he was right.

"The first time I came in," Clemmie said about the first meeting, "when they shut that steel door and they turned that key, I didn't know. Henry and I sat there and I said, 'Ah, Henry, let's pray.' And he said O.K., and so I started praying for protection. Then I said, 'Now if you get an urge or something, call for something; just give me some kind of warning.' He started laughing. He said, 'It doesn't happen like that.' I said, 'Well, don't you get kind of an urge to kill?' I thought it was like an urge to smoke or something. I didn't know."

Henry says that his and Sister Clemmie's first face-to-face meeting took place that very afternoon outside his jail cell. He told Clemmie his story, the story of how light appeared to him in the darkness of his Montague County jail cell, and the voice's telling him to confess his sins. Henry repeated over again to Clemmie the promise he received in the darkness: "If you confess your sins to man, I will forgive you." And Henry explained how he told the voice that he didn't know how to confess, didn't know who to confess to, and didn't know whether he had the courage to face his own crimes. He said that he felt the hand on his shoulder and heard again the promise of the voice that he would not be alone and that his confessions would be his path back out of sin.

Lucas says that this was the first time that Clemmie had heard the entire story. He says that she was impressed and explained to him the story of the conversion of Saul to Paul from the Gospel and described to Henry the voice in the blinding light that demanded from Paul on the road to Damascus, *"Quo Vadis, Saulus?"* Henry says that he was moved by the story and was finally relieved to find someone who actually believed him.

After her first session with Henry, Clemmie says, he wrote her a letter which read: "I cannot put into words how good it feels that I know I would never kill or hurt you." The second time Clemmie saw him, she asked him what the letter meant. "I didn't know if I would still have that in me where I couldn't help but want to do it," he answered her. "There is nothing inside me. That feeling is gone. There's nothing controlling, forcing, pushing me." Clemmie says she listened to Henry and cried.

This was the beginning of a long relationship with Sister Clementine which, Henry says, has sustained him through his years in jail and at the center of public attention. Sister Clemmie visited Henry in jail several times a day and tended to his personal as well as spiritual needs. He says she fuels his religious fire, and she says that she is undoing the damage that has been done to him by

252

his mother. Clemmie herself has been quoted as having said that "a woman wounded him, so the Lord sent another woman to help him heal."

Clemmie also says that she is intent on exposing Henry's death cult, The Hand of Death, and rescuing the children he says he kidnapped and left in Mexico. She is convinced, she says, that he committed his crimes while under evil or demonic influences and that he has been completely forgiven since the time of his conversion. In addition, Clemmie says, Lucas' confessions to crimes in different jurisdictions are actually his own form of personal sacrifice, Lucas' interpretation of *imitatio Christi*. In confessing, Clemmie says, Lucas is admitting to the crimes of other people in order to assume their sins. In his own mind, he is behaving as if he has been given the mandate to assume the crimes of other murderers in order to compensate for the pain he has caused. It is not, Sister Clementine states, an act of suicide.

Eventually, Clemmie says, the jailers quit locking Henry and her behind the cell's heavy door because of one late-night incident. "One time they forgot me. Locked me in 'til past 12 midnight. Now, I couldn't go to the bathroom and we kept banging on the walls and calling, and no one came. Then Henry said 'She will never be locked in again, never. She can't go to the bathroom. I won't ever let her be locked in. It's not right.' So they don't lock me in there. Unless if I come on a

Saturday and visitors are coming, they want to make sure a visitor can't get into that little cat-walk so they lock the door. There are bars between us, but he could kill me. There's just room for a chair, and I sit right next to the bars and he sits there."

"It is hard for me to picture Henry anything but being tender, loving, and caring, because I never saw this other side of him," Clemmie says. "Every day if he wanted to he could kill me. One time I had a crick in my neck, and he was rubbing it 'cause I couldn't move my head. I'm right there, and the bars are wide. There's no problem. I mean he could just kill me."

Clemmie also described Henry's remarks in his cell where she was with him privately following official interviews. "You know," Clemmie claims Henry told her, "I didn't even know that person, and you just wonder how sweet of a person she really was and what was taken from her and what she really meant to someone. I can't dwell on it though, 'cause there's more," and Henry wept and blew his nose. "I just pray that when I confess the last crime that all the memories of everything will be taken from me. But I just have to keep moving on because if I get stuck, I won't be able to finish."

As if to underscore her adamant belief in the veracity of Henry Lee Lucas' conversion, Sister Clementine talked about the time that she and

254

Henry were watching the news together on the television in his cell. The announcer described a man who kept a woman as his sexual prisoner for several years. Clemmie said that Henry listened and muttered, "He's not even a man. That's just terrible that he would treat that woman like that."

Clemmie said that she shot back "Henry, who who are you to talk?"

And she remembers that Henry told her, "I'm not making excuses for myself. I know I was the world's biggest sinner. But that really upsets me now that someone would do that." That, she says, is one of the clearest indications that Henry Lee Lucas is a fundamentally changed person.

Clementine says that she often took her children to see Henry in Georgetown, and her own mother talked to him by phone. Her family is not simply unafraid of the killer, she says, they believe in the conversion he says he has made and consider him a member of the family. "Once Henry accepts you, he's the most loyal person you could know," Clemmie says. She revealed that Henry has even asked her to take possession of his body after he is executed. He has said to her that he is bitter and resentful of his half-sisters who, he claims, would try to capitalize on his notoriety if they could.

Clemmie has also revealed that she purposely said "I love you, Henry," in front of Sheriff Boutwell and Sergeant Prince. She says she is open about her love for Henry Lee Lucas, as she is for all of her prisoners. "Henry knows he's more special, but he hears that you can feel free to say 'I love you' to others." Sometimes, she says, she has asked Bob Prince, right in Henry's presence, " 'Bob, did you give Henry his hug today?' " She says that Prince has answered "Miss Clemmie, I think that's carrying it a little bit too far." Then, Clemmie says, she hugs Henry, saying, "He has to have a hug every day to be told that he's loved."

The entire time that Henry Lee Lucas was held at the Georgetown jail, the task force members and their prisoner functioned according to an unspoken, complicated arrangement. As Bob Prince put it, "Henry is obviously an institutionalized person. He knows how to make the system work." Henry was happy there not only because he postponed death row and received public attention, but because he liked and respected Prince, Boutwell, and Texas Ranger Clayton Smith. He knew what they wanted — his cooperation in clearing cases — so Henry Lee Lucas willingly obliged. In return he got to pal around, work, eat, and travel with them. In effect, they became his family, the family he really never had. And they made a few concessions: his own cell and some personal belongings, his "office," his files, and his social calendar. They gave him a job and made him part of their team. But most important to him was the time he spent with Sister Clemmie.

She was given total freedom to come and go as she pleased, to play a key role in Henry's life at the jail. She calmed him when he grew moody, arbitrated squabbles between them all, supervised Henry's correspondence with victims' families, and dealt with the media. Her influence was indispensable, and they all knew and accepted that. Henry needed her calming reassurance. He desperately needed the sense of self-worth that she encouraged. And the immediate members of the task force realized that it was Sister Clemmie that was keeping Henry and the investigation going.

Chapter 14

"I Never Killed No One But Mom."

Henry Lee Lucas' confessions rocked the nation for over a year and set a parade of reporters beating a path to his Georgetown jail cell door. As case after case was "cleared," that is, taken off the books and considered "solved," by Texas law enforcement agencies and other investigators from around the country, new doubts began to surface about the ability of a single person to have committed so many murders in so many different states in so short a time. These doubts about Lucas' veracity weren't new. Even Texas Rangers Bob Prince and Clayton Smith had suggested when the task force was first organized that they were suspicious of some of Lucas' confessions. Prince said he went so far as to tell visiting investigators that Lucas was a practiced liar who would test them or would just downright lie for fun. Rangers who briefed investigators before interviewing Lucas were equally forthright about Lucas' propensities to manipulate the people he was dealing with.

However, as the investigation grew and the natural skepticism of the Texas Rangers became first obscured and then obliterated by the amount of media coverage, small voices began to question whether the Rangers themselves were behind the runaway freight train that was the Lucas task force. Were the Texas Rangers trying to use Lucas and his confessions to enhance their own reputations during a time of shrinking budgets for law enforcement? Were the Texas Rangers trying to justify their budget by turning the Lucas case into a "confession machine" and providing a steady stream of headline-making cases that were solved with each passing week? As sensational as these claims might seem now, in 1985 they began to cause doubts among Texas law enforcement professionals.

The opening shots in the Lucas backlash were fired in early 1985 when McLennan County District Attorney Vic Feazell, according to a Texas Department of Public Safety report, first contacted Texas Attorney General Jim Mattox and "provided him with information indicating that Lucas confessions to three murders in McLennan County were, at best, highly suspect." In one case, the report states, "Lucas claimed that Ottis Toole had actually committed the murder, but evidence showed that Toole was in jail at the time the crime was supposed to have been committed. Ultimately, District Attorney Feazel requested help from the Attorney General to investigate Lucas' background.

Specifically, the McLennan County District Attorney's office raised a number of questions about the procedural nature of the Lucas confessions and suggested that Lucas had been deliberately or inadvertently seeded with facts to crimes he initially denied having committed, only to confess to them at a later date using facts that were presented to him originally. For example, the District Attorney's report pointed to Lucas' confessions to the Dorothy Collins and Rita Salazar murders and said that Lucas had at first denied having committed them. During the interview, the investigator raised specific facts about the case for Lucas to deny. When he was being interviewed about the cases by a different officer, Lucas used the facts from the first interview to convince him that he had murdered Collins and Salazar. The report says that this is a "significant" fact about many of the Lucas confessions.

In April, Texas Attorney General Jim Mattox ordered Henry taken from the Williamson County Jail and moved to Waco, Texas, in McLennon County, effectively cutting Henry off from the task force that was working with him and cutting him off from Sister Clemmie as well. Henry was now alone in a strange situation and had to adapt to the demands and expectations of a new set of jailers and investigators. Like the chameleon he was, Henry began to reconfigure himself to the new situation.

Mattox also directed Vic Feazell and the McLennan County grand jury to investigate the Lucas task force itself. It was said that Henry had actually gone over the top in his confessions. Nobody in a hundred years could have killed that many people, the Attorney General believed. Maybe it was the nature of media hype surrounding Lucas from the very beginning that generated this natural reaction, but the tide was beginning to turn against the task force. As the pressure began to build behind a re-evaluation of the corpus of the Lucas confessions, *Dallas Times-Herald* writer Hugh Aynesworth reported that in an early interview Lucas once said that he had never killed anybody but his mother. Suddenly "I never killed nobody but Mom" became a watchword among Dallas-based Texas law enforcement officials who had originally been flabbergasted at the extent of the crimes Henry had claimed he'd committed. A true backlash had begun to set in.

Sheriff Boutwell and Ranger Bob Prince claim that they had always been ready for the backlash. It was just a natural thing, they still believe. First of all, the two of them had been around long enough to know that when there's enough press behind a certain issue, a level of public skepticism is just bound to build up. It just happened that the skepticism had been slower than usual in catching up with the pace of the investigations. Indeed, Boutwell and Prince still say that long before any Attorney General or District Attorney voiced any doubts, the Sheriff and the Texas Rangers were the first to say that some of the Lucas confessions wouldn't hold up. Boutwell and Prince also said that much of the responsibility for the value of the Lucas confessions had to rest not on the task force, but on the visiting detectives.

Task force members Boutwell, Prince, and Clayton Smith reminded the Texas law enforcement authorities that when the McLennon County investigation was opened up in 1985, the Lucas task force was originally never charged with the actual "investigation" of the Lucas cases. It was empowered to "coordinate" the hundreds of different investigations in hundreds of different jurisdictions, most of which were out of state. Therefore, investigating the task force for improperly investigating Lucas was to ask of the task force something it had not been empowered to do. The task force's only mission outside of the cases in Williamson County was to coordinate the prisoner's schedule so as to make him available to visiting investigators. It was the visitors, Boutwell and Prince always maintained, who were responsible for the conduct and integrity of their respective investigations.

But that argument, although it appeared reasonable on the surface, didn't make so much as a dent in the counter-press that was building against Lucas. Newspapers called him a hoax. Newspapers called the task force a hoax, too, because they perpetuated

Lucas on the unsuspecting public. What made matters worse was that the newspapers and Texas investigating attorneys were able to point to concrete cases which were poorly managed. "There were some questionable cases," Prince reported. However, he said, those cases eventually were cleared for specific reasons and could stand on their own merits.

Among the most highly criticized of the Lucas confessions was one for the stabbing death of Deborah Sue Williamson in Lubbock. The victim's mother and stepfather, Joyce and Bob Lemons, were convinced that Henry was not responsible for the crime and cited inconsistencies between the facts of the case and Lucas' recorded statements. Henry described his victim as 5'4" with light brown hair and a weight of approximately 135 pounds. He said she was at least twenty years old. However, the Lemons said, their daughter was a 5'7" platinum blonde eighteen-year-old who weighed only 110 pounds. Clearly the height, hair color of the victim, and weight are significantly different physical characteristics which would be hard to mistake.

In Lucas' version of how he committed the crime, he entered through a sliding glass door of a white house. But in fact the victim lived in an olive house and her father had secured the door so it wouldn't slide open. Henry said in his confession that he and Ottis Toole chased the woman inside the house, caught her, stabbed her to death, and raped her. The facts, however, suggest the murder actually took place in the carport and not in the house. Additionally, the Lemons told reporters that they believe that police officers were coaching Henry Lee Lucas about the location of the crime while Lucas was supposed to be directing them to the crime scene purely out of his own memory.

The date of the crime posed another problem for them. August 22, 1975 was only two days after Lucas' release from the state prison in southern Michigan. Could it have been possible, the Lemons asked, for an ex-convict who was free for only two days and who said that he hadn't met Toole until years later in a Jacksonville soup kitchen to have killed this woman? Therefore, people began to ask, did the Lubbock police officers purposely "fix" the case? The Lemons were particularly distraught over what they saw as a disparity between the confessions that the police were using to prosecute Lucas in the murder of their daughter and the facts of the case as they understood them. Newspapers carried stories about altercations between victims' families and the police and complaints that because the police were attempting to clear murder cases through Lucas' confessions, the real murderers were doing unpunished and perhaps other lives were being put in danger. But of all the complaints raised, the task force strategy, the "fixed" confessions charge generated the greatest outcry.

The Deborah Sue Williamson case took on national significance in 1985 when Bob Lemons, the victim's stepfather, went on "60 Minutes" to criticize the Lucas task force and complain about what newspapers referred to as "misconduct" by the Texas Rangers. This brought the work of the task force and the complaints against the task force into the national media as "60 Minutes" profiled the story of Lemons' complaints. Lemons was also quoted in the *El Paso Times* as having complained that the Texas Rangers "fed" Lucas information about the murder of his stepdaughter. Bob Lemons told the press that he wanted to see the Texas Rangers "pay" for what they did and that he wanted to see Rangers Bob Prince and Clayton Smith "prosecuted for the way they used Lucas to clear cases."

The Lubbock Police eventually responded to the charges that they had rigged Lucas' confession in the Williamson murder case. In a 1985 interview in *Third Coast* magazine, Detective Sergeant Travis Lincecum of the Lubbock police responded to charges of confession-rigging by saying that "we have no doubts that Lucas is the one who committed the murder." He explained that some of the facts of the case are known only to the police investigators and that's the way it had to be for the time being because the case is pending and all details couldn't be released. He said that the facts of the case that went beyond the confession provided by Lucas were the basis of the department's pursuit of the investigation. The grand jury brought an indictment against Lucas on the basis of more than simply his confession, the detective continued. "Whatever the details . . . they were sufficient to satisfy a grand jury and persuade the district attorney to file capital-murder charges."

The controversy over Lucas still raged in the days prior to his removal from the Georgetown jail as other examples of factual difficulties with his confessions continued to arise. In another case, Henry had confessed to a murder he said he committed on November 6, 1981 in which he killed a clerk behind a "Mom and Pop" store in Little Rock, Arkansas. One of the prosecuting attorneys in the case produced a receipt for the purchase of an insurance policy that, he said, proves that Henry was actually in Florida at the time he said he committed the murder. In 1984, there was a court hearing in which Henry's confession was challenged, but Lucas stuck to his story. He said that the receipt was probably dated wrong and that as far as he was concerned, he had murdered the clerk. "If people don't want to believe it, that's their problem. As far as I'm concerned," he was quoted as saying. "It's over."

Henry's ex-wife, Betty Crawford, whom he left in Maryland after she said she suspected him of molesting her daughter, disputed Lucas' confession to the murder of Elizabeth Ann Price. The murder took place, according to case records, on April 10, 1976, in Lubbock Texas. But on that day, Crawford says, Lucas was living with her in a mobile home on lot C-3 at Benjamin's Trailer Park in Port Deposit, Maryland. They lived there from January, 1976, investigation records cite Betty Crawford has having stated, to June, 1977. Those same records indicate that Lucas was gone from the area only twice: a one-day trip to Virginia, and a twenty-four hour trip to Rhode Island. This was another example of how evidence uncovered after a confession was touted in the press, not only casting doubt on the confession itself, but on everything Lucas was saying in general.

As more and more reporters and investigators began hunting for discrepancies in the Lucas story, more and more discrepancies showed up. In the Orange Socks case, for example, the one case for which Lucas has been given an actual warrant for his execution, Toole's confession that he committed the murder rocked the press. But the Toole confession, although Boutwell taped it in the Williamson County jail in 1983 — three months before Henry's trial — was never admitted into evidence even though the prosecution knew it existed.

Bob Prince always likes to point to the facts supporting Lucas' confessions. With each of the 190 case confirmations, there are as many as 100 pieces of evidence, and the prisoner was a primary source of it all, he explains. "There are some questionable cases," he says. "But there are reasons that each one is cleared."

Jim Boutwell expresses private reservations about Toole's confession. He says that despite what Toole said, he believes that Henry Lee Lucas did kill the victim. He also says that in the Lucas cases he investigated he's sure that Lucas was the killer. But he also says that Lucas was deliberately misleading other investigators and that, despite Boutwell's clear warnings, they went along with what were spurious confessions. The task force, he claims, could not be responsible for the police work of other jurisdictions. He adds that if another task force were convened to reinvestigate and recoordinate all of these confessions, they'd probably do no better than the original task force. He explained that Lucas is a manipulator and would manipulate anybody he could. Bob Prince described the Lucas case to a *Third Coast* writer by saying that "I don't think we'll ever know how many people he killed." And Lucas' own defense counsel, Don Higginbotham, was quoted by that same writer as saying that his client probably would go down in history as "the biggest liar in history."

The description of Lucas as the most consummately institutionalized person in the world is probably the most apt. Lucas is adept at playing any role he perceives assigned to him, even when he must change his role for different people in the same room. People who've interviewed him or seen him respond to group pressures have remarked that his abilities to sense out what's expected of him and to conform to those expectations are uncanny. He literally reconfigures himself to fit into each situation. And prison is especially easy for him, because he need make no decisions—all he has to do is react.

The task force system in Georgetown was so conducive to Lucas, his attorney Don Higginbotham once said that "If you were to open the front door of that jail and try to kick Henry Lee Lucas out of there, I don't believe he'd leave. He's where he wants to be. But that's not saying that if something goes wrong, like if Sister Clemmie has a heart attack and dies, some hot-shit cop comes in there and tries to rubber hose him, or something happens to Sheriff Boutwell, or something goes awry—in my opinion, he's liable to grab the first pistol that's stuck in front of him and decide to try and shoot his way out of there. I don't know . . . that's the problem. I never turn my back on Lucas . . . I don't care how pleasant the conversation."

Through all of the doubts and the charges of hoax that were raging in 1985, Lucas maintains that it was the story of The Hand of Death that gave people the most problems. Anybody can be wrong about a date, he said. A clerk writing the wrong number on your receipt, a typist's hitting a wrong key, somebody who can't understand a date you mumbled over a telephone all make for factual mistakes. But, he said, The Hand of Death—that really gave people a problem. The cult and what the cult did were considered off-limits, even by people on the task force, he says.

"Nobody wants to know about a cult," Henry said. "They don't want to know it exists, because if they do know it exists, they don't feel they have the power to stop it. This is what all law enforcement's afraid of. I've sent them back, and they found a lot of stuff, but they never found a cult. I told the FBI whereabouts to look for a cult, and they found four to five million dollars worth of opium. But they didn't find the cult. They found our whole factory, but they didn't find anything. And I told them where to go to look for the warehouse, and they went there and looked for it, and found nothing but guns. But yet they said it don't belong to the cult. I mean, I don't know why. I can't have no idea why. I know Bob. He's trying. I don't put all the blame on Bob, but I push him maybe a lot more than a lot of them do."

Henry was right about one thing: the fantastic nature of Henry's confessions became too flashy, too big, and too public. He became too much of an asset to whoever was managing his cases. Thus, the Attorney General's office moved in to sort out details. In the process, they wound up investigating the investigators as well as Lucas. Even reporters and writers lined up on different sides of the issue. Henry had become so valuable, and he was so willing to change his story to fit the environment, that anybody who had him had a person willing to confess to the facts as they were presented to him.

The problem with Henry Lee Lucas' veracity is the problem with serial killers in general. Serial killers are a phenomenon almost no one understands. The killer rarely fits a single stereotype, his crimes are so "unreasonable" because the motive is internal, not explicit, and he is motivated by an animal lust. Therefore, the serial killer's crimes always seem incomprehensible to reasonable people.

A characteristic behavior of a serial killer is a distortion of the truth as a means of survival. Lucas fits that particular profile. He also controls others around him through his submissiveness. He tells everyone exactly what they want to hear: for Sister Clemmie it is the power of religious faith; for the task force it was his details of the crimes, for lawyers it is his legal savvy, and doctors get Henry's first-hand accounts of his symptoms and years in Ionia State Mental hospital. He feeds these people their own thoughts and words and tells them what he wants them to believe and what they have told him they want to believe. He even believes what he's saying at the time he's saying it. Each interviewer comes away happy. And when there are discrepancies in his stories or he appears to know impossible things, he calls up his explanation of a sixth sense, talks about divinely inspired communication, and says he is able to know some things other people can't. And Henry is mercurial—he even provides surprises to liven up an otherwise tediously procedural homicide investigation.

When Lucas was in Waco for the McLennan County investigation in 1986 he had begun to recant his confessions. Finally, he went public and said "I never killed nobody excepting Mom." Suddenly the most prolific serial killer in history became the most prolific recanter in history. From hundreds of "cleared" cases and hundreds more "claimed" confessions, he had switched to the side of the McLennon investigators and said that he had only killed his mother. Which side of Lucas was telling the truth: the killer or the person who said that he had been forced to confess by the task force?

Once a person better understands Henry's reasonings, the prisoner's actions during the two investigations are easier to rationalize. During the task force phase, Henry claimed some of Ottis' cases because, he now says, he may have recalled some information reported by his fellow cult members from the Everglades. Maybe he recalled something Ottis had said to him or even something another police investigator had said to him inadvertently. Whatever the reason, what is true is that he told officers amazing details from many of the crimes even though he did make factual errors. The problem is that the real facts that can be corroborated were obscured by the willingness of officers to believe many more facts that could never be corroborated and later returned to haunt the investigation. Aspects of the truth were obscured by the fantasies that were also there.

During one Texas case in which Henry was the suspect, for example, he selected the correct photograph of the victim from a picture lineup and then described the manner of death. He directed officers to the house next door which was similar, and named the room in which they had found the mur-dered woman. But because he did not mention steal-ing the car and leaving it on the railroad tracks, these officers refused to blame Henry for the crime.

This could easily have been one of the situations in which the facts that Henry provided and his sub-sequent confessions convinced police that he was tell-ing the truth even though he forgot about the car. However, the very fact that he'd forgotten the car could cause a solid legal challenge to his testimony. However, because Lucas was not charged in the case, there was never any dispute.

"There have been a few officers who were anxious to clear their cases," Boutwell says. "But they have been in the minority." There is no statute of limita-tions on homicide, and law enforcement admires books that are clean, so it seems possible, even prob-able, that some portion of the 1,000 officers who in-terviewed Henry inadvertently slipped him too much information—say a glance at a photograph or too many hints about the MO—or simply disregarded an excess of errors due to overzealousness or a ca-reer need. The tragedies lies in these mistakes be-cause the cases may be forever lost and the real killers may have remained free.

In Waco, the McLennan County grand jury put Henry—the diagnosed schizophrenic—on the stand and grilled him for hours on the details of his cases. Then when he was unable to remember details and consistently changed his story, they asked him if he had lied about the cases. When he said he had lied, they brought the media in and Henry admitted his lies to the media. Sister Clemmie said that Henry was made to perform for the public. She claims that Henry was coached by prosecutors in Waco to the point where he was "brainwashed." She says that at one point Henry didn't know what was true and what was false.

Down in Waco, Sister Clemmie said, she repeatedly asked Henry to tell the truth about the murder cases. Finally, she said, "Henry, you know I love you. Did you or didn't you kill those people?" And she said that Henry felt divided. She claims that he actually didn't know which story he was supposed to regurgitate. He looked at her and replied, "I thought I did it, but now I don't know. I don't know." The fact that he had told the media people that he hadn't killed anybody except his mother should have surprised no one. He was simply trying to survive the moment by figuring out whom he was trying to please.

Bob Prince has called the Waco hearing a publicity stunt. "The only time Henry was not accessible to law enforcement was while he was in Waco," Prince said. "Law enforcement officials were completely cut off. Even the FBI was denied access. California officers came all the way here, but they couldn't talk to him. Why the news media? He was available to any news media who wanted to see him. Henry's just saying anything. Ninety-nine percent of any prisoners getting the death penalty want a person in a position of authority to believe they didn't kill anybody.

Sister Clementine said the entire Waco hearing was Henry's greatest hour of need because it eroded whatever sense of reality and self that she had been able to help him find when he was in Georgetown. She said that she became most concerned when she believed that Henry was threatening suicide. "I'm in a big black hole," Sister Clemmie says he repeatedly told her. "And the hole's getting smaller and smaller. Pretty soon there's going to be nothing left of me." She also says that she begged Jim Boutwell to rescue Henry and made a tape recording of her fears about Henry's treatment and possible suicide. She gave the tape to Boutwell, and a San Antonio federal attorney followed up Sister Clemmie's charges with an investigation of her own: an investigation of the investigation of the investigation. The federal attorney made certain that Lucas had a legal counsel and that a doctor was called in to examine the prisoner and attest to the status of his health. Sister Clemmie says she finally told Lucas in Waco: "Henry, you're crazy as a loon." She says he answered, "I know I am."

Henry wrote to Clemmie in an April 28, 1985, letter that was smuggled out of the McLennon County jail by a minister. In that letter he says he feels "betrayed" by the Texas Rangers who have not stood up for him since he was removed from Georgetown. "When I was in Georgetown they stood up. But since I came up here they get their captain to say I am only a lyer [sic]. That made me feel like they have betrayed me, so I went on the TV and told that I haven't killed anybody except my mother. How else am I going to fight them when I can't tell you any different because if I do, they will make it harder for me to see you."

In the letter, Henry claims that he was both enticed and pressured to recant his serial murder confessions. But the way he was behaving in Waco, conforming to what was expected of him was really very similar to the way he had conformed in Georgetown when he was deprived of his coffee and cigarettes. The same people who said that Lucas was threatened and bribed into making confessions may themselves have been committing the same kinds of coercion whether inadvertently or not. If Henry's letter can be believed and he was threatened with not ever being able to see Sister Clemmie again, his claims that he would have said anything to see her have a ring of truth. Henry will say whatever people want him to say to earn the rewards that are being held out for him.

"No matter what you hear, don't let anyone tell you what your hart (sic) knows is right, because I cannot stop these people," Henry writes. "I have to do like they want me to do. I'm here and have no one that I can get help from. I even have tried to make Jim and the Rangers mad at me by tellin' that they gave me the information, to get them to fight." Lucas seems to be saying that he wanted the Texas Rangers to fight for his return to Georgetown. He says that he felt betrayed by the state by being moved to Waco and that he went on TV to recant in order to get back at everybody. But his biggest reason for recantation, he says, is that he is afraid that if he refuses to recant, Clemmie will never be able to visit him.

"Do you want me to stop even if they come up with these phony dates?" Henry writes, possibly referring to the conflicts in dates that the McLennan attorneys cited in their investigation of the original task force confessions. Even though he says he "killed some people," he says that the recantation of all his crimes is what the grand jury wants from him before they will allow him to see Clemmie.

"When I need to talk this out, I can't without making it so I can't see you and visit you. Which means my life, not to see you. When they take you away from me, how can I love. My love for you is all that I want to live for. God has been my shoulder so far, and I need you. When you are sad and get sick with the hurt they are causing then I want better for you. Will you please understand me. I have no choice as long as I am here, but to do as they want. I can't say in words what I want because they have a way to listen to what I say to you, and they have the upper hand on me because everyone

277

has turned their backs on me."

Lucas both recants and supports aspects of his recantation when he says that he may have admitted guilt to some of the crimes he didn't commit, but that he isn't sure which ones because he really did commit some of the homicides. "Maybe I have excepted [sic] some that are not mine, but how can I say which ones? I don't know. I told you the first day, when I came here, that I did kill some people, but how can I keep telling you over and over without them finding out."

Lucas also denied in the letter that he was shown crime scenes by officers to encourage his confessions. "Look at the facts, they know they didn't show me the places. I took them there. But if they aren't going to fight for the truth, then why hold me? Turn me loose, since I haven't killed anyone like they say here." And in a final postscript, written to Jim Boutwell, Lucas says that what is happening in Waco is an attempt to silence him. It is, he says, what he predicted would happen once he began telling the full story of his crimes. The crimes were too fantastic, they implicated a conspiracy, and they implied that one person and the cult he belonged to were able to elude the police too well. He says that he is being provided with false information to back up his recantations, recantations he will keep on making to protect Sister Clemmie. "You are safe as long as I do as they say," he writes. "I know they have the power to do what they say. They have given

278

me false records everywhere now and I can't stop it."

People have asked whether it can ever be determined which version of the story was actually a hoax? A more appropriate approach may be to focus on which cases are true and which cases are false and understand that both true and false may have equal weight in a personality as fragmented as Henry Lee Lucas'. Psychologists who work with serial killers should know that serial killers live in a world of delusion and fantasy. Dichotomies such as real and fantasy, true and false, good and bad do not have the same meaning for serial killers that they do for their therapists and investigators. Serial killers easily take a little bit of truth, mix it with a little bit of fantasy, mix that with whatever they believe people want to hear about them, and come up with a finished product that may change from moment to moment. This is called "confabulation" and Henry Lee Lucas is a skilled confabulator.

To believe that Henry's confessions and the work of the Boutwell/Prince task force was a hoax is to believe that a thousand professional law enforcement officers, including the Texas Rangers and the FBI, and over a hundred trips to different crime sites should be suspect. For this to be the case, most, if not all, of these officials would have had to have been in cahoots or fooled by a demonic genius who kept each of his facts straight. The conspiracy would have had to have taken place before live television cameras—each of Henry's interviews was videotaped—and would have had to have been aided and abetted by the FBI. Worse, the actual pieces of evidence that were located through sources other than Lucas would have to be discounted as somehow "planted" by the police. It just doesn't make sense that hundreds of agencies and the federal government would "conspire" with one another to create a Henry Lee Lucas.

The sanest answer to whether Lucas is a fraud or whether he is telling the truth is to believe in the evidence which points to the veracity of his confessions and throw out the confessions that are clearly untrue. That's what the task force was trying to do from the very start, Prince and Boutwell have said. The problem is that the fantastic nature of some of Lucas' confessions have all but obliterated the accuracy of his truthful confessions.

When the Waco investigation ended in June, 1985, Lucas was sent back to Georgetown. He was given an execution date for the murder of Orange Socks and remanded to Huntsville to await an execution that was originally scheduled for December 3, 1990. That execution was stayed on a procedural appeal, and Henry was transferred to Florida where he will be investigated by a grand jury in a number of capital murder cases that he has confessed to in that state. Sooner or later, Henry may actually be put to death for one of these crimes.

But whether it was for a crime he actually committed or a crime he falsely confessed to may no longer be the issue for him.

If Henry is executed for a crime he did commit and confessed to, then, in his mind, he will have been forgiven and he will be reunited with Becky. If Henry is executed for a crime he didn't commit then he will be executed as a martyr and as a martyr he will be reunited with Becky. If, as Sister Clemmie has explained it, Henry is executed because he took on the sins of someone else, then he will have been emulating the example set forth in the New Testament and, he believes, will also be reunited with Becky after death. If he simply stays in jail for the rest of his life, confesses to all of his crimes and his several life sentences are his punishment, he believes he will simply be forced to wait longer to see Becky. Any which way you choose, Henry winds up with what he says he wants the most: salvation in his own death.

Chapter 15

The Specialists

Henry Lee Lucas' confessions drew more than police investigators and reporters to his cell in Georgetown, later in Waco, and finally Huntsville. Among the supplicants looking for some acknowledgement from Lucas were teams of lawyers, representatives of families with missing children, politicians, evangelists, spiritualists, photographers, and doctors. There were plenty of doctors. There were psychologists, psychiatrists, neurologists, pathologists and experts from various specialized fields of criminology and sociology. There were so many experts that even the Georgetown jail team was surprised at the number of different experts the Lucas case was attracting. All of them were willing to line up, sometimes for hours, for the opportunity to sit across the battered table from the curly-haired man who was being so cooperative in answering their questions. And everyone of them came away happy. People remarked that no one could satisfy so many different types of people, many of whom seemed to have diametrically opposing views about the Lucas case, unless he were simply giving them the answers they wanted to hear. And that's exactly what Henry Lee Lucas was doing. He was enjoying himself.

Some of the experts came because they were so ordered by local courts or law enforcement agencies for "expert" opinion and testimony. Others saw in Lucas an opportunity to assist legitimate research projects and possibly learn more about the aberration Lucas seemed to illustrate. Others came because they wanted to further their own reputations by associating their work with the excitement of the new "find." But only the author retrieved samples of his blood and his hair for biochemical studies on the man or to corroborate the biochemical predictions other experts had made about him.

Lucas was generally cooperative with all of their efforts in spite of his antagonism toward individuals he perceived as authority figures and therefore threatening. He submitted to lengthy interviews with psychologists, researchers, and others. He seemed to answer their questions openly and frankly, albeit with a situational sense of honesty. In other words, he would make sure that his honest answer conformed to the situation he was in and the way he was feeling at the time. Lucas didn't seem to have the same sense of right and wrong or honest and dishonest that other people had, and this made him even more of a phenomenon.

Lucas also seemed to want to learn from the experts about the things he had done wrong. If he was sick, he wanted to know the cure. If there were things he was supposed to do, he wanted to know them. It was as if Lucas himself, who had lived underground most of his life, had discovered his own version of a "brave new world" and wanted to learn more about it from the strangers who were visiting. He also seemed more than fascinated by the spiritual side of what was happening. He had already fallen under Sister Clementine's influence, as she had fallen under his, and his cooperation began to take on religious overtones as well. He was a soul whose salvation many people wanted to facilitate.

To be sure, there was a legitimate motivation in studying Henry Lee Lucas, and there continues to be even as his sentence in the Orange Socks case is stayed and he is sent off to Florida to face a new set of capital indictments. If Henry Lee Lucas is a serial killer of staggering proportions, people want to know why. What was it in his background or early life that set him on a path that most human beings find abhorrent? If the "bad seed" or flawed gene could be discovered; if the precise moment in time when a critical adult turned against him, or even if the path through Lucas' brain could be mapped, maybe scientists would then formulate the magic bullet that could once and for all eradicate the Henry Lee Lucas syndrome. If we knew what made Henry Lee Lucas, we could possibly prevent future Henry Lee Lucases from coming into existence.

But scientists wanted to know more. Was Henry Lee Lucas different from other serial killers? Was he horribly unique? Was he similar to other serial killers and so could become part of a serial killer profile. More to the point, could a profile of a serial killer or a potential serial killer be constructed? And if it were possible to construct such a profile, would we then have an instrument that could predict the possibility of dangerousness and be used as an alert for physicians, law enforcement agencies, or corrections professionals. How far could we take such an instrument and was the study of Henry Lee Lucas, therefore, the means to an end?

Lucas gave police and doctors many different versions of his past history, changing a few facts here, embellishing facts there, depending upon the circumstances of the interview. It is also obvious that he doesn't always remember what he told one person and may tell that person something else or may tell a different story to another person. When the two stories are compared, discrepancies usually rise to the surface to confound the experts. But the essential outline of his early life has remained fairly constant over the course of the stories that have been written about him and the interviews he has given.

His childhood history reads like a textbook prescription for how to make a serial killer. In a cause-

and-effect-world, Henry's extreme hatred for his mother in particular and probably for certain unsubmissive women in general, turned him into a lust killer whose M.O. is to murder his female victims before having sex with them. In his own words, he was "stretched" to the breaking point.

Because Lucas has been institutionalized in reform schools, state mental facilities, federal prison, and state penitentiaries for most of his life, he has grown used to dealing with prison psychiatrists. He knows what they look for and he knows what answers to give to the various interviews. He has also discussed his own psychiatric reports and profiles and knows what most psychological evaluators will say about him. In short, Lucas belongs to a certain type of post-Freudian individual who is so at home in a psychiatric environment, he actually knows how to manipulate it.

"I have heard the questions so many times," Lucas has said. "I know what they're going to ask before they ask it."

Other psychologists and profilers have raised hosts of questions about Lucas' background and the standard Lucas story that since his mother was a prostitute he kills any woman what reminds him of a prostitute. One psychologist questioned whether prostitution is really an issue in Lucas' case. According to the argument, how much prostitution could there really have been in the Virginia hill country and just how attractive could Viola Lucas have been by the time that Henry would have realized what was going on?

286

The standard answer is that precisely because there was very little of what we understand to be modern prostitution going in the Virginia hills in the late 1940s and early 1950s Viola Lucas was made that much more attractive, no matter how old or homely she might have been, to her johns who didn't have much of a selection in the first place.

Viola Lucas might have been a common figure of her time: a woman who took in boyfriends that were procured for her by someone just like Bernie. Anderson Lucas or "No Legs" as Henry says people called him, might have been an older man who had been a boyfriend but now just lived in the shack because he had nowhere else to go. Whether he was actually Henry's father or not is, even according to Henry, purely conjectural.

The point is that issues regarding Viola are largely irrelevant as the primary or sole causes of Henry's homicidal aggression. She was certainly a factor in his hatred of women. Henry refers to her as a factor, and medical records and reform school reports generally support the information that Henry has provided. He has said that any woman who slapped him, tried to beat him, or challenged him in any way reminded him of his mother and caused an almost instantaneous reaction. His mother's beating him caused him to strike back at her. Becky's slapping him similarly, he says, caused him to strike at her. He attacked both women with a knife.

Henry Lee Lucas, despite later statements to the

contrary, had killed his mother after they fought in a bar in Michigan. Henry was charged with her murder by the police, and he confessed to it when he returned to Michigan from Virginia where he had fled. He had said, and looking at it purely from his perspective he might have even been right, that he really didn't intend to kill her. He only defended himself against her when she beat him with a broomstick handle and in the process, nicked her with a knife or a razor blade. She fell forward and he fled the motel room, driving all the way back to Virginia to wait for her to come and punish him. However, because she bled to death from the wound that Henry inflicted, he was charged with and pled guilty to manslaughter in her death, was convicted, and served prison time in Michigan.

Shortly after his being charged with the Orange Socks murder, Dr. Tom Kubiszyn, an Austin psychologist, wrote a psychological evaluative report on Henry Lee Lucas on referral from Jay Fogelman M.D., in order to assist in Lucas' competency evaluation. Police wanted to know if Lucas was mentally competent to stand trial for the murder. Kubiszyn reviewed material from Ionia State hospital, interviewed Lucas, and performed a full-scale battery of standard evaluative psychological assessments. He administered the Wechsler Adult Intelligence Scale-Revised, the Bender Visual-Motor Gestalt Test, projective drawings, a Rorschach Ink-Blot Test, and other basic instruments.

Kubiszyn noted Lucas' previous criminal history,

his murder of his mother, his suicide attempts, his history of alcohol and drug abuse, and his medical history. The amount of head traumas Kubiszyn refers to is extensive. Besides citing the famous incident in which Lucas was beaten into a coma by his mother for not bringing wood for the stove, the report also refers to the injuries which resulted in the loss of his left eye, his fall from ladder which resulted in a nail having to be surgically extracted from his skull, and another accident at a construction site in which a sliver of metal from an I-beam lodged in his head and had to be surgically extracted. Lucas also told Kubiszyn about his numerous car accidents, especially one in which the car he was driving rolled over nine times.

Lucas told Kubiszyn about his hallucinations, the vision he had in the Montague County jail, the voices that troubled him during his time in the Michigan penitentiary, and the feelings of floating he had as child when he felt as though he could see himself lift from the bed and float in space. Kubiszyn reported that this type of vision followed Lucas' head injury at age 6 or 7.

Then Dr. Kubiszyn referred to Lucas' spiritual conversion, his relationship with Sister Clemmie, and his recantation of his 140 confessions to murder that had been coordinated through Sheriff Boutwell's and Sgt. Prince's Lucas task force. Kubiszyn reported that Lucas told him that at first, after he'd killed Becky, he was seeking the death penalty because "I just don't want to live anymore." However, after his conversion, he realized that confessing falsely to crimes for the purpose of getting a death sentence was tantamount to suicide. "If I get the death penalty, I'll be lying to get it," Kubiszyn reported that Lucas said. "That would be suicide. I want people to know the truth. It's a sin to take your own life, and so I'm telling the people to do it and then they're responsible and not me."

Afterwards, Lucas again explained to Kubiszyn that if he were to be given the death penalty, then he will go to his death "thinking he has been wronged by the state. In addition, he thinks he will be able to go to heaven." Kubiszyn concludes that Henry's attempts to trick himself into heaven by tricking the state into wrongfully executing him was an example of Henry's illogical and contradictory thinking. From a purely psychological and rational point of view, Dr. Kubiszyn was probably correct, but from Henry's point of view, his attempts seemed to have a perverse logic.

Others have pointed out that because Henry Lee Lucas hadn't gotten much out of life except, perhaps, an understanding of what might lie in store for him if he were to die in a state of grace, it made sense for Henry to pursue a state of grace with the limited amount of understanding that was available to him. Confession of his own guilt was one clear road to grace, in Henry's view of the world. Assuming the sins of others was another clear road. After all, didn't the Bible reveal how the assumption of the sins of humanity was an act of grace in itself? Henry simply applied the same exact logic to himself.

Subsequent to the April, 1984, Kubiszyn evaluation of Henry Lee Lucas, other types of medical evaluations have been conducted and a more complex picture of the killer has emerged. First, Lucas was found to fit into a larger pattern of deviance that has typified most convicted serial killers. He has had a physically abusive and violent relationship with one of his parents, one of his parents traumatized him sexually, he had a very early history of dysfunctional sexual experiences, and he received multiple severe head traumas when he was younger. Lucas, like other convicted serial killers, had been so violated that he never developed a sense of boundaries and appropriate behavior. It was as if his sense of self was completely obliterated under the onslaughts that he confronted growing up. Needless to say, Lucas was deprived of any of the basic nurturing or benevolent physical contact that is a basic necessity for most children. Lucas grew up abandoned and abused and, like the vast majority of other convicted serial killers, he turned the visceral rage of his having been abandoned and abused upon the rest of humanity.

Our seven-month biosocial study of Lucas, called an "n of one" study, which was completed in April, 1985, was one the first comprehensive medical, neurological, biological, biochemical, psychological, and social studies ever conducted on a self-confessed serial killer. Here is what the study found:

Lucas conforms to a set of complex of patterns of behavior and physiology that is so pervasive, it actually eludes any one discipline's diagnostic procedures. In other words, psychologists routinely don't see the extreme biological pathology for what it is and biologists don't see the extreme psychopathology for what it is. His symptoms extend way across the range of specialized expertise and in so doing, challenges the theoretical concepts underlying those expertises. The study found that Lucas' biological motivations for his behavior were so extreme that they challenged the way a traditional psychologist would approach him. This has made it very difficult for anyone to get a real scientific handle on his behavior.

The study found, in fact, that Lucas didn't fit any of the standard psychiatric labels at all, even though he had been diagnosed a schizophrenic by psychiatrist after psychiatrist. Schizophrenia might have been only a starting point, but it didn't even begin to explain the full range of symptoms that made Lucas kill. Lucas also was a chronic drug abuser and an alcohol abuser since the age of eleven. Those levels of substance abuse—he claims that he was drunk or high most of his life and certainly whenever he was killing—creates a severe character disorder all by itself. One need not be a schizophrenic to be rendered completely dysfunctional by a reliance on or abuse of drugs and liquor. Lucas also had significant and possibly debilitating brain damage and suffered from an extreme amount of lead poisoning. Both of these problems also cause delusional states and aberrant behavior.

Lucas was a sociopath—no doubt because of the

type of upbringing he endured and the levels of abuse he experienced — as well as a sadist and masochist. He was used to getting beaten up and learned to dish it out. Moreover, he has suffered from a range of memory impairments — psychological, neurological, and chemical in nature — that resulted in black-out states, states of dream-like memory confusion, and hypermnesia triggered by specific stimuli. No one of these impairments alone can account for the levels of brutality that Lucas inflicted on others, but taken together, they present a composite picture of an individual who had, in effect, been programmed to kill.

The neurological damage that Lucas evidenced in 1985 was substantial and, as indicated earlier, almost debilitating. As was learned from CAT scans, a neuromagnetic resonance test, other forms of ultrasound, and extensive electroencephalograms, Lucas had small contusions of the frontal poles which indicated a frontal lobe injury. There was a loss of cortical tissue at the frontal poles which could have been related to a post head trauma event. The neuromagnetic resonance test specifically revealed that the Sylvan fissures on both sides of Lucas' brain were expanded. This would have caused substantial behavioral impairment.

The physicians and radiologists suggested that the damage to Lucas' brain was probably caused by post-birth head traumas. They estimated that the traumas probably occurred before Lucas was ten and probably after he was five. That would certainly coincide with

Lucas' story of being knocked unconscious by his mother with a board and remaining in a coma for almost thirty-six hours. The extensive damage would also coincide with Lucas' other stories of having fallen from a ladder (Bernie, Viola's pimp, told this story to the emergency room doctor) and of being stabbed through the eye with his brother's knife. Lucas also reported a variety of fights and scuffles throughout his life — almost all of them resulting in severe blows to his head — including one injury in which a woman hit him in the forehead during a robbery and knocked him out. He claims he was found wandering around by police two days later, not knowing who or where he was. He was taken to the hospital, examined and briefly treated, and then released to the Union mission in the area.

Lucas has had a history of brain poisoning from alcohol and drug abuse. Lucas also had three times more cadmium and lead poisoning in his system than an average person. Three signs of cadmium poisoning are a strong body odor, absence of dream recall, and a loss of the sense of smell. Lucas has all of these symptoms. His socks are said to have an abnormally foul odor; he says he seldom remembers his dreams, and during one of his killing sprees, he bragged to Ottis Toole, that he drove for days with a forgotten decapitated head in the back seat of his car without noticing any foul odor whatsoever. He even joked to Ottis that when he passed through a toll booth on an Arizona highway, the toll taker stuck his head in Lucas' window and told him to clean out the garbage in the back seat of his car because it was smelling so bad.

Lucas has had vivid hallucinations and delusions. Among them, which we have described earlier, were his sensations that he was floating above his bed, that he heard voices speaking to him in his prison cell in Michigan, that his mother urged him to kill and keep on killing, and that when he kills, the people he is about to kill become phantoms in his vision. He has said that he knows when he is going to kill someone because he feels a cold chill deep down at the base of his spine and the person he will kill seems to fade away or turn gray. Lucas also said that when he was a child he would go into trance-like states in which he could see demons tormenting him as he lay in his bed and he would be held against his bed or the floor by devils. He described these as frightening experiences, but said he learned to live with them.

Most psychiatric evaluators have interpreted Lucas' symptoms as schizophrenic in origin, but the author has suggested that Lucas suffers from what appears to be temporal lobe epilepsy, a strictly neurological impairment. Although when the "n of one" study was performed on Lucas, traditional epilepsy was not observed on Lucas' EEG, a 36-hour EEG was not performed. Temporal lobe epilepsy tends not to turn up on a traditional EEG, only on a 36-hour EEG, and thus would have not have shown up in the study. The neurologist's suggestion of a temporal lobe problem was based on the evidence of Lucas' symptoms which resembled temporal lobe hallucinations or delusions that occur during recurring epileptic or black-out periods.

Lucas has described his participation in cults and has described his conversion to Christianity as the result of a vision he saw in his Georgetown cell. The extreme shift in religious loyalties can, of course, be explained spiritually. It can also be explained as a condition known as hyperreligiosity. Many serial killers exhibit hyperreligiosity and often shift religious commitments dramatically from one belief system to another. The connecting link is that all of the belief systems involve a pattern of "magical thinking" or the placing of one's reliance on supernatural elements to shape the future.

It is therefore not uncommon at all for devil worshippers to become fundamentalist Christians after the cult fantasy has played itself out. It is as if one set of magical thinking projections has been replaced by another, without affecting the basic pattern of magical thinking. None of this is in any way intended to suggest that any religious belief system, is only a pattern of magical thinking. What we are pointing to is a medical condition in which a person throughout his or her life has consistently not applied any form of cognitive logic to problem-solving, but has been influenced *solely* by sets of supernatural events over which the person has absolutely no control but which the person must obey even at the cost of his life or other lives.

The supernatural events may have no specific identity; they may shift throughout the person's lifetime, or they may change depending on how the person reacts to a new situation and peer pressure from an occult group.

Hyperreligiosity is also a common trait among temporal lobe-damaged people, and it is a symptom evidenced by Lucas to the extreme. His brand of hyperreligiosity is marked by grandiose claims of power, importance, and the ability to inflict harm. His claims are matched by other serial killers who embellish the facts of their own cases and claim far many more lives than they may have actually taken. For entirely identifiable and even diagnosable medical reasons, a hundred or hundred and fifty person killing spree is more powerful and meaningful than a ten person killing spree. The larger the numbers of victims, the more demonic the killer is in his or her own eyes and the greater the level of sacrifice the killer must endure in order to achieve some form of salvation. Maybe the death penalty itself becomes more meaningful or justifiable.

The symptom of hypergraphia is another symptom that people with temporal lobe dysfunction exhibit. They cannot stop writing or expressing themselves verbally and nonverbally. Henry is an obsessive writer. He also paints eight to ten canvasses per week with excessive detail, very little instruction during the actual painting event, and no formal instruction prior to his painting. He just feels compelled to create images. About a month before he was transferred to the Georgetown jail, Lucas began a daily journal of writing down his prayers. And he wrote down one prayer after another and would not stop. While this, to be sure, may be an example of religious devotion — hand-copied books of personal prayers became a form of literature in the thirteenth and fourteenth centuries — the writing itself, when combined with other forms of graphic expression, is an example of hypergraphia.

Lucas, like all serial killers, has a history of bizarre sexuality, and this history has been documented by sources other than Lucas himself. The history includes incest with his sister-in-law and brother, bestiality in adolescence, rape in adolescence, necrophilia and murder in adulthood, and violent masturbatory fantasies which continue. Lucas is also creative both in his fantasies and in his expressions of those fantasies. Simply listening to the bizarre form his confessions took indicates the level of creativity active in him. Most serial killers are extraordinarily creative. They have to be, if only to stay alive.

Lucas demonstrates a particularly wide range of unique memory problems. For example, on the day of his first neurological testing in 1985, Lucas could remember Jimmy Carter's name but could not remember Ronald Reagan's name when asked. On alternate days during the "n of one" study in 1985, Lucas freely remembered that Ronald Reagan was the president. However, Lucas often recalled minute details about some of the crimes he has confessed to. To the aston-

298

ishment of the police that cleared his cases, these details proved to be true. And in these instances the police investigators are adamant that no one leaked any information to Lucas prior to the interrogation.

Lucas, like other serial killers, is overly concerned with his health. This is not surprising at all. Most, if not all, serial killers realize that something is dramatically wrong with them. When asked, many serial killers explain that they don't really feel that they're "there." It is as if they can look down and see their own hands and feet, but do not have the sense of self that "normal" people have. Whether this is true or not is perhaps a matter of perception, but there is a clear difference in self-perception between serial killers and "normal" people. Sometimes this dysfunctional lack of self-perception manifests itself as hypochondria, sometimes as an extreme tolerance or even indifference to pain, and sometimes as an obsessive concern for one's body wastes: sweat, urine, and feces. It is as if by leaving scents and stains, a person with a dysfunctional sense of self-perception can prove to himself that he's really alive.

Lucas had severely deficient nutritional habits when he was a child. These have largely been corrected now that he is institutionalized, but they contributed to a severe form of malnutrition which hampered his development throughout his life. Although no one has thought to raise a "Twinkie defense" for Henry Lee Lucas, in his case it may be appropriate. Severe nutritional and vitamin deficiencies, deficiencies in trace minerals and other nutrients can result in bizarre forms of behavior and sexual aberrations. Sugar reactions, sugar highs and extreme depressions can result; zinc or other deficiencies can result in a skewed sexual response to stimuli, and lack of proteins can result in different kinds of depression and distortions in self-perception. When you consider that throughout most of his life, Lucas was abusing alcohol and drugs, you realize the precarious state of his behavioral control mechanisms. In fact, he had no behavioral control mechanisms and that was part of the problem.

Lucas has a severely dysfunctional sexual confusion about himself. He has lived primarily as a heterosexual, but admitted to homosexual events in prison and in the passive role with his homosexual friend Ottis Toole. Yet Henry steadfastly denies homosexuality. Again, we are not suggesting that there is anything deviant about homosexuality as either a practice or a lifestyle. Nor are we implying in any way that homosexuality is a basic part of criminal behavior. We are only commenting upon Lucas' problems with sexual identity and his *hostility* over his confusion.

Lucas, like almost all other serial killers, has evidenced an escalating propensity for violence throughout his life. By this we mean: he has abused animals, killed them, and had sex with their remains; he has been a fire-starter; he was an adolescent rapist, and he progressed to single-event homicide when he killed his mother. Upon his release from prison, he became a multiple homicide offender, and the violence associated with those homicides, by his admission, escalated over the course of time. Finally, he was not only killing. He was killing, mutilating, dismembering, and having sex with what he'd dismembered. Lucas threatened authorities in his Michigan prison that he would kill if he were released and, he says, he made good on those threats. This escalating violence combined with warnings and threats to people in authority is one of the hallmarks of a serial killer.

Lucas, just like other serial killers, shows a remarkable stability and control once in prison. In fact, he's more controlled in prison than on the outside because the institution itself becomes like a personality skeleton. Because most serial killers never develop their own advanced adult personalities, they use the institutional structure of the prison as their personality. Thus they often become model prisoners while they are incarcerated. When they are released, they may go on killing sprees, surprising the parole officials who released then. It's really no surprise; serial killers belong under strict institutional controls because they are critically damaged and will inflict violence on others unless they are controlled.

Lucas, like other serial killers, has made warnings to law enforcement and mental health professionals about his inability to control his violent rage. He repeatedly told law enforcement officials during previous jail sentences that something was wrong with him and that he would kill if he were released. He could not control himself, he realized, and needed to remain under the supervision of an institution.

The Lucas study revealed the true nature of a classic serial killer personality for the first time anywhere. It helps to explain not just why Lucas killed but what made him into a serial killer. To say that his mother did it is a dangerous oversimplification. Obviously parents play critical roles in the emotional and neurological development of their children. And a parent who decides to create a killer by savagely torturing and abusing a child may just succeed. However, in Lucas' case there was a combination of childhood abuse, brain damage, nutritional deficiency, substance abuse, post-traumatic stress, and maladaptive socialization as a result of his being institutionalized at an early age. As each component came into play, it affected the other components until the constellation of symptoms was so great that it extended well beyond the range of expertise in any one discipline.

Can we learn anything from having studied and examined Henry Lee Lucas? Besides learning how *not* to raise a child, we can see that the problems of violence are not simplistic. Law enforcement officials cannot remedy the problems by carrying a big stick and wielding it against anyone who transgresses. We may just find out by studying Lucas and people like him that prevention may be the only way to stop entire generations of Henry Lee Lucases from being spawned.

This is not a far-fetched scenario. If we take a long, hard look at the generation of crack children about to push through the age envelope into the school systems, we will find that our cities and municipalities are about to be overwhelmed. The amount of care and attention these potentially dysfunctional, abused, and angry crack children may demand will likely drain all of our system's resources. Henry Lee Lucas may seem like a bizarre nightmare, but compared to what may be coming down the pike, Henry may seem like the good old days.